"I LOVE YOU, SABRINA,"
DAVID WHISPERED

When there was no response he moved closer to her sleeping form. "I said 'I love you.' Doesn't that get an 'Oh' or a 'That's nice'?" he teased.

Sabrina opened one eye and smiled over at him. "I love you, too," she said softly.

"So what are we going to do about it?" he asked, snuggling up to her.

"Do?" She had a sinking feeling of what was coming next and wondered why she wasn't filled with joy.

"Well, we could take out a full-page ad in the *Greensboro Chronicle*, or have it skywritten over New Orleans...or get married." The last was offered on a hopeful note.

Sabrina didn't know what to say. She loved David with all her heart. But there were far too many unanswered questions between them....

ABOUT THE AUTHOR

Because of a special love of history, particularly
that of the American south, Kelly Walsh has spent
many vacations touring historic sites and
antebellum homes from Virginia to Texas. A
recent trip to New Orleans fueled the idea of
setting *Of Time and Tenderness* in Louisiana.
When Kelly isn't traveling, she can be found hard
at work at her new word processor. Readers will
be delighted to know there's a new Superromance
in the works by this talented author.

Books by Kelly Walsh

HARLEQUIN SUPERROMANCE

Don't miss any of our special offers. Write to us at the
following address for information on our newest releases.

Harlequin Reader Service
901 Fuhrmann Blvd., P.O. Box 1397, Buffalo, NY 14240
Canadian address: P.O. Box 603,
Fort Erie, Ont. L2A 5X3

Kelly Walsh

OF TIME AND TENDERNESS

Harlequin Books

TORONTO • NEW YORK • LONDON
AMSTERDAM • PARIS • SYDNEY • HAMBURG
STOCKHOLM • ATHENS • TOKYO • MILAN

Published December 1987

First printing October 1987

ISBN 0-373-70286-8

CHAPTER ONE

SABRINA STORMED INTO HER APARTMENT and plopped the white pastry box onto the dinette table. "Hi," she mumbled to her friend and apartment mate, Ina, who was sitting on the sofa, watching her with hesitant humor in her eyes.

"Hi to you. One of those days, I take it."

After setting her briefcase on the sideboard behind the table, Sabrina shrugged out of her beige suit jacket and draped it across the easy chair opposite the sofa. Her movements were restless and irritable. "The worst."

Ina put down the magazine she'd been reading and went to the table. She peered into the white box and innocently asked, "A four-éclair evening?"

Sabrina turned quickly, and the shoulder-length auburn hair that had been tousled by the New Orleans September breeze whipped around behind her. Her hazel eyes sparked the way they always did when she was upset. In a voice lower than usual, she said fiercely, "I should have gotten *eight* of them."

Ina started toward the kitchen. "That bad, huh?"

"Eight!" Sabrina repeated, grabbing the back of the easy chair and swinging around it. "It's corporate sexism—overt and intentional."

Gathering napkins and two plates, Ina asked, "Want to tell me about it now, or do we polish off these caloric delights first?"

"I don't want to go!" She moved spread fingers through her hair as she walked toward the table, and sat down.

"So don't go," Ina suggested, placing an éclair on each of their plates. She sat down and looked over at Sabrina, noting that her brows were pulled together in a defiant frown. Curious, she asked, "Go where?"

"Greensboro," she answered in a voice muffled by the cream-filled pastry.

Her mouth similarly occupied, Ina asked, "What's in Greensboro?"

"Some broken-down mansion." Sabrina wiped the corners of her mouth with a napkin. "It's to be renovated, made into a paying guest house."

Ina's tongue flicked at a dab of chocolate on her lips. "What's sexist about that? You work for an architectural firm."

Sabrina swallowed another bite. "Greensboro is almost two hundred miles north of here. I'd have to spend weekdays there. What about Michael?" Her head turned toward her son's room. It was too quiet. "Where is he?"

"In the back garden with a jar, waiting for the fireflies to do their thing."

Sabrina rose and walked over to the rear window of their second-story apartment. Looking down into the garden, she saw him sitting patiently on a wrought iron chair, holding an empty mayonnaise jar in his little hands. She leaned against the window frame and said quietly, "I want to be a success in a hurry, Ina. I need to make money—lots of it—for Michael's security... and for mine, too." She glanced at her friend over her shoulder. "Do you know what four years' tuition is going to cost at a good university?"

With wide eyes, Ina declared, "The boy is only seven years old, for God's sake!"

Returning her attention to her son, Sabrina asked in a troubled voice, "What if he became seriously ill or had an accident?"

"What if you remarried and found yourself wealthy?"

There was a bounce to Sabrina's steps as she rejoined Ina, her mood suddenly lighter. "What if it snowed here in New Orleans in July?" She reached into the box, took another éclair and bit into it enthusiastically. Seeing Ina look longingly at the sole remaining one, she offered, "Help yourself."

Ina did. "Why does something so delicious have to be so fattening?" As she bit into it, she eased out a long, contented "Mmmmmm" and then asked, "So, why don't you want to go? How often do you get out-of-town assignments?"

"This is the first, but it'll take months. I'd only see Michael on the weekends."

"You can't take him with you?"

Sabrina shook her head and licked a blob of chocolate from her finger. "Don't want to do that to him. His school term's just started. I can't just pull him out and take him away from the friends he's made. Michael has had to make too many adjustments already—the move from Connecticut, the divorce. Besides, his father gets custody next month."

"The shared custody bit," Ina commented a little caustically. "You told me your ex backed out the first time he was supposed to have his son for six months.

What makes you so sure he's planning on taking him this time?''

Sabrina looked over at Ina and thought how fortunate it had been that she'd met her this past summer. Ina had been hired for a summer clerical job at Delta Associates, Architects & Interior Design, Inc., the firm that Sabrina worked for. She had immediately taken a liking to Ina; most everyone at the office had. Hers was a cheerful and optimistic personality, in spite of the fact that she wasn't finding it easy to finish the last bit of her graduate work in music. She was a cellist. Her family lived in Mississippi and they hadn't been able to help much with the cost of her studies, but she had plugged away, taking jobs wherever she could find them in order to study with the cellist of her choice in New Orleans. When her temporary job at Delta Associates had ended the month before, Sabrina had offered her the third bedroom in her apartment in exchange for looking after Michael part-time. It had been difficult ever since the divorce two years ago. She welcomed Ina's help and friendship, and Ina appreciated the financial assistance gained by free living quarters.

Sabrina had already shared much information with the young woman, regarding her life to date, but not everything. Ina's question about her ex-husband repeated itself in her mind. Sabrina leaned her elbows on the table while she wiped her fingers with a napkin. "Todd backed out because he'd just gotten married again." She chuckled. "He's the kind of man who's going to keep getting married until he finds a woman who will put up with his idiosyncrasies. Anyway, he didn't think Ann would appreciate a made-to-order family on her honeymoon. There was all that getting-adjusted time he needed with her." Sabrina smiled wickedly. "And I loved every minute of having Michael with *me*."

"Well, until his father takes him, I could watch over Michael while you're gone."

"Thanks, but what would you do? Strap him to your back while you lugged that cello of yours to nighttime rehearsals with the symphony? It's enough that your schedule allows you to keep an eye on him until I get home from work and when I have night classes."

"I'd manage something."

Sabrina watched as Ina picked up the empty pastry box and headed for the kitchen to throw it out. She was constantly impressed with the young woman's determined focus on her career, although she had to stifle laughter whenever she saw the five-foot-one-inch Ina carting her cello in and out of the apartment, her brown eyes glowing, her long straight chestnut hair streaming down her back.

Ina emerged from the kitchen and curled up in a corner of the sofa across from the dinette area. "So what's with this corporate sexism business?"

With her elbows still on the table, Sabrina rested her chin on clasped fingers. "My boss, *Mr.* Sadler, explained why the qualified men in our firm couldn't be sent. *They* have families." Her eyes glowered. "What do I have? A pet? And even though I have seniority over Jack Myers—who happens to be very single—I was told I was *it*, the chosen one." She stood up. "So much for equality in corporate America!"

"I take it you can't go to your boss's boss."

"A basic canon of corporate conduct," Sabrina recited as she moved to the sofa and sat down, "is to pay attention to the chain of command and respect the hi-

erarchical rank system. In other words . . . no, I can't."
She kicked off her pumps and tucked her legs under
her. "Besides, my interest lies in modern architecture
and interior design, not in refurbishing old bedrooms
into new ones, and Sadler knows that. I didn't work my
tail off getting my degree to do that, and having this
assignment thrown at me is going to put a screeching
halt to my work on the postgraduate degree I need to
get anywhere in this business."

"Tell me about it," Ina agreed, twisting the ends of
shiny strands of hair around her index finger. She
shifted her eyes toward Sabrina and studied her for a
moment. Then she asked, "Sabrina, has it ever crossed
your mind that you're trying to do an awful lot at the
same time—trying to be everything to everybody? It
doesn't leave much time for Sabrina."

A comfortable silence settled over the two friends for
a few moments. Sabrina nodded. "I know. I don't have
the time I'd like to have for myself. Sometimes I do feel
tired, and sometimes I worry, but I've trained myself
not to dwell on things."

She rose from the sofa and went to the rear window
to check on her son. Then she turned. "Ina, I will ask
you to do me a favor, though."

"Ask away."

"Would you be able to look after Michael the rest of
this week—just this week—while I go up to Greensboro? Sadler wants me to give the woman who owns
the house an estimate on the renovation costs before
Delta takes on the project."

"It's not definite, then?"

"Not exactly, but Sadler told me she's anxious for
the work to begin, says he's pretty sure she'll agree to

whatever is necessary. He's spoken with her on the phone several times."

"No problem...except for Friday night, the symphony rehearsal, but I could—"

"I'd be back early Friday," Sabrina said quickly.

"Then there's definitely no problem."

Sabrina combed her fingers through her hair. "If Delta does get the project I'll talk to Todd and see if he'll take Michael a few weeks sooner." Just the thought of that caused an aching sensation in Sabrina's heart.

She gazed down into the garden again and watched as her son waved the mayonnaise jar in the air frantically. She worried about Michael: worried about his lacking a live-in father, worried about not being able to give him all of her time, worried about the prospect of his being shuttled back and forth between parents. Yes, as she had told Ina, she certainly worried sometimes.

"Assuming that Todd will take him," Ina suggested, "maybe you could finish your night course on an independent study basis."

Sabrina faced her. "I haven't even had time to think of that possibility. I'll talk to Professor Rawlins in class tonight." She glanced at her watch. "God, look at the time! Bless whoever invented the microwave. Ina—" she started toward the kitchen "—be a doll and try to capture the young one for me while I produce instant lasagna."

IT WAS A LITTLE AFTER eleven o'clock that evening when Sabrina returned home after class. Her steps were less sprightly than when she had come into the apart-

ment earlier in the day. She was bushed, understand-
ably.

She put her briefcase on the dinette table, went to
Michael's room and quietly opened the door. Her eyes
shone with obvious love, and she smiled softly as she
studied the sleeping form hugging his favorite stuffed
tiger.

She slipped inside his bedroom and partially closed
the door behind her so that the light from the living
room wouldn't shine across his face. At the side of his
bed, she leaned over and gently ran her fingers through
his blond hair, hair that was just like Todd's. His eyes,
however, were hazel, like hers.

In the soft glow of the night-light by the bed, she
examined the freckles that dotted his cheeks and nose
and wondered if they would disappear with age as hers
had. After adjusting the lightweight cover over him,
she kissed his forehead and left the room, quietly closing the door behind her.

For a while Sabrina paused outside his bedroom
door, mulling over her half-formed decision to look for
another job rather than be separated from her son in
the coming months. Even though he would be going to
live with his father eventually, he would still be in the
same city. And even though it was going to positively
break her heart when Michael did go to Todd's, she
had long decided that she wanted her son to have a
solid relationship with his father.

But now this Greensboro business, almost two
hundred miles away.

Pushing herself from the bedroom door, she went
into the kitchen to put some coffee on, then returned
to the living room and sat down at the table. She

opened her briefcase, took out some papers and began to review the evening's notes.

A groggy-eyed Ina, in an "I love Bach" nightshirt, waddled into the living room. Sabrina looked up. "I didn't mean to wake you. Sorry."

"You didn't. I got hunger pains." She glanced down at the papers Sabrina had spread out on the table and went into the kitchen. As she took the milk out of the refrigerator, she said, "Your father called this evening."

"Damn!" Sabrina threw her pen down. "I forgot about that."

"Were you expecting him to call?"

"No, but I promised him when we talked last that I'd bring Michael up to Connecticut to visit for a long weekend when I finished the Cosgrove project." She began a tapping motion with her fingers. "Now that's out, too. What else can go wrong?"

"Don't tempt fate," Ina advised as she put a glass of milk and a piece of leftover Italian bread down on the table. "Coffee's ready. Want a cup now?"

"Would you, please?" As Ina moved away, Sabrina asked, "What did he have to say?"

She stuck her head outside the kitchen doorway; her voice took on a highly dignified tone. "'A mother's place at night is at home with her child. Please ask my daughter to phone me *if* she has the time.'" She brought Sabrina's filled coffee mug out and set it down in front of her. "What's with him? Does he always needle you like that?"

Sabrina wrapped her fingers around the warm cup. "No...just since the divorce. I'm afraid I've disappointed him." Her eyes stared at the steam rising from the coffee. "He thought I should have stuck to my vow of 'for better or for worse,' regardless. Now he can't understand why Michael and I don't return home for good."

Sitting down, Ina commented, "Connecticut could be better than Greensboro."

Sabrina took a sip of the hot coffee. Then she said, "It's not as simple as that. Todd is settled here in New Orleans, and there's no way I could stay in Connecticut and send Michael here for six months at a time...no way." Just the thought of that possibility caused Sabrina's mouth to become a line of grim determination.

"Have you told your father that?"

"Yes, but he doesn't want to hear it." She rubbed her thumb up and down against the mug. "Staying here, I'll also get to see Michael every weekend when his father does have him...just as Todd does now. Well, most weekends he finds the time." After another sip she added, "Then there's my job here. All may not be rosy, but I've got the opportunity for a lot of experience a woman with only a B.A. might not get with another firm. And besides, I like New Orleans."

Her eyes took on a sense of conviction. "And going back to Connecticut would be giving up the battle for independence I've worked so hard to achieve... independence from my father and from Todd. It would be like retreating, and that's unacceptable now, when victory is so close."

Ina glanced down at the papers on the table again, then she studied Sabrina's face as she sat there holding the coffee mug tightly. "You look a little tired, kiddo, and it concerns me. We've only known each other for a few months, but even so, I can tell you're a woman dancing too fast. Ever think about slowing down?"

Manufacturing an easy smile, Sabrina tried to put her friend's concerns to rest. "Not as long as the éclairs hold out." To change the subject, she asked, "How is it going with you and Eugene?"

Ina let loose a dissatisfied moan. "He still acts as though I don't even exist. All he thinks about is that bassoon of his." She scratched under the collar of her nightshirt. "How does a woman compete with a bassoon?"

Sabrina's low laugh brightened both their faces. "Just remember, you have a few advantages over a bassoon."

"Tell that to Eugene."

"You're really stuck on him, aren't you?"

Ina's big brown eyes shimmered softly, and her voice took on a dreamy quality. "Yeah, I guess I am—have been ever since he joined the symphony this year. He came here from Arkansas." She rested her chin on a cupped hand. "I can still see him walking onto the stage that first night. The overhead lights made that red hair of his shine like burnished copper. He's tall, Sabrina, and he walks with a kind of swagger that makes me crazy."

"You do have it bad."

"Oh well," Ina philosophized as she picked up her bread, "he's just shy. I'll bide my time."

Much later, after Ina had returned to bed, Sabrina gathered up her notes and placed them in a drawer in the sideboard. She snapped her briefcase shut, and let an exhausted sigh slip past her lips. "Well, Sabrina . . . another day."

DAWN CAST a gray-blue light over Sabrina as she lay in bed. She was only half awake when she suddenly felt as though she had a mouth full of fuzz. Something was pressing against her face.

"Wake up, Mom! Say good morning to Stripes."

"Morning, Stripes," she mumbled to the stuffed toy, "and to you, too, Tiger," she added, using her favorite pet name for her son. She yawned and forced her eyes open, smiling warmly at the tousled-haired boy standing at the side of the bed. "How'd you sleep?"

"Good . . . and you did, too."

"What time is it?" She glanced over at the alarm clock, saw that it was ten after six and vaguely remembered pressing the Snooze button when the alarm had gone off earlier. Reaching over, she hit the Off button. "Why does every day have to start in the morning?" she complained, raising herself up on her elbows. "How about a kiss for your mom?"

Michael's smack on Sabrina's lips was quick and moist. His blue pajamas were covered with the image of a red-haired cartoon figure from a TV program he watched on Saturday mornings, and Sabrina's eyes were drawn to the bright spots of color. Michael's own hair was almost as wild looking. Gently she smoothed down the wayward blond strands.

"Mom, Eddie's dad got him a new model rocket—the kind you gotta put together by yourself. Can I go over and help him tomorrow after school?"

"Sure, if you've been invited. I'll call—" Sabrina interrupted her own words, remembering that there was every possibility she'd be in Greensboro tomorrow. Sadler hadn't said just when she was to go, but he had told her the client was in a hurry for the estimate. Maybe she could put off going until next week, she thought.

"You don't have to call. Eddie's mom was right there when he asked me after school yesterday."

A renewed wave of guilt tore at Sabrina when she pictured Eddie's mother picking her son up at school every day. No matter how often Sabrina reminded herself that millions of children rode the bus to and from school, it didn't seem to help. The worst part of it was the guilt she felt at not being at home when Michael finished school.

She reached over and cupped his chin. "We'll work something out. Now, what do you two want for breakfast?"

Morning chores taken care of, Sabrina rushed to work. Her boss had asked her to gather up the material on the project she was currently working on in order to turn it over to Jack Myers, who would take charge of its completion, freeing her to devote her full efforts to the job in Greensboro.

"Sure," she muttered to herself as she retrieved the structural layouts of the office complex and art gallery that was her pet project, "after I've done the heavy work."

On the one hand she seethed, realizing that as a woman in a field dominated by men, more was expected of her. But on the other hand, she knew she had gained a great deal of experience at Delta Associates and had made many invaluable business contacts during the past two years. She'd had the opportunity to hone all the skills she had been developing ever since college back in Connecticut. When Delta took on a project, it took on the entire package: the structure of the building, the interior design and the landscaping.

On top of the layouts she was holding, she piled the final designs and working drawings she had done showing the exact dimensions of every portion of the building, including the locations of all electrical outlets, fixtures, plumbing, heating and air-conditioning facilities and windows and doors.

She had labored hard over the drawings and had worked closely with the engineers in determining what materials were to be used, considering the climate and soil of New Orleans. She had made certain that everything she had chosen conformed with local and state building and design regulations. The only thing left to do was obtain approval of her plans in accordance with zoning laws and fire regulations.

Cosgrove, the client, was an easy man to work with, which wasn't always the case. She'd already assisted him in the letting of bids to construction companies, and she'd been looking forward to working with the specification writer and the estimator, who would convert her drawings into instructions for the contractor and subcontractors who would build her building.

Her building. Sabrina permitted herself a moment of pride when she glanced down at the drawings she'd made, but she also experienced a sense of loss, hating to turn the project over to someone else. It was almost as though she were giving a child up for adoption.

She forced that thought out of her mind quickly, telling herself that the landscaping decisions would be minimal, since there wouldn't be that much land around the office complex once it was built, and although Jack Myers wasn't one of her favorite people, she knew he'd do a first-rate job of guiding Cosgrove through the furnishing of it.

With the bulky folders and working drawings under her arm, she went to Ralph's office.

"Ah, come on in, Sabrina," he drawled from behind his desk, where he was hanging a wooden plaque on the wall next to other awards the firm had garnered. "Chamber of Commerce Award of the Year," he read, adding, "a lot of credit goes to you and the work you did on the new Afton building."

"Thanks, Ralph," she said dryly, walking toward his desk. "Here are the plans for the Cosgrove project. Don't let Jack mess with the energy efficient earth-sheltered walls or the passive-solar-collecting loft rooms. Cosgrove wants them as is."

She searched for a particular folder, opened it and spread out her drawings of the pedestals that would support sculptures in the loft. "The only thing Cosgrove hasn't seen yet are these. He was thinking in terms of unadorned contemporary shafts for the art gallery, but I think he'll like these geo-prismatic pedestals. They're far more interesting than the standard columnar types he was talking about. I checked with Brice Industries in town. They can make them in glass or in polished or satin stainless steel."

"My guess is he'll go with the glass."

Sabrina disagreed. "I'd advise the satin stainless steel." She handed him another folder. "Here's the file on the proposed Dodson project. I recommend you turn it down."

Ralph opened the folder. "Why?"

Leaning against his desk, she rested her hands along its edge. "When I was checking for financial limitations, I found that one of his backers used to own the Yearby Construction Company."

Pale gray eyes registered recall. "The one that had the fire a few years back?"

"Exactly. The same Yearby who stole equipment from his own company and collected insurance on it."

"Then set fire to his own office in an attempt to cover up evidence when the insurance investigation zeroed in on him."

"Right, and since we can't handle all the business that's being offered now, why ask for trouble?"

"Glad you checked, Sabrina." He walked over to the coffee maker. "Care for a cup?"

"No, thanks."

He sent her an intimate look that started at her well-shaped legs and rose slowly—and smugly—over her turquoise suit and up to the hazel eyes that met his with aversion. After taking a lingering swallow of coffee, he smiled. "I can't get you to even have a cup of coffee with me, let alone an after-work drink."

Having been through this with him before, Sabrina told him, a little impatiently, "Ralph, you're not paying me to have coffee or martinis with you. Now, what about this Greensboro assignment? Why this firm?"

"The lady wants the best," he answered as he walked back over to his desk with his coffee and sat down in his oversized leather chair. "Her name's Hester Devereaux. We were recommended to her. I told her you'd phone. She doesn't think the house will need a lot of structural work, but you'll be able to tell better when you get up there tomorrow."

"Two hundred miles up there," Sabrina reminded him. She was just about to try for a postponement, but he changed her mind.

"That's what I like about you, Sabrina...your spirit of cooperation...team player and all that. I also like the fact that being a woman, you don't come in here and say 'I can't do this or that because I'm a mother with outside responsibilities.'"

Sabrina wasn't feeling at all like a team player just then. Besides her annoyance at this latest assignment, and at Ralph's crude overtures, she knew she was being paid less than the men in the firm who were doing comparable work. Trying desperately to keep her cool, she reminded herself that once she earned her master's degree, she planned to shake the dust collected at Ralph's firm from her high-heeled sandals and move on.

For now, she asked, "Am I going to have to cope with the comings and goings of a large family if I wind up overseeing the tearing up of the house?"

"Uh-uh. You lucked out on this one. The Devereaux lady lives at the place—" he flipped open a folder "—called Belleamie, all by herself. Just one body to make sure the ceiling doesn't fall on . . . hers."

Sabrina forced a semblance of a smile. "Things *are* looking up. I'll phone her this morning."

"And tell her you'll be up there tomorrow," he reminded her.

Again she checked the words that struggled to form on her lips. Ralph Sadler was no bargain, but, she reminded herself, he was no worse or no better, for that matter, than some of the men she'd come in contact with in her chosen field. But what about Michael? Maybe Ina would take him over to Eddie's and pick him up.

Ralph said, "As soon as you come up with the estimate, and that may take a day or two, give me a call."

"Mrs. Devereaux's home is that big?"

"Yeah, but I'm not sure if it's Mrs. or Miss." He smiled condescendingly. "Or Mzzzz."

Sabrina dug one heel into the carpet. "I'll let you know what Hester Devereaux prefers to be called." Then she asked, "Did you already check for financial limitations?"

"She's solid. Inherited the place from her aunt; been living there for over twenty years."

"By herself, you said."

He shrugged his shoulders. "She does now, anyway. At least that's what she told me."

Sabrina pondered that for a moment, then asked, "How old is she?"

Ralph checked inside the folder again. "Forty. Why?"

"Just wondering." She started toward the office door.

"Oh, Sabrina." Turning, she saw him direct a detestable leer at her. "We guys are gonna miss you. You're a nice decoration around here."

One, two, three. She calmed herself, vowing that before she left the firm she was going to tell Ralph just what she thought of him and the "guys." She gathered her poise. "It's always nice to be respected for one's abilities, isn't it, Ralph?"

She closed the door behind her with a little more force than usual and started back to her own office at a good clip. With a clenched jaw she fought against the lump stuck in her throat. She didn't need the man's stupid innuendos, didn't need this damn trip to Greensboro and most of all, she didn't need this forced separation from her son. *It's not fair!* she screamed silently.

A little voice in her brain retorted: *So? What's "fair" got to do with anything?*

CHAPTER TWO

WEDNESDAY MORNING BEGAN like any other weekday for Sabrina, but in spite of the usual rush, this Wednesday was very different. For the first time she would be putting an enormous distance between her and Michael.

The evening before, when she had returned home from work, she had had a careful talk with him and had explained why it was necessary for her to leave, and that she would be back on Friday. As she did, her heart had been in her throat. She had felt somewhat disappointed when her son had voiced his main concern: Was he still going to Eddie's to assemble the rocket?

In order to squeeze in every possible moment with Michael before she left for Greensboro, Sabrina decided to drive him to school, rather than let him take the bus as he usually did.

Her heart grew heavier and heavier as her Bronco approached the red brick building. School buses were lined up in the circular drive, so Sabrina parked along the curb a little distance away.

She pulled the emergency brake and looked over at Michael. "I'll phone you this evening."

"I'll be at Eddie's, Mom," he said insistently, "dinner and everything."

A smile found its way through her concerned expression. "Well, you're not going to spend the night there. When I talked with Eddie's mother, we agreed that seven o'clock would be enough for you future aeronautical engineers. Ina will pick you up—and remember, no trying to con her. Seven, right?"

"Jeez, you'd think I was just a little kid," he complained as he pumped his legs, anxious to leave and find Eddie.

"Seven," she said again.

"Seven," he repeated and reached for the handle of the car door.

"Hey, hey, Tiger! Aren't you forgetting something?"

Michael glanced down at his books and then up at his mother. He knew what she was waiting for. His hazel eyes swept the area outside the car. "Not here, Mom!"

The sudden realization that her "baby" was growing up too quickly for comfort hit her heart with a thud. *Damn Sadler, damn Greensboro, damn Todd and everyone and everything else,* she moaned inwardly. She heard the distant ringing of a bell.

Michael did, too. "I gotta go or I'll be late," he told her hurriedly and reached for the door handle again.

"What if I bend down?" she suggested. "Real low?"

She did and Michael joined her, giving her a quick peck on the cheek. Then he forced the handle down on the car door, hopped out and disappeared into the crowd of schoolchildren.

"Thanks, Tiger," Sabrina whispered, watching him as long as she could see him.

As she sat there wiping her eyes, she berated herself for behaving so ridiculously. She reminded herself that soon Michael would be going to live with his father for six months. And someday he'd probably go off to camp—and eventually he'd be off to college. What would she do when he went off and got married?

"Cry, that's what," she said out loud, slamming the stick shift into gear and taking off.

As she drove north from New Orleans, Sabrina tried to get her mind off Michael. It settled on Todd Hutchins, his father.

She had long been thankful that he had insisted she take the newer of their two cars when they'd divorced. The added space for carting in the Bronco came in handy when she had building models and bulky construction samples to haul.

Todd. She tried to remember all the good things about him, and there had been good times during the six years they'd been married, but after Michael was born, it seemed their marriage started a slow downhill course with a certainty of never reversing itself.

She had regretted that, but was forced to face the fact that Todd had some kind of "primary" fixation. His wanting to be considered number one in her life seemed natural in the passion of their early love when she was studying architecture at Wesleyan University in Connecticut and he was studying marine biology at Yale. They'd married in her senior year and the following year Michael was born.

That was when she had first begun to notice the change in Todd. She hadn't understood it, but he seemed to resent the fact that her child had become the most important person in her life. Todd could never accept that her love for the infant was not deducted from the love she'd had for him. It was a new source of love she had discovered within herself when Michael was born. It had started the instant he was handed to her, and had surged when his tiny fingers had clutched at her face and when he had nursed at her breast for the first time.

Matters worsened between her and Todd when, a year after Michael's birth, Sabrina began taking courses toward obtaining her master's degree in architecture. Todd was busy with his doctorate work and then with his first job in Hartford, but he began to complain that he was having to share her with her school work as well as with Michael. He'd told her she was always "so busy with everything but him." Sabrina knew that wasn't true, but she stopped taking courses to placate him. Two years later, however, she did take a part-time job with an architectural firm in Hartford, much to Todd's chagrin.

When Michael was five years old, Todd accepted the position in New Orleans, and the family relocated, settling in the apartment she now lived in. Michael soon started school, and she and Todd had bitter words when she told him she had decided to embark upon the career for which she had studied so diligently—and had set aside during Michael's early years at Todd's insistence. Knowing that to reach the goals she had set for herself she would have to complete the work toward her master's degree, she enrolled for one night course after landing the job at Delta Associates.

That really set Todd off—irrationally so, Sabrina believed—and soon they were constantly arguing about *her* responsibilities, none of which he would help her take care of. So, they decided that— The muffled bang of a blowout jarred Sabrina from her thoughts. She saw the car ahead of her go into a skid and veer off the highway. She rammed her foot on the brake and pulled up behind the disabled vehicle to see if anyone had been injured.

As she was getting out of her Bronco, she saw a tall, dark-haired man scurry from the driver's side of the brown Jaguar. He checked his watch, then kicked the front tire—which was definitely flat.

"Are you all right?" she asked, noting that there were no passengers in the car.

He looked up at her, and she saw the concern in his face. Obviously he was late getting somewhere, she decided. In the next moment, a remarkable thing occurred. As he looked at her, his expression, which had been contorted with anger, transformed slowly into an inquiring pleasantness. The lines that had furrowed his brow smoothed out; his lips, which had muttered a low curse a moment ago, eased into an attractive smile. Yet, it was his eyes that were most compelling: as she watched they seemed to lose their darkness, and transmuted to a beautiful azure, a color not unlike that of a clear morning sky.

"You are all right?" she asked.

"Uh…yes," he finally answered, not taking his eyes from hers. "Thanks for stopping to check."

Sabrina liked his voice, liked the soft, southern-style prolongation of the vowels, the pleasant sonorous tone to it and its warm melodic rhythm. She found herself staring at him, and he at her. "Good…I'm glad you're not hurt," she said.

His rather full lips parted in a slightly wider smile, exposing white teeth that would make a movie star envious. Then, as though reminding himself of something, he glanced at his watch again. His eyes shot back to the flat tire. "Damn!"

"Do you have a spare?"

As he leaned down across the front seat to retrieve his car keys, he said, "Yes, but I needed this like a hole in the head. I'm already late for a board meeting. This hasn't been my best day." He pulled a folded piece of paper from his shirt pocket. "Speeding ticket," he told her and tossed it on the car seat.

Sabrina smiled in sympathy. "Well, good luck." She started back to her car.

"Wait!" he said, and she turned. After a momentary pause—as though he were trying to think of something to say—he offered, "Thanks again for stopping. Not everyone would have."

"No problem," she told him, realizing that he was studying her face. She wondered why her feet felt anchored to the grass, wondered why he seemed content to just stand there looking at her. His interest seemed unusually keen. Hadn't he just said he was in a hurry? Then it occurred to her to ask, "Have you checked the air in the spare lately?"

His brow furrowed slightly once again. "No, I've never had to use it." He went to the trunk, opened it and lifted the tire out of the back. Sabrina watched as he pushed down on it. It was definitely soft. His eyes rose to meet hers. "You had to mention it," he said half jokingly and began rolling up his shirtsleeves.

"Not to worry," she told him. "I've got an electric air pump in my car. It'll operate from your car's cigarette lighter socket. You get the flat off, and I'll take care of the spare."

She went back to her car and returned with a plastic case the size of a lunch box. As he jacked up the car, he glanced over at her. "Name's David Mansfield."

"Sabrina Hutchins," she told him as she leaned into his car to plug the end of the double-wired electric cord into the cigarette lighter socket.

As she bent a little farther, one of her feet left the ground and David couldn't help but notice that her legs were long and slender, her calves shapely and muscled and her ankles slim. He'd always liked high heels on women: they added elegance, he thought. And that tan-colored skirt she was wearing—it had an eye-catching sheen to it, and he found himself staring once again.

When Sabrina ducked her head and backed away from the car door, he returned his attention to getting the flat tire off. Soon, though, his eyes sought her out again, and he watched her efficient movements as she removed the spare's valve cap and attached the black air hose to the tire valve with the snap connector.

Without looking at him, she asked, "How much air do you use?"

"Thirty," he told her, seeing that she was watching the gauge intently.

He liked the way her auburn hair looked so soft, the way it hung in casual waves, framing a face that didn't need—and didn't seem to have—a lot of makeup on it.

"Thirty exactly," she said as she removed the air hose. "That should get you where you're going."

David carried the flat tire to the rear of his car and put it in the trunk. As he did, he saw Sabrina rolling the spare toward the front of his car. He found himself smiling again. Then he reached into the car and removed a white handkerchief from his inside jacket pocket. Giving it to her to wipe her fingers, he remarked, "You're a handy lady to have around. Thanks again."

"Women can be more than decorations," she said, recalling Ralph's parting shot at her.

"In your case, definitely," he responded, thinking that her reaction was a little strong. "What made you suppose I thought you were only a decoration?"

She returned his handkerchief and replaced the wires and air hose in the plastic case, chuckling more at herself than him. "Not you . . . something my boss said to me yesterday."

"And he is . . . ?"

She snapped the case shut. "Mr. Ralph Sadler of Delta Associates, a New Orleans-based architectural and interior design firm."

"You're a designer?"

Why did that always have to be the first supposition? she wondered. "You guessed wrong . . . an architect."

His dark brows rose in a complimentary gesture. "I'm impressed. Where're you headed?"

"Greensboro."

A light twinkled in the depth of his blue eyes. "So am I. I live there."

The suggestion of a smile played at the corners of Sabrina's mouth, and in that moment she felt that something was different between her and the man she'd just met. Seconds ago he had represented only a brief, chance encounter, but now, with the possibility of seeing him again not too farfetched, she became more interested in him. The prospect of being in the same town with him caused a slight twinge of excitement.

"Visiting?" he asked.

"No. On business at the Devereaux estate. Delta may be taking on a refurbishing project there."

"You'll be staying at Belleamie?"

Sabrina heard the surprise in his voice, saw the inquiring look in his eyes. She gave him a gentle nod. "Temporarily, yes."

He glanced at her ring finger—no wedding band. That pleased him, just as the look of her graceful hand did. He had a sudden impulse to caress it, but checked himself. "We'll be neighbors . . . literally."

She felt that odd twinge again, and a quick swallowing sensation caught at her throat. "That will be nice. I won't feel like a total stranger. Well, goodbye, Mr. Mansfield. I hope you're not too late for your board meeting."

She was about to turn away when he extended his hand to her. It was strong looking, strong enough to take whatever he wanted, she thought. His forearm seemed powerful, and she noted the light spray of dark hair over tanned skin. Sabrina eased her hand into his and was instantly aware of the warmth of his palm as his hand caressed hers and then took possession of her fingers. Seconds passed silently, and she wondered how long he was going to hold her hand in his firm grasp. Not that she minded.

In that low, musical voice, he said. "You have me obligated to you, Sabrina Hutchins. First you stop in an act of mercy, then you help me put my car in good order."

The twinge of excitement that still lingered soared to a delightful sensation. Wondering at her reaction to this stranger, she eased her hand from his and averted her eyes from his steady gaze. "Not obligated, Mr. Mansfield . . . just your thanks is enough. I'm happy I was able to help."

"David," he suggested. "Remember, we'll be neighbors—close neighbors."

A warning voice whispered in her head. It warned against the eager affection in his voice, against the vitality he radiated, against his compelling, magnetic eyes. The silent whispers also hinted at her own sudden feeling of vulnerability in the face of his masculine strength. Her lips settled into an unconscious smile, and she headed back to her car—quickly.

David leaned his arm on the top of his Jaguar as he watched her drive away. His index finger moved slowly over his lower lip as he murmured, "Obligated, Sabrina Hutchins... and happily so."

Looking in her rearview mirror, Sabrina stole glimpses of the tall, dark-haired man leaning on his sports car. As the image became smaller and smaller, she felt a slight vibration coming from the steering wheel, but then she realized the vibration—the tingling sensation, rather—was originating in her right hand, the hand David Mansfield had held for so long.

She shook her head and laughed. "Sabrina, you've been too good for too long. A man shakes your hand to introduce himself, and you start to hear violins."

To distract herself from thoughts of him, she glanced out at the landscape along the highway. It was a sea of greenery—lovely, but she missed the blazing autumn golds, reds and oranges of the woods she had left behind in Connecticut. Autumn here was so—green. The palms, the marshes and the flatness of the land she was driving through now only heightened the memory she had of the dazzling autumn colors of home.

Checking her watch, she realized it had already been four hours since she had left New Orleans. Then, up ahead on the right, she saw the sign indicating she was entering Greensboro, population 31,984. "Eighty-five, now," she mumbled, scanning the neat rows of what she guessed were soybeans.

As the highway diminished to two lanes, she took in the features of the outskirts and decided that little had probably changed in this century. The farm houses and the few country stores she passed were neat, but they gave her the feeling that she'd left modernity somewhere behind on the road. She pulled up at the stop sign at a road crossing and smiled. There wasn't another car in sight—only several Jersey cows behind a wire fence studying her Bronco as they chewed their cud.

Continuing, she passed a sand and gravel plant, a chemical plant and a poultry farm before she saw the sign that told her the downtown district was to the left. She turned off the main road. Soon she could see hints of civilized life. The occasional pine trees gave way to tall oaks that had at some time in the past been planted in rows along the street; ribbons of clean white sidewalks lay in front of well-kept lawns and modest homes; and then she spotted the first stoplight.

Sabrina noted that the people she saw looked just like people in any small American city. There was a conservatism about their dress and an unhurried attitude in their steps.

After turning right she found herself in what she imagined was the town square. The red traffic light gave her a few moments to glance around. Her impression thus far was that the town was small, sleepy and ridiculously backward; but at the same time there was a charm about it. She looked across the long, manicured park facing the town courthouse. It was white and neat, and like so many Southern towns, the centerpiece of the square. The focal point in the park was a large gazebolike platform—for bands, she imagined.

The streets to the left of the park were lined with old but neatly cared for one- and two-story buildings. The charm about the stores lay in the merchants' attempts to give them a similarity of design by the use of colorful canvas canopies that offered shoppers shade as they walked along the plant-studded sidewalk.

Yet, opposite the casual, old-fashioned shops that covered a three-block span stood an ultramodern steel-and-glass mall. It was handsomely landscaped, yet it seemed to laugh at the street on the other side of the park.

Following the instructions Hester Devereaux had given her when she had telephoned her yesterday, Sabrina drove through Greensboro and followed U.S. 157 north. This, she decided immediately, was apparently the "right side of the tracks" in this town. The homes were old, aristocratic and imposing, set far back on large lots; the automobiles parked in the long driveways were new and shiny. Even the leaves of the oaks that shaded the street seemed to sparkle in the afternoon sunlight that filtered down through them. But, in just a few blocks, she came to countryside again.

Mrs. Devereaux, or Mzzzz. Devereaux as Ralph had suggested, had told her to turn right after she crossed the railroad tracks north of town. She watched, and several minutes later felt the bump of them rock the Bronco. After another short drive, she turned off the road at the sign marked Private Property—No Trespassing.

She steered the car along a wide, curved road bordered by pink crepe myrtles and darkened by aged oaks. An anticipation began to take hold of her, and she straightened up in the car seat. Rays of light filtered through the massive branches overhead that formed an archway like a cathedral, but then the oak canvas suddenly disappeared, and there, on a gently sloping hill, set against the clear cloudless sky, was Belleamie.

In another time, in another generation, Sabrina knew the stately Doric columns of the mansion would have glistened in the bright afternoon sunlight, but as she surveyed the huge house, she could see that time and neglect had grayed the columns and cracked the paint on the elegant edifice.

She parked the Bronco in the weed-filled driveway, got out and just stood there for a moment—a smiling woman with sunshine in her hair. With hands on her hips she gazed up in awe at the massive two-story antebellum house. She was impressed with the haunting beauty of the structure before her; with its tall windows protected by heavy green shutters and the haughty Greek colonnade that rose to support a long balcony on the second floor. The roof supported a large octagonal cupola poised like a crown over the tree-shaded grounds. Her eyes scanned the tall cedars and oaks draped with shining garlands of moss, the overgrown box hedges, the crepe myrtles and the oleanders.

Yet, an uneasy feeling began to seep through her. It was almost as if the air was alive, foreboding, threatening, daring her to proceed. She tried to shake the inexplicable feeling and returned to the veranda and the carved double doors. "So," she murmured, "this is what I'm supposed to perform miracles on."

She started up the steps leading to the double doors, unaware that she was being watched by a lone figure peering at her from behind the heavy draperies of a second-floor window. Sabrina took hold of the dulled brass knocker, tapped and waited. No response. She knocked harder, but still no one answered. *Odd*, she thought; Hester Devereaux was expecting her. She tried the handle, and the door begrudgingly creaked open.

Cautiously she stepped inside and was confronted with a spectacular octagonal entry hall bathed in an eerie yellow-gold light. As she gazed upward, Sabrina saw that the octagonal pattern was repeated on the second floor, and in the attic and the cupola as well. The space had a verticality she usually associated with religious structures, but the atmosphere of the house closed in on her with anything but a peaceful or comforting feeling.

She noted that the moody light was coming from the cupola windows high above. It filtered down to cast brooding shapes on the dark wooden wall panels, panels that were richly carved and fluted. Ahead of her, a great walnut staircase curved gracefully up to the next floor. Above her, dangling from a heavy chain that hung from the top of the cupola, was a tarnished chandelier dripping with dull, yellowed crystals that had obviously been neglected.

"Mrs. Devereaux," she called lightly, taking a nervous step backward. She jumped as the house echoed her words. Directing her next inquiry toward one of the side rooms, she tried again. "Mrs. Devereaux?"

The response came from above. "*Miss* Devereaux." The woman's voice startled Sabrina, and when she turned to see her standing at the top of the walnut staircase, she was even more startled. Hester Devereaux's brown hair lacked luster and was severely pulled back from her pale, unsmiling face. The only thing bright about her was the small white collar on her faded mauve dress.

She slowly descended the staircase, the golden light from the cupola shining over her. Sabrina saw that her stoic face was dominated by unshining, cool blue eyes, eyes that told of loneliness and suffering, of the austerity of an ascetic life devoid of laughter and perhaps even of love. Ralph had said Hester Devereaux was forty, but the woman coming toward her looked older. Perhaps it was the pallor of her complexion, the lack of makeup.

She reached the bottom of the stairs and stood erect, her hands folded in front of her—hands that struck Sabrina as incongruous with the rest of the woman. They were extraordinarily lovely, slender and well manicured.

Recovering from her initial surprise, Sabrina politely explained, "I knocked, but I assumed you didn't hear me."

"I was upstairs, Mrs. Hutchins," came the response in a weak voice, "preparing your bedroom."

She seemed exceedingly formal, but that didn't bother Sabrina. What did was the way the woman was looking at her—as though something was upsetting her. With an uncertain smile, Sabrina asked, "Is anything wrong, Miss Devereaux?"

The woman's lashes flickered nervously. "No...it's just that I don't have many visitors here at Belleamie."

Sabrina followed her into the parlor off the entry hall. The long room was wide with a high ceiling that had mahogany roses in each corner. Sabrina scanned the walls and ceiling and noted that they appeared to be sound structurally, just as the outside of the house did.

The chairs resting on the faded, flowered carpets were covered in red damask, their curved rosewood backs decorated with wreaths of laurel leaves on top. They were in good shape, she decided, and would only need reupholstering. The aged damask drapes over the French windows were formal and looped. They would have to be replaced, but the style should remain the same, she thought decisively.

Over the fireplace of Egyptian marble, hanging majestically, Sabrina saw the portrait of a beautiful young woman in a white dress, a woman who resembled Hester.

The older woman noted Sabrina's interest in the painting. "Lenore Devereaux," she told her and then looked up at the portrait. "My... aunt. She was a true lady, a vision of loveliness and grace when she was young, a bright light whose existence set ablaze an admiration in all who knew her."

Sabrina's eyes went from the painting to Hester and then back to the painting. "There's a striking resemblance between you and your aunt," she commented. "When was the portrait done?"

Hester whispered the answer. "It was painted in 1946." Her tone darkened. "It was to have been a wedding gift to Shelby Mansfield."

Mansfield, Sabrina repeated silently, recalling the name of the man who had had the flat tire—*David Mansfield*. She wondered if there was any connection.

"We'd best get your luggage, Mrs. Hutchins, and then if you like, I'll show you the rest of the house. It's to be made suitable for guests, but I don't want any major changes."

The two women retrieved Sabrina's suitcase and garment bag from the car, and then Sabrina followed Hester upstairs to the second floor.

"I've readied these rooms for you, Mrs. Hutchins. They were my aunt's."

Sabrina stepped inside, not seeing the older woman's smile as she noted the expression of delight on Sabrina's face. The bedroom was a vision of soft green and gold; the furniture, a lustrous mahogany, with shiny brass hardware. Adjacent to the bedroom was a comfortable sitting room. The green-gold brocade of the chairs and love seat matched the drapes around the French doors that led to the second-floor balcony. Sabrina walked through the sitting room and onto the balcony from which she could survey the disarrayed gardens below. They, too, would have to be worked on, she thought. Again she noted the sad condition of the outside of the house: the paint on the columns had cracked terribly, and there was a depressing dullness to the whole place.

In her mind she estimated the minimum cost of the renovation. She had a secret hope that when the woman heard how expensive it would be to restore the house she would cancel the project, and then Sabrina could return to New Orleans and Michael.

But when Sabrina told her, Hester merely commented, "I see." Then, as though oblivious to the run-down appearance of the estate, she said, "This used to serve my aunt as a pleasant, cool retreat on warm evenings."

Sabrina returned to the sitting room. In contrast to the rest of the house, the bedroom and sitting room were quite cheerful. They were spotless, well kept, glistening, and filled her with a sense of well-being.

"Hester," she said enthusiastically, "it's absolutely lovely in here." As an afterthought, she asked, "May I call you Hester?"

As though unused to friendliness, the woman hesitated, but then nodded.

Sabrina glanced around. "It's thoughtful of you to let me use your aunt's rooms while I'm doing the detailed estimate. Mr. Sadler, the man you talked with at Delta Associates, told me it might take two days to complete, and now I agree with him."

"Come," Hester suggested, "I'll show you the other bedrooms, the ones the guests will use." She stopped at the doorway. "Of course, this one will remain untouched."

Sabrina followed her around the second floor where doors led into bedchambers and sitting rooms, but here again existed a heaviness, a somberness caused by years of disuse. As they went from room to room, Sabrina spot-checked the ceilings, walls and floors, looking for cracks or evidence of termite infestation that would necessitate reconstruction or repair. She was pleased that even the ornamental trim in the bedrooms appeared to be in good condition; the less work needed on the house, the faster she would be able to get the job completed and return to New Orleans permanently.

She knocked on the walls, found them solid and decided the original plaster had been applied directly to masonry, not lath. "Repainting will be necessary, Hester. As for the oak floors, although they would be beautiful refinished, I suggest a cleaning and the installation of wall-to-wall carpeting, since it's more comfortable for guests."

The bathrooms were another matter.

"Lenore's father," Hester said, "had them installed in each of the bedrooms in the late twenties. The rooms were even larger before that was done." Her face took on an expression of wistfulness. "Lenore used to speak of her childhood in this house and how it was filled with guests and laughter." The wistfulness turned into listlessness. "Not that it's been like that since I arrived here."

Sabrina tried to dismiss her eerie reaction to the woman's morbid tone. She turned on the water in the old enamel sink and then in the claw-footed tub. The water came out in spurts with an unhealthy water hammer accompanying it. "You're going to have to have the water and drainage systems thoroughly checked. Are you hooked up to the public utility system?"

"Yes, several years ago."

"In the long run, you'd be better off having new bathroom fixtures installed. I'd suggest one of the new plastic tub-shower combinations rather than the porcelain enamel for the bath, but the sinks should be enamel...takes stronger cleaning better." Using her pocket calculator, Sabrina estimated the cost of remodeling the upstairs bathrooms, told Hester what she came up with and jotted the figure down in her notebook.

In the last of the five bedroom suites that guests would use, Sabrina punched figures into her calculator and came up with an approximation of the cost for quality bedding and new draperies. "The existing furniture can be used. It's soiled, but will be all right with cleaning and polishing," she assured Hester.

As they started up the curved stairway leading to the next level, Hester said, "That's the attic, but there's no electricity, only a window at either end. I leave a kerosene lamp just inside the door. You will want to check it, won't you?''

Sabrina opened the door and looked in at the shadowy darkness. An unpleasant, musty odor rushed into her nostrils. "Yes, I need to check for possible leakage from the roof, but let's wait until the morning," she suggested and closed the door. "I'd like to see the cupola."

Hester raised her eyes. "It's up there." Then she looked down over the railing to the entrance hall below. "This central space acts as a thermal chimney for the entire house. It draws the hot air up to the cupola windows—" she glanced upward again "—and out of the house. The summers here can be very warm."

Sabrina followed her up the flight of smaller curved steps that led to the cupola. It was quite wide and its eight sides all had large windows, each with shutters on the outside. Under alternating windows was a cushioned bench. Scanning the roof, she noted that in several places the blue slate was missing, exposing the roofing felt that had been applied over the wood base. Also, the roofing cement was gone over many of the exposed nailheads of the slate.

"The drains will have to be replaced, Hester, but overall it's not in bad shape. The builders of the house must have been craftsmen of the first order. I imagine, though, that some repairs must have been made over the years."

"Some," Hester allowed.

The cool, fresh air that was coming through the open window felt good on Sabrina's face. She exhaled a deep breath and realized she was quite tired. It had been a long day what with dropping Michael off at school, the four-hour drive from New Orleans and then the lengthy tour of much of the house. She checked her watch: six-twenty. Then her attention settled on the grounds around the estate.

"This reminds me of the widow's walks we have in New England," she remarked wistfully. "When their men were out at sea, women would keep watch while they waited for them to return."

Hester eyed her curiously, and as if almost forcing herself, she confided, "My aunt used to come up here in the evening to wait for someone to return. She came up here every night of her life until she could no longer climb the stairs. Then she would send me up to watch...to wait."

Sabrina followed Hester's eyes as they swept to the left. There, off in the distance on another hill, was a large house. The words "neighbor" and "David Mansfield" triggered her next question. "Is that the Mansfield property, Hester?"

The woman's face hardened. "How did you know that?" After Sabrina briefly explained the afternoon's events, Hester said, "Yes. Shelby Mansfield lives there with his son, David, the man you met, and his daughter, Julie."

Venturing on, Sabrina asked, "And Shelby's wife?"

"Dolores." Hester paused, but then said quietly, "She died ten years ago, not long after my Aunt Lenore." With her right hand, she made a slow, sweeping gesture over the terrain below. "At one time my aunt owned as far as the eye can see from up here, but then we had to sell acreage off little by little for maintenance and taxes." Her eyes darted back to the neighboring house. "But no matter who we sold it to, Shelby Mansfield wound up with it." She faced Sabrina, her blue eyes resolute, as she said, "But I'm determined he'll never take possession of her home, of her things. That's what he wants. That's why I've sold more land, in order to pay your firm to refurbish this house. I'll sell more if necessary."

Sabrina suggested, "To bring in income to preserve it."

"To bring in income, yes, but mainly to keep Shelby Mansfield away."

CHAPTER THREE

As Sabrina followed Hester down the stairway, she wondered at Hester's strong reaction to her mention of the Mansfields, and she wondered, too, about Shelby Mansfield. His son, the man she'd met earlier today, had seemed quite nice—charming, even. There was nothing to dislike about him. Just the opposite. But, of course, she really didn't know him at all; yet, the brief time she had spent with him had left an indelible impression on her. She was, in fact, hoping she would see him again.

Hester turned when they reached the attic landing. "Would you like some tea, Mrs. Hutchins?"

"Please, Hester, call me Sabrina," she suggested, adding, "I'd love some."

Again Sabrina thought it was odd that Hester hesitated to be on a first-name basis. That wasn't going to make the job any easier, she decided as they continued down the stairway. And she was hoping Hester hadn't heard the gurgling growl that came from Sabrina's stomach. She was hungry, since she hadn't eaten since breakfast, and that had consisted of only coffee and toast. She'd been too upset about leaving Michael to get anything else down.

The large kitchen was in the back of the house. Looking around with her professional eye, Sabrina immediately decided it would require a massive overhaul. While Hester put on the kettle, Sabrina asked, "Hester, do you plan to serve meals to your guests?"

Her prospective client's expression changed from the usual stoic mask to one of confusion, leaving Sabrina with the impression that perhaps she hadn't fully thought out all the ramifications of opening a guest house. After long moments of awkward silence, she asked, "Were you thinking of a bed-and-breakfast arrangement, maybe?"

"Uh...yes," the older woman replied uncertainly.

Sabrina eyed the old gas stove and the aged refrigerator. "You'll want to plan on modernizing this kitchen. Its size is a plus, though."

Hester reached up into a cupboard for cups and saucers. "That will be expensive, I imagine."

When Sabrina gave her a quick approximation, she knew what the woman's response would be. She was right.

"I see."

Sabrina realized that she'd have to change the impression she'd gotten when Ralph Sadler had first told her of the client who lived alone and wanted to convert her home into a paying business venture. Sabrina had guessed she would be a dynamic and self-assured lady, but Hester Devereaux didn't fit that image at all. She seemed just the opposite—and slightly strange. Sabrina had to wonder if Hester would really make it on her own. That thought stirred up a feeling of sympathy for the woman.

After readying the teapot, Hester turned to Sabrina. "I'm sorry, but I didn't think to ask you if you'd like something to go with your tea. You did have lunch, didn't you?"

"Actually, I didn't," Sabrina confessed, appreciative that Hester had brought it up.

"You must be starved, then. I was planning to heat up a stew I made yesterday. Would you like some...if you don't mind leftovers?"

"Mind?" Sabrina laughed softly. "When you work and have a seven-year-old mouth to feed, you plan on leftovers."

"You have a child?"

Sabrina's face lit up. With unabashed pride she told her, "A boy. His name is Michael."

For moments Hester observed her silently. Then she said, "Mr. Sadler told me you would be here to oversee the work that needed to be done...but I suppose your husband will look after the boy."

"No, I'm divorced, but if you decide to go ahead with the project, I would plan to be here during the week and return to New Orleans each Friday around noon."

Again Hester was silent as she lit the oven and went to the refrigerator to retrieve the stew. When she did sit down at the kitchen table and begin to pour tea for both of them, she glanced at Sabrina. "There's plenty of room here if you want to bring the boy."

Sabrina sat down across from her. "Thank you, Hester, but there's the matter of his schooling, and—" she decided she didn't want to mention the business of joint custody "—and there are other reasons." Accepting the cup offered, she was surprised at Hester's next remark.

"Life is never simple, is it...especially when there are children involved."

Sabrina nodded her head slowly in agreement and then checked her watch, deciding it was still too early to phone Michael. Just the thought of him renewed the anxiety she felt at leaving him. And now that the project seemed to be becoming more definite—She searched quickly for something else to think about. "You're not on the best of terms with the Mansfields, are you, Hester?"

The answer came instantaneously and definitely. "No."

Chancing it, Sabrina asked, "Do you mind if I ask why?"

Hester raised her china teacup and took a sip. Still holding it, her lips parted as though to say something, but she paused, as if censoring her almost-spoken words. With nervous eyes she glanced over at Sabrina and then set her cup down. "Shelby owns a chemical plant just outside of town—Mansfield Chemicals— produces insecticides. One of the plant's by-products is hazardous waste material. It's so dangerous that it has to be transported out of state to be dumped in EPA approved landfills. I don't much like living so near a plant like that."

Sabrina didn't believe matters were that simple as far as Shelby Mansfield was concerned, not after the look she had seen on the woman's face up in the cupola, but she decided the matter was none of her business. She sampled the tea. "This is delicious."

"Herb tea, just a touch of mint in it."

Sabrina smiled inwardly as her mind's eye flashed the image of a tall, dark-haired man with beautiful eyes. Then she asked, "Does his son work at the plant?"

Hester rose and adjusted the temperature knob on the stove. "No. David's never wanted to. I'll give him that...he's worked hard to establish and build his own company. Too hard, maybe. I'd call him a workaholic. Something to do with electronics and computers, that sort of thing—computronics, they call it, I think. He has an office complex in the new mall in town."

Remaining by the stove, she crossed her arms. "The idea of his not wanting to take over the plant has never sat well with Shelby. He always wanted David to take over as president, especially after Shelby's heart problem got worse."

"Oh," Sabrina said softly, thinking that that was probably where David had been rushing to earlier—his own board meeting.

"Stew should be warm enough pretty soon. You can wash up right here at the sink if you'd like."

Sabrina glanced at her watch again, deciding that Ina and Michael should have returned home from Eddie's by now. "Hester, would it be all right if I made a collect call to New Orleans?"

Pot holder in hand, Hester gestured toward the kitchen door. "Go right ahead. There's a phone on the table in the hall, the one next to the parlor."

Ina and Michael had returned, and as Sabrina spoke with her son, her mood became buoyant. She listened with honest interest when Michael explained in detail the problems he and Eddie had had in beginning to assemble the model of the Titan III rocket. He was quick to tell his mom that Ina had already agreed to take him to Eddie's again after dinner tomorrow evening. After briefly talking with Ina, Sabrina hung up, and her mood lost some of its exuberance as she returned to the kitchen.

Hester's stew was delicious: the chunks of beef were tender, and the gravy was rich with subtle seasoning and fresh, tasty vegetables. After being talked into a second helping, Sabrina assisted Hester with the dishes, and again they set to the task of evaluating the costs of the restoration of Belleamie. This time they focused on the rooms downstairs.

They were in the library across from the parlor when the sound of the door knocker reverberated throughout the entry hall. Hester's eyes shot toward the library door, and Sabrina almost felt the wave of apprehension that emanated from Hester as she stood there, immobile.

Again Sabrina wondered how she was ever going to manage opening her home to strangers when she appeared too meek and frightened to even answer the door.

The knocking started again. Sabrina asked, "Aren't you going to see who it is, Hester?"

"Yes—of course—but I wonder who it could be at this hour?"

Sabrina's smile was tentative as she told her, "There's one way to find out."

She watched as Hester cautiously went to the front door and slowly opened it a little. From where she stood at the library doorway Sabrina saw her accept a flower box from a young man and close the door quickly.

Looking up from the box, Hester said, with obvious surprise in her voice, "They're for you."

Surprised herself, Sabrina went over to her and took the box. She read the typed name on the delivery card: Sabrina Hutchins, Belleamie.

For a few seconds the two women just stood there in the entry hall: the younger with a confused smile on her face, the older with a look of only confusion. Then,

Sabrina set the box down on the table near the door and opened it. She removed the small envelope on top of the green florist's paper and uncovered what had to be at least two dozen long-stemmed yellow roses. Her eyes engaged Hester's for a moment and then she removed the card from the little white envelope. It said, "For the greatest lady mechanic in Louisiana. Much thanks. David Mansfield."

"David Mansfield," Sabrina repeated quietly, feeling an unexpected, quickening of her heartbeat.

Suspiciously, Hester said, "I thought you just met David."

Sabrina couldn't understand the woman's troubled expression. "I did...just as I told you earlier. These are his way of thanking me for helping, I suppose. I think it's a very nice gesture on his part." She inhaled the sweet scent of the rose buds. "Hester, could I trouble you for a vase to put these in?"

Following her into the kitchen, Sabrina saw Hester go to an adjoining storage room and return with a crystal vase. As Sabrina filled it with water and began to arrange the roses in it, she suggested, "These would look nice in the parlor."

"I'd rather you took them up to your room."

"Certainly...I only thought that—" She didn't finish, hit with the sudden realization that anything to do with the Mansfields was apparently anathema to Hester.

Feeling tired, Sabrina told her she would like to turn in early, that tomorrow would be a busy day for her if she were to complete the estimate. Hester politely agreed, saying that she was certain an arrangement would be made with Delta Associates and that she hoped the assignment would be to Sabrina's liking.

As she went up the wide walnut staircase, Sabrina began rehearsing what she would say to Todd about taking Michael a few weeks earlier. Even more troublesome to her was the thought that the boy might feel he was being shifted to his father because he was in the way.

After getting ready for bed, Sabrina mulled over the day's occurrences. They had certainly been strange—and so was Hester Devereaux. But she managed a smile as she thought of David Mansfield while brushing her hair. She glanced over at the vase filled with roses and again breathed in the aromatic sweetness that permeated the room. She felt certain they would be in good enough condition to take back to New Orleans Friday. Her smile broadened. *Ina will die!* she mused. A handsome man sending her roses. Sabrina momentarily thought of Ina's bassoonist. Knowing Ina, she guessed the man didn't stand a chance.

She set the brush down on the vanity, switched off the light and slipped under the coverlet on the four-poster. Her thoughts drifted to Michael and the unwelcome knowledge of how quickly he was growing up. She tossed, thinking that perhaps Ralph wouldn't approve the estimate she would be giving him. No, there was little chance of that. She yawned and rolled over onto her stomach. Soon her eyes closed.

She didn't know how long she'd been sleeping—an hour?—two?—but suddenly her eyelids flicked open, and her head shifted on her pillow. She listened. Was someone walking around? There it was again. The steps were soft, but the wooden floors in the old mansion betrayed them. She peered at the travel alarm clock she'd placed on the table next to the bed. It was almost midnight.

Silently Sabrina put on her robe and eased her feet into the low-heeled slippers beside the bed. With cautious steps she went to the closed bedroom door and listened. Again she heard that stealthy treading. Then all was silent. Opening the door a crack, she looked out. Now the sound was coming from downstairs; it was faint but very real.

She opened the door a little more and scanned the walkway around the second floor. All the doors except for the one to Hester's room were open. The moon sent eerie streams of gray-silver light through the bedrooms to meet the soft rays flowing in from the cupola windows high above.

Curious now, she made her way to the top of the staircase and started down—slowly, keeping close to the curved wall. Halfway down she stopped and pressed her body against the wall. Had she imagined it, or had she seen a shadowy figure break the ray of moonlight that fell across the library door?

She took a few more steps and was near the bottom of the staircase. All was quiet. Sabrina felt her throat tighten as she moved toward the library. She whispered, "Hester, is that you?"

A harsh banging sound resounded in the library. Sabrina jumped back as a whoosh of sweet jasmine filled the entry hall.

Her heart racing, she summoned all her courage and slowly entered the library. There was no one there, but ahead of her she saw the sheer panels over one of the French doors being blown by the night wind. Quickly she closed and locked the door. She turned—and let out a startled cry.

Fear, stark and vivid, glittered in her eyes, then subsided when she realized it was Hester. "Ohhh," she moaned, spread fingers on her chest. The low laugh that followed was halfhearted. "I didn't hear you come in."

"I'm sorry if I frightened you."

Sabrina thought how different Hester looked in her long light blue robe. The color lent a softness to her. She also noted that her brown hair, which now hung loosely about her shoulders, seemed to have a natural wave. With only a little care, Sabrina thought, Hester could be an attractive woman.

"I thought I heard someone down here," Sabrina explained, "and then the wind blew open one of the French doors. I locked it."

"That was careless of me. I usually check them all before going to bed." Her brows drew together in a tormented expression. "At times I find it difficult to sleep."

Gently touching the woman's arm, Sabrina said sympathetically, "Sometimes I do, too. Maybe some warm milk would help?"

Hester shook her head.

"We should both try to get some sleep. Perhaps you'll be able to now."

"Yes," she agreed listlessly.

Together the women returned upstairs and went to their rooms. Thankfully, the remainder of the night was uneventful.

In the morning, after a breakfast of sausages, eggs, and homemade buttermilk biscuits, Sabrina concluded that Hester was indeed a good cook. *Bed and breakfast might not be all that bad here,* she decided when the dishes were done. Hester followed Sabrina around outside the house, where she checked the con-

crete foundation and woodwork for cracks and signs of
termite damage. They were there in abundance.

She pointed to one of the larger cracks. "Hester, cement masons will have to be called in to repair the
foundation." Next she pulled off a rotted sliver of
wood from just above the concrete. "A termite treater
can assess the extent of the damage already done."

Back inside the house, they discussed the general
plans for the rooms on the first floor. Although Sabrina's interest was in modern architecture, her studies
and early job experience had given her a deep appre-
ciation for the design and furnishings of Belleamie. The
place was rambling and formal at the same time, filled
with English tables, French mirrors and Italian arches,
all imported from Europe, Hester told her, and
brought up the Mississippi by riverboat from New Orleans when the house had been built in 1852.

The long dining room was particularly compelling.
Sabrina ran her fingers over the carved cherrywood
furniture and examined the heavy brocade draperies.
On one side, set into the wall, were three huge mirrors
framed with gold leaf. Under the middle one sat a remarkable oval side table decorated with inlaid marble
held stoutly by carved birds.

"Their eyes were once jewels," Hester said and then
looked up at the large hand-carved punkah that hung
over the long dining room table. "In the old days, a
servant created a breeze by pulling the fan back and
forth with this cord. It would make the room quite
comfortable."

"It certainly is lovely, and the workmanship is extraordinary." She studied the room again. "I think
only the carpet and the wallpaper will have to be

changed. The draperies haven't faded; they should hold up under careful dry cleaning.''

The large solarium was next. "Hester, all this wicker furniture should be replaced, but when this room is remodeled, it will be a lovely room for your guests to lounge in.''

Sabrina wasn't looking forward to it, but the attic was their next stop. She could still remember that unpleasant musty smell that had attacked her nostrils when she had opened the door the previous day. Hester brought up a second kerosene lamp, and they entered the long room that ran the full length of the house. As Hester had said, there were only two windows, one at either end, and even now, at midday, the huge area had a dismal solemnity about it.

Sabrina raised her lamp and looked up at the massive pegged attic beams, checking for signs of water infiltration; then she lowered it and spot-checked various parts of the wooden floor, noting that there was no apparent leakage.

While opening the second window, Hester told her, "I really have forgotten just what is stored up here.''

They then began to take stock of the contents in the attic, examining the rows of covered furniture and the items that had been placed on rows of wide shelves long ago. Together they uncovered bolts of damask, silks and velvets, along with numerous objets d'art. ''Lenore's grandfather had an interest in collecting porcelain,'' Hester told Sabrina.

"Looks like French Empire period.'' Sabrina uncovered several occasional chairs and ran her fingertips over the back of one, tracing the initial N that was surrounded by a laurel wreath. ''Napoleon,'' she said quietly and moved toward one of the shelves. ''He must have had eclectic taste. The china and silver is from the Georgian period, I think." She indicated a cluster of furniture they had previously uncovered: "Those, I know, are Chippendale and Hepplewhite pieces."

She reached up on the shelf and removed an object from its large velvet protective covering and held it closer to the kerosene lamp. "Hester," she murmured as her eyes inspected a beautifully crafted swan centerpiece. Although it lacked luster, having gathered so much dust, she believed that the four curvaceous swans and the tulip-motif candle holders were solid silver, and she could tell that the bowl in the center was hand-carved crystal. "This is exquisite!"

Looking at it, Hester told her, "I don't remember ever seeing that before." She slowly glanced around the attic. "But then, it's been so long since I've had any reason to come up here. Lenore never did."

Sabrina replaced the centerpiece in the velvet bag. "Once this attic is wired for electricity, we'll do a complete inventory and take photos. You should have it for insurance purposes. And I suggest a lock for the attic door. If we're going to have workmen all over the place, we don't want any of them wandering around in here."

Then she recalled Hester's saying she would sell more acreage if necessary to pay for the work to be done on the estate. "Hester, you have some extremely valuable pieces up here. Some could be used in the house . . . in fact, the two Aubusson rugs would be ideal for the parlor, but all of these things—" she made a sweeping gesture with her hand "—would bring in good money from antique shops in New Orleans, if you wanted to part with them."

Hester's eyes roamed over the long, wide room. "I'd never thought of selling any of Lenore's things, but I guess they'd just stay piled up here forever, gathering more dust. It might be wise to sell them. Then Shelby Mansfield wouldn't be able to snatch up any more of her land."

Sabrina observed one of the first smiles she'd seen on the woman's face. Diffidently Hester asked, "Would you possibly be able to handle that for me . . . with the antique dealers, I mean?"

"Certainly. I know several of them in the French Quarter on a professional basis."

As they continued what took on the feel of a treasure hunt, Sabrina found herself becoming more enthusiastic about her present assignment. The house needed a lot of work, but now it seemed as though there was much to contribute toward its rehabilitation. In spite of the semidarkness and the looming shadows created by the light from the kerosene lamps, she now felt nothing resembling the foreboding about the house that she'd experienced when she'd first arrived. It seemed that as her interest in restoring the house to its former splendor increased, so did the odd feeling she experienced of being welcomed by the place.

A little after three o'clock in the afternoon, Sabrina phoned Ralph Sadler at Delta. He was surprised by her enthusiasm as she peeled off the estimated costs of materials, labor and her own time, assuring him that Hester Devereaux knew the figures were just that—estimates.

"Good, Sabrina. Get her to sign the estimate papers and we'll get a contract written up."

"Will do, and I'll check to see if there are any local firms available to contract for the jobs."

"Right on top of it, just like always, aren't you?"

She smiled snidely into the receiver. "Ralph," she reminded him, "don't forget to include my travel expenses, including mileage to and from New Orleans each weekend, in the contract."

"Like I said . . . right on top of everything."

Sabrina had only taken a few steps away from the phone in the hall when it rang. She knew Hester was busy in the kitchen, so she answered it.

"Hello?"

"Sabrina? It's David . . . David Mansfield."

His mellow voice sang with eagerness, and an unexpected ripple of delight rushed through her. "Yes, David," she said, trying not to let her feelings show in her tone.

"How's my favorite car mechanic?"

Her friendly chuckle was followed by, "Fine, and how is my favorite computronics expert?"

"Uh-oh, you've been checking up on me."

She rested her shoulder against the door frame behind her. "All good mechanics do." She remembered the flowers. "Of course, not all mechanics receive beautiful roses for the loan of an air pump."

"You liked them," he ventured.

"Love them . . . it was thoughtful of you. I plan to take them back to New Orleans tomorrow."

"You're not staying on at Belleamie?"

"I'll be back on Monday. Miss Devereaux has hired us on."

Sabrina could hear the smile in his voice when he commented, "I was hoping she would."

His words brought a relaxed smile to her lips, and she began to toy with the phone cord. Mentally she could see his clear blue eyes and his disarming smile.

Playfully she asked, "Afraid you're going to have more trouble with your car?"

"Uh-uh...afraid you'd run away before I could take you to dinner."

She straightened up.

"You do eat dinner, don't you?" he asked following the momentary silence.

"Why, uh, yes."

"Then how about tonight? Is it a date?"

A date! The word reverberated in Sabrina's brain. It had been a decade since she'd had a date. Certainly none of the business dinners she'd had with clients in the two years since her divorce could have qualified as that. And she'd been married to Todd for eight long years! What could she wear? She hadn't brought anything appropriate with her from home. She certainly hadn't planned on dating! She wanted to say yes, but something—fear, perhaps?—made her hesitate.

"Sabrina? Still there?" he asked.

"Yes, David," she answered softly, her fingers pulling a little harder on the phone cord, "I'm here. It's just that I don't know about tonight...there's so much I have to do before I leave tomorrow."

Quickly he reminded her, "You have to eat. I'll get you back early. I could pick you up around six-thirty...better make that seven." Before she could object further, he lowered his voice. "I'd really like to see you again...please? A quick dinner for old times' sake?"

Again she found herself smiling at him. "Old times' sake? You're crazy, David Mansfield."

"Better humor me, then, Sabrina Hutchins. I'll pick you up at seven. Bye now."

The click on the line resounded in her ear before she could say another word. She peered into the receiver. "Well, Sabrina, looks like you've got a date tonight," she said aloud. She was thoughtful as she set the phone down onto its cradle. Turning, she saw Hester standing nearby.

On her face was an expression Sabrina couldn't define, but when the woman spoke, her voice was a warning.

"Be wary, Sabrina, for your own sake. The Mansfields are not like ordinary people. They're takers, the lot of them. Shelby ruined Lenore's life, and given the chance, David will—" She stopped midsentence and looked at Sabrina with eyes full of regret. Then she rushed back toward the kitchen.

"Hester!" Sabrina called, but the woman didn't stop.

CHAPTER FOUR

SABRINA PICKED UP HER WATCH from the vanity in her bedroom. A quarter to seven. Nervously, she adjusted the clasp at her wrist and took a last look in the mirror. The navy linen suit would have to do, but she wished she had brought along at least one of the more feminine dresses that hung in her closet back in New Orleans. Recognizing her increased anxiety, she tried to remember if dating had always caused her this much turmoil. No, she couldn't recall having felt so tense when she'd first dated Todd.

She never wore a lot of makeup, but she had applied what she did use with special care this evening. And she had given her auburn hair extra strokes with the brush. After checking her watch again, she admonished herself for having spent so much time getting ready. She grabbed her handbag and left the room.

Her steps were hurried as she descended the walnut staircase, but halfway down she stopped. Hester was at the front door letting David in. Sabrina saw him smile at her and offer a greeting, but Hester hardly even looked up at him. She quickly disappeared into the parlor, leaving him standing there alone in the entryway.

But when he saw Sabrina, David took long strides toward the staircase. He moved with such grace, she thought, and he looked incredibly attractive in his dark brown suit. When he reached the bottom of the steps, he gazed up at her. He just stood there, looking tall and broad-shouldered. The light from the chandelier behind him framed his masculine form with a soft yellow glow.

The anxiety she had felt earlier quickly disappeared and a feeling of combined contentment and exhilaration took its place. His smile widened, indicating that he approved of what he saw, and Sabrina felt her own lips part slightly in reciprocation as she started down the stairs once more. As she did, their eyes held each other's, and she experienced a sensual awareness that she hadn't felt for some time. The feeling was welcomed, yet it caused her momentary confusion. When she reached the bottom of the staircase, she took the hand he extended and felt his fingers tighten around hers.

His hand was warm and comfortable, as she knew it would be, and the pressure it exerted was just right. For what seemed like long moments to her, they stood there as David continued to hold her hand and search her face, as though trying to read her thoughts.

Finally she eased her hand from his and said softly, "You're right on time."

His smile lingered. "I'm not only thoughtful, I'm punctual as well."

Lightly she asked, "A man with no faults?"

He took her arm and they started toward the front door. "Not on the first date," he told her.

There was that word again, bringing with it a return of her earlier nervousness.

As they passed the parlor, Sabrina glanced into it quickly to see if Hester was in sight. She wasn't. Aware that the woman disapproved of David, Sabrina quickly reminded herself that her approval wasn't necessary. She was, after all, a client, not a close friend. Yet, she had to admit, it *was* Hester's home that was being invaded by a Mansfield because of her.

As David's Jaguar pulled away from Belleamie, Sabrina asked him about his firm.

"It's called Mantek, and it's a personal computer research and development corporation. Unfortunately, it seems to be running my life right now." He glanced over at her. "I don't have much time to enjoy myself like this." He directed his eyes back to the road ahead. "See, I'm thanking you for something again."

Studying him, Sabrina admired his attractive profile and his dark shock of wavy hair. She wondered if it were as soft as it looked. "You do that very well."

He looked her way again. "Do what?"

"Make me feel obligated when you're thanking me. The roses are still lovely...and now dinner."

An easy laugh exposed his bright teeth. "I'm glad you're enjoying the flowers. It's the truth though," he insisted. "I do need to thank you again. I can't remember a dinner out that wasn't tied to business somehow."

Sabrina doubted that. David was too handsome a man not to have an active social life, but that just made his invitation all the more flattering.

Not long after, he turned the car onto a paved circular driveway in front of a modern colonial building. Sabrina noted the sign: Greensboro Country Club.

An attendant parked the car, and David led her into the opulent lobby, quiet except for soft strains of pleasant music coming from hidden speakers. A svelte hostess welcomed David and introduced herself to Sabrina, then escorted them into a lounge. It was long and wide, plushly carpeted, more like a vast living room than a bar, with its scattered modules of soft sofas and easy chairs arranged around marble-topped cocktail tables.

Sabrina eased herself onto a sofa, and as David did the same he asked, "What's your pleasure, Sabrina Hutchins?"

"Bourbon and water in a tall glass," she responded and listened to his deep voice with pleasure as he ordered the same for himself. Her eyes followed his easy movement as he leaned back next to her, the soft indirect lighting doing wonderful things to his tanned face.

"Well," he asked, his blue eyes gleaming with interest, "how do you like Belleamie... and Hester Devereaux?"

Thoughtfully she told him, "I've certainly got my work cut out for me. To put it mildly, there's a lot to be done before she can open the house to paying guests."

"Is that what she's up to? Think she'll actually do it?"

The way he asked the question caused Sabrina to look deeply into his eyes. In them she saw only innocent inquisitiveness... or was it concern? She wasn't sure, but she did remind herself that as a client, Hester had every right to confidentiality. Suddenly she wondered how far David would go with his questions regarding Hester. Was he asking as an interested neighbor or as one of the Mansfields Hester seemed to despise so much?

"I'm almost certain she plans to."

Their waiter brought their drinks, and as Sabrina lifted her glass, David touched the edge of his to hers. "Here's to old times' sake," he said with humor in his eyes.

They both sipped, but before David could continue his questions about Hester, Sabrina asked, "What exactly is it you're researching and developing right now at Mantek?"

He had been intent on studying her face: her shining hazel eyes, slender nose and lovely symmetric lips. Distracted by her inquiry, he answered, "Right now we're involved in a networking project, trying to solve the need for better computer-to-computer communications—" his face moved closer to hers "—trying to come up with a standardization of hardware for data compatibility between firms."

Her unblinking eyes locked with his and she managed to whisper, "Yes . . . that would be nice."

Just then a slender female hand settled on David's shoulder. Sabrina glanced up. Looking down at her was a raven-haired beauty, a year or so younger than Sabrina herself, and she was dressed exquisitely. A blond-haired man, somewhat older, was standing next to her.

"So, David," the woman said in a crisp, affectionate voice, "this is why you couldn't have dinner with us." Her eyes swept back to Sabrina. "I don't blame you."

David smiled at her and leaned back against the sofa. "Sabrina, my sister, Julie, and her fiancé, Brian Forestall." To them he said, "I'd like you both to meet the best car mechanic north of New Orleans, Sabrina Hutchins."

They exchanged pleasantries, and then Julie asked, "Sabrina, are you really a mechanic?"

Sabrina sent David a wry smile and replied, "Not exactly. I'm employed by an architectural-interior design firm in New Orleans. We're taking on a project at

Although she was curious to learn more about Shelby Mansfield, Sabrina decided this was not the right time to ask David about his father. She settled back against the sofa. "The short version goes like this. Born in Connecticut, architectural degree from Wesleyan University, married, one son, divorced."

David rested his arm on the back of the sofa; his fingertips inched toward her shoulder. "How old is your son?"

A soft and loving expression lit up Sabrina's face. "Michael is seven. He's a wonderful boy... bright, friendly, healthy. I don't know what I'd do without him."

His fingertip touched her shoulder and moved in a slow, circling motion. "Does he know he's got a great mother?"

As gentle as the movement was, Sabrina could feel the pressure of his finger underneath her jacket and blouse. She looked at him in a sideways glance. "I think he does.

In a quiet voice, David asked, "How could what's-his-name have let you get away?"

"Todd," she told him, enjoying his attentions. "It was by mutual agreement."

"This Todd... he ought to have his head examined. What's his problem?"

Sabrina didn't want to talk about Todd, not now. "Another time, maybe. Let's eat. I'm starving."

They finished their drinks, and he led her into one of the elegant dining rooms. Over dinner their conversation was general, mostly about their work. Sabrina found herself thoroughly enjoying David's company and liking the way he thought about things. She was particularly impressed by the sense of fairness that ruled his judgments. She was already too aware that she liked the way he looked and the way she felt when he was close.

After dinner he drove her back to Belleamie, and once the car was parked in front of the house, he rolled down the windows and switched off the ignition. For a while they sat silently as jasmine-laden air permeated the car. Through the windshield, off to the side, she could see the top of the white gazebo in the garden. Night birds called to others in the stillness.

Sabrina had never quite accepted the idea of "chemistry." When she'd married Todd, she had loved him, of course, but she had never experienced that "magic" that other women talked about. In later years she began to wonder if she hadn't married young in order to create a family to replace the one she had lost: first her mother dying and then the cooling of her relationship with her father. She had never understood why that had happened; she and her father should have been drawn closer to each other after her mother's death, but instead, he had withdrawn from her.

And then Todd. At first she had been happy with him, and ecstatic with Michael. Again she'd had a family. But magic? No.

As she sat with David now, she thought more about the idea of "chemistry." What else could be making her feel the way she did at this moment? She wondered if he felt the same excitement she did. On one hand she wanted to think so, yet on another she didn't. She had her hands full at the moment: she was a mother, a homemaker, and a career woman working hard to earn her postgraduate degree. *Chemistry or not,* she warned herself, *the only way I could fit in a romance now would be to give up sleeping!*

David adjusted his body and leaned back against the door on his side of the car, the better to see her. "You do wonderful things for the moonlight, Sabrina."

The sound of his voice was doing wonderful things to her, she decided as she looked back at him—too wonderful. "It's late, David, and you've more than made up for the use of my air pump. The compliments are appreciated, too, but I'd better go in now."

Slowly he ran the back of his fingers up and down her arm. "Have to?" he asked.

She nodded.

"All right," he said, disappointment obvious in his tone, "but tell me you really don't want to...if it's the truth."

All of Sabrina's hesitation and confusion welded together in a sudden upsurge of yearning. The semi-darkness only seemed to sharpen David's attractive features. She was forced to recognize that he had a powerful aura that sent her pulses hammering and awakened feelings and emotions in her that she believed were best left to rest. There was so much of him that was unknown, that intrigued, that promised to be fascinating. She was pulled to him.

As the tumble of confused thoughts and desires assailed her, she heard him repeat, "The truth, Sabrina."

She attempted a steady tone. "I do have to go now...but...no," she admitted, "I really don't want to."

"Good," he said as he gently brushed the back of his fingers across the silky strands of hair below her ear. "That you don't want to, I mean."

She felt his fingers touch her shoulder, and then the full warmth of his palm settled on it. The pressure of his hand increased, making her uncomfortable with eagerness to enjoy his touch. As his hand moved slowly from her shoulder down over her back, she whispered, "David—" But her next words were left unspoken.

His warm breath tingled on her earlobe and sent a shiver rippling down her neck and across her breast. Another surge of pleasure charged through her body when his knee touched her thigh, but those intimate sensations paled when she felt the slow movement of his lips on her ear.

Drawing in a much-needed breath, Sabrina let the air ease from between parted lips and tried again. "David—"

He kissed her cheek once and then again. "Just a few more minutes," he pleaded.

After another soft kiss he slowly sat upright. His eyes appeared darker; they glowed with an inner fire that spoke of need, of desire, of passion.

Only chemistry, Sabrina told herself. *Nothing more.*

For excruciating moments their eyes remained fixed on each other's, and then she saw his tense features relax. Taking hold of her hand, he stroked it. "Now I'm the one who thinks you should go in."

With a gentleness in her voice, she said, "I enjoyed dinner. Thank you."

"My pleasure," he assured her as he quickly got out of the car to open the door on her side.

He walked her to the door and as she was about to enter the house, David thrust his hands into the side pockets of his trousers. The motion caused his unbuttoned jacket to open further, and Sabrina couldn't help but notice the attractive curves underneath his tapered dress shirt. His slender waist made his broad shoulders appear all the more powerful, and the yellow overhead light gave his tanned face a golden hue.

She wavered a moment, but then, as though ordering herself to do so, she said, "Good night, David." However, the battle within her was not at all decided, and she added, "Perhaps we can have dinner again...my treat next time."

"Perhaps," he said, his eyes set intensely on her features. "Sleep well."

After Sabrina closed the door behind her, David stood in silence and then took slow steps across the veranda to one of the columns and leaned against it. His eyes drifted back to the closed door, then out over the gardens.

Chiding himself, he smiled wryly. Here he was, he thought, a man of thirty-four, acting like a teenager. What was this woman doing to him? Why was he letting her get to him—or did he really have any control over that? He'd just have to control the situation, he told himself. He always needed to feel in control. But this Sabrina, maybe she really was as different from other women as she seemed. Maybe she would be able to understand the commitment he'd made to make a success of the firm he had created all on his own. Maybe she would understand that it was sometimes necessary to break dinner engagements, that business necessitated many trips out of town, and that he'd have to— Hell, why would she be any different?

He looked up at the stars and breathed in the sweet smell of night-blooming jasmine, but even that strong fragrance couldn't erase the way Sabrina had smelled when he'd been so close to her in the car. Had it been the perfume she was wearing? Her hair? Just her? He inhaled a deep breath of the night air, trying to ignore the reaction he felt building in his loins. Why was it that the women he thought he'd been serious about in the past now only seemed like nameless faces?

He shrugged out of his jacket and hurried down the steps, smiling at his own reflections, thinking, *You're losing it, David! One dinner with the lady, and you're sounding as though you're about to jump in feet first. Knock it off!*

After opening the car door, he looked up, hoping to see a light appear at one of the windows. He wondered which room was hers, wondered what she was doing this minute. In spite of himself, he hoped she was thinking of him—aching a little, just as he was.

CHAPTER FIVE

AS SABRINA SIPPED Hester's strong black coffee at the breakfast table, she tried to quell the pleasant memories of last night's date with David. She had enjoyed the entire evening. Their last minutes together still teased her thoughts, demanding to be acknowledged, to be recalled as one would an unexpected pleasurable gift. But, if his attentions were a gift, it was one she wasn't certain she could accept.

It was with a certain pride that she reminded herself she had pulled back the reins of the emotions that had almost gotten out of hand, and she complimented herself in facing up to the fact that she had responsibilities, Michael being the primary one. Thus far she was performing the balancing act of a single parent perfectly.

"More coffee?" Hester asked, and Sabrina looked over to find the woman examining her distracted features.

"Uh...no, thank you," she said quietly and glanced down at the empty cup she'd been holding in her hands. She set it down. "I'll be leaving early today, Hester, but before I go we should decide how much work you want done on the grounds."

Hester rose and began to collect their breakfast dishes. "There's a man in town—Mr. Fundy—who has a landscaping business. I thought I'd see if he could take on the job." At the sink, without looking back at Sabrina, she said, "He's quite capable. He created the botanical gardens in Greensboro and also did the landscaping at the new mall."

Sabrina thought she detected a new tone in Hester's voice as she spoke of Mr. Fundy. She carried their coffee cups to the sink and asked, "Would you like me to contact him and discuss what he would charge?"

The older woman glanced over at her briefly, and Sabrina thought she saw a warm glimmer in her blue eyes, a brief shining light that was accompanied by a sudden flush of color on her pale cheeks. "No...no," she said falteringly. "I know Mr. Fundy's work, and he's a fair man."

"Fine, then. I'll concentrate on the house. This weekend I'll work up a master schedule for your approval, and when I return on Monday I'll contact firms in town to get bids on the work that needs to be done."

Hester turned off the water faucet and reached for the hand towel draped on a hook by the sink. "Sabrina," she asked hesitantly, "do you think we could really get a good price for some of the things stored in the attic?"

"I'm positive. Some of the pieces are quite unique, especially that swan centerpiece. Are you certain you want to part with it?"

"Oh yes. Besides, it's so humid in these parts, I'd wind up spending most of my time keeping the silver pieces polished."

"Well then, I'll contact Rudy this weekend. He's one of the antique dealers in the French Quarter."

"Good...and of course you'll receive a commission on anything he does sell."

Sabrina thought she detected a wavering moment just before Hester had responded, giving her the impression that she would be parting with her aunt's things with great difficulty. Obviously, the financial strain of keeping up the house and grounds around Belleamie had worn heavily on the woman. In one sense Sabrina admired Hester for dealing with it all, but at the same time she began to feel a concern for her new client's burden.

"We'll discuss commission later, Hester," she told her and went to the workroom to recheck her figures, but she couldn't quite get Hester Devereaux off her mind.

Sabrina had always felt it necessary to get to know her clients and their life-styles; many of the decisions she would make regarding a project were based upon that knowledge. Getting to know Hester, however, would not be easy. The woman had encased herself in a protective shell—for whatever reasons—that seemed formidable. Yet her vulnerability was painfully obvious as was the air of mystery that surrounded her and the house itself. Sabrina couldn't help but wonder why a woman would live such an isolated existence, alone in such an imposing home. It seemed to her that Hester thought of Belleamie as a fortified castle, its drawbridge to be lowered only at great risk to herself, and that saddened Sabrina. She wondered if the woman would really be able to cope with strangers crossing the figurative moat.

A little before noon, Sabrina's Bronco headed south toward New Orleans. The sky was clear and blue, and as she drove, listening to soothing music from the car radio, she caught a whiff of the still-sweet aroma of David's yellow roses. Before leaving the house, she had carefully wrapped their stems in paper towelling soaked with water and had covered that with plastic wrap.

He was indeed a thoughtful man, she mused as she went onto the double-lane highway. And attractive. Her smile broadened, and with a touch of self-satisfaction she concluded that her first foray onto the singles scene had not been all that bad.

The singles scene. She hadn't given it much thought before last night. Immediately after her divorce, dating had been the last thing on her mind. Not that she had the time to even entertain the thought of it now. Time—there never seemed to be enough of it.

She drove through Winnfield and checked the car clock, telling herself she would be back at the apartment long before Ina would have to leave for symphony rehearsal. Then her thoughts eased back to the new Sabrina Hutchins—the one who was dating again. What had Ina said to her a few evenings ago? What if she were to remarry and find herself wealthy? She recalled having said something about it snowing in New Orleans in July.

She thought about marriage. She had been happy those first years with Todd, had luxuriated in the feeling of being so totally feminine. He had introduced her to the sensual intimacies possible between a woman and a man, and with him she had learned of her ability to excite by touch and tender caresses. Doing so had given her a sense of power as well as pleasure. But then Todd had changed, and the pleasure had diminished and finally ebbed away. She had to wonder if she would ever feel that way again.

Still, if pleasure had diminished, the memory of having been part of a family unit had lasted, and lingered with her even now. Remarriage? How it would change her life! Would she be wiser this time? Would she marry for the right reasons: to bring a good role model into Michael's life, a dependable husband into her own, and a feeling of security to both their lives?

A strong, sweet smell tickled her nose, and again she glanced down at the roses, but she decided to roll down the window to let the air clear her thoughts.

"What about Michael?" she asked herself in a half murmur. She wondered how he would feel if another man did enter her life. Would he understand her loving someone other than his father? He seemed to have finally adjusted to the fact that Todd had married again, although he rarely spoke about Ann, Todd's wife. Of course, he didn't know her that well. Apparently, she had lunch with Michael and Todd only occasionally.

"Marriage...remarriage!" she blurted out. "You're being a complete idiot, Sabrina. You've got your hands full now. Once burned and all that. Right? Right."

Over the drone of the Bronco's tires on the highway, she thought of her son's excitement at going to Eddie's house to help construct his rocket model, and she decided she would stop in Alexandria to hunt down a rocket model that Michael would have for his own.

She finally arrived home, and wasn't certain which one of the two people who greeted her was more excited: Michael, because of the rocket model, or Ina, because of the roses.

"Boy, Mom, this'll be neat! It's even bigger than Eddie's."

Sabrina watched as he placed the box on the dinette table and tore into it. Was she imagining it, or had he grown in the two days she'd been gone? All she really wanted to do was hold him in her arms for a while, but she knew in seconds he'd be wriggling to get at the model.

With playful curiosity Ina asked, "Want me to put the *roses* in water?"

Sabrina noted the raised eyebrows and the probing query. "Would you?" she asked and teasingly added, "Pretty, aren't they?"

"We'll talk later," Ina informed her and went into the kitchen with the flowers.

The thud coming from the area of the dinette table got Sabrina's attention. "Tiger, let me put a cloth on the table, and then I'll help you with that."

Michael's face took on an insulted look. "I can do it . . . it's easy."

Sabrina felt a lurch in the pit of her stomach as she removed a tablecloth from the sideboard. "Well, if you want some help, I'm right here." She saw the tube of glue Michael shook out of the box. "How about I get you a clean rag? If that's space-age glue, your fingers will be sent up with the first launch."

With Michael settled at the table, Sabrina went into the kitchen where Ina was waiting impatiently. She was standing by the sink, her arms crossed, fingers tapping.

"Long-stemmed yellow roses?" she asked. "And you've only been gone two days. They must have some welcome wagon in Greensboro."

Sabrina smiled as she reached into the fridge and took out a diet cola. "Want one?"

"Uh-uh. I want to hear about the yellow roses."

Sabrina slid down onto the bench in the corner breakfast nook and popped open the cola. After a swallow she looked over at Ina. "All right, Miss Nosy, they were a thank-you gesture from someone I helped on the highway.''

Ina stepped closer. ''You picked up a hitchhiker?''

''Of course not. A car in front of me had a flat, and I helped the driver with my electric air pump.''

''Driver...as in man?''

Sabrina nodded and took another sip of cola, enjoying every second of Ina's inquisitiveness. She watched with amusement as her friend flicked her long dark braid over her shoulder and sat down on the adjacent bench in front of the small table.

''And?''

''And what?''

Ina sent her a restless sigh and crossed her arms on the table. ''You're not going to make this easy, are you? Is he single? Good-looking? Employed? Are you going to see him again?''

Sabrina's grin flashed mischievously. ''Yes, very, yes and maybe. His name is David Mansfield,'' she said softly, and just saying his name caused her hazel eyes to brighten.

Ina noted it and after a thoughtful moment asked, ''Young, old?''

''Just right.''

''So what's wrong with him?''

''Nothing!''

Raising her hand, Ina asked, ''What's this 'maybe' business? Of course you're going to see him again. Does he live near Greensboro?''

''Right next door to Hester Devereaux's place.''

''You'll be neighbors?''

''Uh-huh, and he owns his own computronics firm.''

With one hand flattened against her breast, Ina murmured, "Be still my heart." She jumped up. "I think I will have a cold cola."

Sabrina's laughter followed her to the refrigerator. "Calm down, girl. We haven't quite set a date yet."

Ina turned. Her eyes were sharp and assessing. "But you've already been thinking about it, haven't you?"

Her friend's question struck recall with Sabrina as she remembered her earlier thoughts as she was driving back to New Orleans. But she certainly hadn't been thinking about David Mansfield then—just men in general. A little too forcefully she said, "Ina, no one in her right mind thinks of marrying a man after having only one dinner date with him."

"You had dinner with him, too?" Ina squealed.

Sabrina nodded again and commented casually, "Yes, that meal we all have between lunch and breakfast."

Ina slipped back down onto the bench, her smile eager. "It's serious, isn't it?"

Sabrina just stared at her. "Ina, you've been playing too many high notes on that cello of yours. I met David the day before yesterday, and I am not husband hunting. I don't have time for it."

Looking down at the cola can she was tapping with a fingernail, Ina declared, "Pity." She glanced up. "You could make time."

Amusement flashed in Sabrina's eyes. "Are you unhappy with our living arrangements here? Have I done something to make you want to get rid of me?"

Ina smiled and inclined her head. "Course not, but I'm dying to attend a wedding."

"Make it your own," Sabrina suggested.

"No such luck...not in the foreseeable future, anyway."

"Luck," Sabrina told her decisively, "has nothing to do with love, nor are women who fall in love always lucky." She rose and placed her half-finished cola on the counter top, next to the vase of roses.

Following her with her eyes, Ina said, "I guess that's why the expression is 'fall in love' and not 'climb in love.' No guarantees of avoiding the dangers."

Sabrina turned back against the counter and crossed her arms. "Are we talking about Eugene again?"

"Who else? Tonight I'm going to make my big move."

"You have a plan, I take it."

"Kind of. I'm torn between telling him, 'I love you and I want to bear your children, but I don't want you to feel trapped,' and walking into rehearsal tonight stark naked. I think that would get his attention."

Sabrina laughed. "For a sweet farm girl from Mississippi, you have some pretty brazen ideas. Why don't you just ask him out for coffee after rehearsal? And I'd skip the lifelong plans when you ask him."

"You have a point there."

Sabrina glanced up at the clock on the wall, then took one of the roses that was still in good shape from the vase. "Tell you what, why don't you wear this tonight to rehearsal. Maybe Eugene will notice it." She handed the bloom to Ina and opened the door to the freezer compartment.

Ina knew what Sabrina was looking for. "There's some beef stroganoff for you and Michael, microwave ready. There's also a surprise in the white box in the fridge."

"Bless you," Sabrina said gratefully. She was about to open the refrigerator door when she heard Michael's call.

"Mom! This stuff's all icky!"

"Space-age glue," Sabrina said, moaning, and went into the living room.

LATER THAT EVENING Michael sat down once again with his rocket. This time he let his mother help. As they worked together they talked about various things—school, fireflies and then his friend Eddie. Sabrina listened as he became more animated when he spoke of Eddie's father and his job as a firefighter. When she asked if Michael had told them about his father's work as a marine biologist, the boy said he hadn't, claiming that he didn't know much about it, really.

It was then that she casually asked Michael what he thought about Ann, Todd's wife.

"She's all right, I guess," he said noncommittally.

"Well, I think Ann is very nice, and she loves your father very much."

"I s'pose." He checked what his mother was doing. "No, that goes here—" he showed her "—like this."

Sabrina watched as his small fingers deftly attached a piece of wood to the model. The tip of his tongue stuck out between his lips in concentration. "You know, Tiger, when your father and I decided it would be better to live apart, I was the lucky one." Michael didn't respond, so she gently brushed his blond hair with her fingers. "Because I had you with me. But your father didn't have anyone, and now he has. That should make you happy for him."

The seven-year-old tilted his troubled expression up toward his mother. "I would have been happier if he hadn't left."

Sabrina died a little inside. "I know," she said softly, understanding his feeling of loss, "but sometimes it's for the best when two people who can't get along divorce. That may be hard for you to understand right now, but someday you will."

For moments he was silent. Then, without looking up, he asked, "You won't ever divorce me, will you, Mom?"

Fighting against the tears in her eyes, Sabrina leaned down and kissed her son's head. "Never, never, and you remember that, Tiger, all right?"

"Right," he said more cheerfully and smiled at her. "Can we have an éclair now?"

"And some milk."

In the privacy of the kitchen, Sabrina wiped at her eyelids. This was the first time her son had ever voiced the insecurity he felt, and it pained her deeply that he was still so deeply affected by the divorce. Lord knows, she had tried to make that marriage work, but she had always been the one to give in to Todd—almost always. And the man's constant naggings and arguing! Living like that had eventually worn her down, and she knew instinctively it had been harmful for Michael. Now, although she had been doing her best to raise him alone, she began to think her best was not good enough. Would it ever be?

After she had gotten Michael snugly into bed, Sabrina put some clothes into the washing machine and checked her watch. She had planned to phone her father. It wasn't too late, but she was tired, and conversations with him were rarely pleasant. He just didn't want to understand why she and Michael wouldn't come "home" to live in the house she was raised in. She couldn't tell him that his house was no longer "home" for her. And now she had to explain why she wouldn't be bringing his grandson up for the promised visit. She decided to write instead.

With that chore taken care of and the clothes placed in the dryer, Sabrina sat down to hit her Structural Theory book, telling herself that things were back to normal.

Normality also reigned Saturday morning. Sabrina was the first to rise, and after readying the coffee she began to set up a master schedule for the work to be done on Belleamie. First to be considered was the extensive rewiring that would have to be done, and following that, the installation of a modern plumbing system throughout the large house. Then she set down tentative dates for work to start on the exterior and the interior of the various rooms, all the while making copious notes for future reference.

After breakfast, while Michael continued to work on his rocket model, Sabrina sat down in one of the easy chairs in the living room and started in again on the master schedule. But Ina's curiosity regarding David Mansfield wasn't yet satisfied.

Speaking softly, she remarked, "Sabrina, you suddenly seem to be quite enthusiastic about the assignment that had you so ticked off a few days ago." The vase of yellow roses, now fully opened, sat on a small table by the window. Ina leaned down to sniff them. "Anything to do with your new friend?"

"David?" Ina's smirk said yes, David. "You're stretching the facts, Ina," she told her, but in her heart Sabrina knew that he had a great deal, indeed, to do with her newly found optimism about working in Greensboro. She'd already admitted to herself that their dinner together had brought with it the realization that what she was missing in her life right now was love.

But Hester, too, had played a big part in making Sabrina enthusiastic about restoring the estate. And she had been strangely affected by Belleamie itself, both the spirit and the shell of the place. It was like a unique piece of silver that had been sorely neglected, whose tarnished surface obscured its original craftsmanship and beauty. And she felt a stirring of pride at the thought that she would be the one to coordinate the step-by-step renewal of the house to its former elegance.

Wanting to change the topic with Ina, though, Sabrina asked, "Did Eugene notice the rose you wore to rehearsal last evening?"

"I thought you'd never ask. I owe you, Sabrina. Not only did he notice, he also asked me out to dinner tomorrow night. From now on, I adore yellow roses."

"Good. I take it you didn't mention your plans for the future."

Ina chuckled. "No...I'm saving that suggestion until at least the third date."

She saw Sabrina check her watch. "Lunch with Todd and Michael again?"

"Uh-huh," Sabrina replied and ached a little inside when she glanced over to the dinette area where Michael was totally preoccupied with his model. Knowing he couldn't hear them, she said quietly, "I've got to see what Todd thinks about Michael going to live with him a few weeks early."

Ina sat down in the chair next to Sabrina's. "Have you told Michael about it?"

Sabrina shook her head. "Not yet. I want to see what Todd's reaction will be. I'm afraid that if he says no—for whatever reason—Michael might take it as a rejection. I'll try to talk to him alone before we sit down, and if he agrees, I'll bring it up at lunch, tell Michael the reason for it and treat it as a family conference. That's the way I used to try to handle situations. I wanted Michael to know that his feelings were important to both Todd and me."

"And if your ex has another excuse ready?"

"That possibility has already crossed my mind. I guess I'd have to have Michael transferred for the rest of the term, or else look for a new job."

Sabrina glanced toward the dining room again and studied Michael's blond hair, deciding that he'd soon need a haircut. And it seemed to her that his hair was beginning to darken somewhat. He was kneeling on a chair and had his elbows propped on the table top as he worked. She realized she'd have to buy him larger jeans. *He's growing so fast,* she thought.

"Tiger," she called to him, "time to get washed up. We'll be leaving soon."

"Okay, Mom . . . just a minute more." He raised his hand to brush back at the strands of hair that fell over his forehead.

When Michael did leave the room, Ina said, "It's good that you and Todd get along better than most divorced couples."

After a throaty chuckle, Sabrina admitted, "Better than the last few years we were together." She closed the folder she held on her lap and placed it on top of others that lay on the table beside her. She looked directly at Ina. "I don't ever again want to have to try to convince a five-year-old that he's not responsible for his father's moving out. That's one reason why I believe these lunches with his father are so important for Michael. He's got to know that his father still loves him."

"Good luck," Ina said. She then went into her bedroom and closed the door. Minutes later the pleasing sound of a cello echoed throughout the apartment.

As Sabrina gathered up her folders, she tried to prepare herself for the inevitable, but try as she did, she knew she hated the idea of actually asking Todd to take her son away from her.

CHAPTER SIX

SABRINA SET THE FORK DOWN on her plate and chewed the last of her broiled pompano, trying to appear nonchalant, all the while thinking it true that the best-laid schemes often got screwed up. Hers certainly had.

Each time she'd had lunch with Todd and Michael, there had always been an opportunity to speak with her ex-husband before they actually sat down to eat. Today had been the first exception. So much for her plans to talk to Todd privately about his turn at custody.

She glanced down at her son as he worked away at his cheeseburger and then over at Todd, who sat steely-eyed, watching her.

Conversation during lunch had centered on Michael: his school work and friends, his recent dental checkup and his current interest in becoming an astronaut. Todd's attempt to interest the boy in sediments and living creatures recently scraped from the floor of the Gulf of Mexico had been less than successful. Michael's interest lay in the opposite direction—up.

After their waiter placed caramel custards in front of them, Todd set his green-gray eyes on Sabrina again. "Something's on your mind. I can tell. It's my new mustache, isn't it? You don't like it."

With little interest she examined it again, taking time to put off the inevitable. "It's nice . . . suits you."

His eyes narrowed somewhat. "You never did lie very well. No matter. Ann likes it. What about you, Michael?"

His son raised his hand, and Todd leaned down to let him feel it. "It's neat...just like Eddie's dad's, but his is thicker."

"Mine will get thicker, too. Just takes a little time, but in a few weeks we'll be able to watch it grow together, right?"

Sabrina's spoon of custard was halfway to her mouth when she realized that Todd wasn't going to back out this time. The spoon went back down and into the custard cup. "That's what I want to talk to you two about," she said quickly. "I've got a problem." She smiled at Michael. "I need you two guys to help me out."

Through a spoonful of custard Michael chimed in with, "Sure."

Todd asked, "What *kind* of a problem?"

"A work problem. I've been assigned to a project in Greensboro, upstate. It'll take months, and I'll have to spend weekdays there. What I need to know is how you both feel about—" the words came hard "—well, about Michael's spending his six months with you, Todd, starting tomorrow."

During the silence that followed, Sabrina took a spoonful of custard and forced it down. To herself she screamed at Todd, *You're supposed to sound delighted, you jerk!* When she looked up she saw Michael watching his father's face as though waiting for a cue from him. Todd was staring at her. Finally, his mouth twisted into a sort of smile, and he glanced over at his son.

"Fine with me. How about you, Michael?"

Michael's clear hazel eyes blinked a few times, and then he turned to his mother. "Will that solve your problem, Mom?"

His question stabbed at Sabrina's heart. It would solve one problem, but she didn't want him to know that it would create a greater one for her—missing him. Yet, she knew he would normally be going to live with his father in just a few weeks anyway. She felt a momentary panic as she heard herself say, "It would right now, but I'd see you each and every weekend. I'll be back here in New Orleans every Friday."

Michael's eyes shifted to his father and then back to Sabrina. "Okay."

Todd reached over and tousled his son's hair. He spoke with affection. "It'll be just like old times. We'll be buddies again."

That pleased Sabrina. She could always tell when Todd was being sincere and when he wasn't. "Todd, I'm sorry to spring this on you so suddenly. What about Ann? I hope this won't change any of her plans."

With obvious satisfaction in his voice, he informed her, "In my house, I wear the pants. Ann understands that."

So much for warm feelings, Sabrina said to herself.

"Well," Todd told Michael, "if we're going skating, we'd better finish up and be on our way." To Sabrina he said, "If you want, why don't you pack Michael's things, and we'll pick them up later on."

Her response came in a rush. "No!" Calming her voice, she added, "Tomorrow will be fine. In the afternoon, all right?"

Later, Sabrina watched as Todd's car left the restaurant parking lot. She knew he'd be bringing Michael back to the apartment before dinner time, but as she stood there by her Bronco, she felt that she was rehearsing the scene that would take place tomorrow afternoon. It wasn't a pleasant feeling.

Instead of going straight home, Sabrina dropped off the estimate forms Hester had signed at Delta Associates and then drove to the French Quarter to tell Rudy about the items Hester had decided to sell. Antiques did very well with the tourist trade, and Rudy said he'd be happy to take the pieces on consignment. With a strangely heavy heart, she drove back to her apartment.

ON SUNDAY MORNING Eddie rode his bike over, and he and Michael talked of the day when they would make their first stellar flight. As the boys devoured the lunch Sabrina prepared for them, she filled her eyes with images of her son. Meanwhile, hands on the clock moved closer and closer to the time when Todd would arrive to take him away.

The time came and went—too quickly. When he was gone, Sabrina started to take out the leftover meat loaf she was going to reheat for dinner, but she took one look at it, put it back and closed the refrigerator door. Eating was the last thing she felt like doing. And she couldn't even share her thoughts with Ina, who was preparing for a big date with Eugene.

Work—there was always work to be done. She got out the master schedule for the Devereaux project and sat down at the dinette table, but found herself making mistake after mistake and finally tossed the pencil down. She glanced at her watch. "Ina! It's almost five."

"I'm hurrying!"

Sabrina erased the wrong month she had jotted down and disciplined her thoughts.

"How do I look?"

Turning in her chair, Sabrina perused the younger woman and nodded. "Not bad . . . not bad at all. That dress looks great on you." She gazed admiringly at the lovely material and the ruffles at the neckline and wrists.

Ina's fingers went to her ears. "Are these red hoops too much?"

"No, I don't think so. Where's Eugene taking you?"

"Tokyo Sam's. He's got a thing for sushi."

"Sushi? I didn't know you liked raw fish."

"I didn't know either. Actually, I've never had it, but I'd eat live fish if I had to. Eugene's so shy I don't think he'd ever get the courage to ask me out again if I don't grab at this chance."

"Got your key?" Sabrina asked, returning her attention to the schedule.

Automatically checking her purse, Ina said, "Maybe I'll be able to change his eating habits after he realizes what a wonderful person I am."

Sabrina turned and rested her arm on the back of the chair. "I wouldn't plan on changing him if I were you. I didn't have any luck changing Todd. And I don't think Ann's doing much better than I did. You'd better make sure you'll be content with the Eugene of *now*. What you see is probably what you'll have to put up with fifty years down the line."

"Got the key," she reported just as the door buzzer sounded. "Lord willing I'll be late getting home," she said hopefully and went to let her date in.

Ina introduced Sabrina to Eugene, and she decided that although the young man would not turn every woman's head—he was tall and lanky, with undisciplined shocks of rust-colored hair looming over horn-rims—he did have a nice, friendly handshake, and his Arkansas accent was pleasant on the ears.

"Ina told me how much you've been helping her, Mrs. Hutchins. We're beholden to you."

We, Sabrina repeated mentally, thinking that perhaps Eugene had noticed Ina more than she knew.

"Ina's the one who's been helping me."

Sabrina noted the sparkle in her friend's eyes when she said, "Eugene's going to be playing the solo bassoon part in *Peter and the Wolf* when we play it at the children's concert next month." She looked at Eugene. "He's a wonderful musician."

The young man's momentary embarrassment gave way to a disarming grin that, Sabrina thought, immediately put him in the category of a man any woman would be proud to take home to mother.

Now he concentrated totally on Ina, and Sabrina felt that the two of them didn't even know she existed. His voice took on an affection that was warm and honest. "You're the wonderful musician, Ina. God! the way you play the swan selection from *Carnival of the Animals*... well, it just about melts my heart." Sabrina decided then and there that if any two people were well matched, it had to be these two.

After they had departed for Tokyo Sam's, she realized that her happiness for Ina was only magnifying her own depressed mood. Her attention settled on the yellow roses David had sent her in Greensboro; they, too, looked tired, like her. Her fingers touched one fully opened bloom; the petals shattered under her touch and fell to the floor. She knew the night would be a long one.

ON MONDAY MORNING, when Sabrina parked her Bronco in the driveway at Belleamie, she saw Hester in the garden, speaking with a man. He was wearing jeans and a plaid shirt with the sleeves rolled up. As she neared them, she noted Hester's animated gestures as she pointed toward the gazebo at the far end of the gardens, but the man seemed more interested in looking at Hester.

Something else caught Sabrina's attention. The color of the dress Hester wore was a pretty shade of peach. It wasn't particularly stylish, and on any other woman the color might be considered ordinary, but on Hester, it was a nice change. For the better, Sabrina thought, and its cut showed that the woman had an attractive figure.

"Morning," Sabrina offered, noting the healthy flush on her client's face.

"Oh, Sabrina…I didn't even hear you drive up. Mr. Fundy and I were just discussing what to do with the gardens." She seemed a little flustered. "Uh…Mr. Fundy, I'd like you to meet Mrs. Sabrina Hutchins, the architect I told you about. Sabrina, Mr. Fundy."

Sabrina extended her hand to him and liked the firmness of his handshake. Although his hair had already gone gray, it had a silvery luster that was quite attractive. His metal-rimmed eyeglasses covered dark brown eyes that were youthful in their brightness; his smile was catching, and she found herself returning it broadly.

"Real happy to meet you, Mrs. Hutchins. I was just telling Hester we oughta clear away some of those boxwoods in front of the gazebo, maybe put in some young magnolia trees—" his hands went out to demonstrate "—in a semicircle on either side. After we spruce the gazebo up, it'll be a pretty thing, could be a nice focal point from the main walkway. Shame to hide it like it is now.''

Sabrina watched as he took several quick steps one way and then the other as he outlined what his workmen would do to the various areas on the Belleamie grounds. His movements were energetic and she imagined that it was his work outdoors that had kept him trim and tanned.

As the three of them walked through the gardens Sabrina wondered at the almost secret smile that brought an amazing softness to Hester's features as she listened to Mr. Fundy talk. She found herself wondering just how long Hester had known the man and in what capacity.

''Hester,'' he suggested, touching her shoulder lightly, ''I have some real healthy camellias that would do well on the east side of the house. As I remember, you always took a liking to the pink ones.''

The older woman cast an almost embarrassed glance at Sabrina, then she looked back at Mr. Fundy. ''That'd be nice, but you just do what you think would be best.'' Her eyes lowered momentarily, then rose to his smiling face. ''I do trust your judgment, Mr. Fundy.''

''And I've always respected yours, haven't I, Hester?''

Sabrina couldn't help but notice that when Mr. Fundy was about to leave, he held Hester's hand between his for an inordinate length of time, causing the woman's cheeks to flush once again. It was then that Sabrina politely excused herself, telling Hester she was going to take her luggage from the car to the house.

When she did return downstairs, Hester was in the room across from the solarium, the room that Sabrina had suggested could be used as a temporary workroom and office while the house was being refurbished. Hester was just setting down a tray that held a pot of coffee and two mugs. Sabrina was more than curious about her relationship with the man she had just met but decided that Hester would bring up that subject if she wanted to.

As they sipped coffee, Sabrina showed Hester the master schedule she'd prepared and gave her suggestions for color schemes for the upstairs guest bedrooms. And she told her that Rudy would take whatever antiques Hester wanted to sell on consignment.

Although Hester seemed deeply appreciative of all of Sabrina's efforts, she had the feeling it was all overwhelming the woman—that too much was happening too soon. Her eyes were confused and her hands trembled slightly. In an effort to reassure her, Sabrina reminded her that she would be right there to take charge of matters.

After Sabrina contacted selected firms in town by phone to set up estimate appointments, Hester served lunch for the two of them in the solarium. The large room was a horticulturist's nightmare in its present state of disarray, but the sunlight streaming through the large jalousie windows that had been cranked open insisted on a cheerfulness.

"Delicious sandwich," Sabrina praised as she reached for her glass of iced tea. "I love chicken and cheese."

"Lenore did, too." Hester then quickly asked, "How is your son? I imagine it was difficult to leave him."

Sabrina forced a smile. "Yes. He's fine, growing so fast. Michael will be staying with his father in New Orleans while I'm here."

"I'm glad. I was concerned about that. Children need their parents. They need to know they're loved, especially when they're young."

Lowering her eyes, Sabrina felt a flash of longing for her son, but a sudden idea brought a smile to her lips. "I've some pictures of Michael in my handbag. I'll get them if you like."

When she returned and handed the snapshots to Hester, the woman was generous in her comments.

"What an attractive boy! You can see the intelligence in his eyes." Glancing at Sabrina, she added, "He takes after you."

Sabrina's smile broadened, and in her heart she felt a mixture of love and pride as she herself gazed at one of the pictures. "Michael has his father's hair, but he does have my eyes."

When Hester returned the snapshots, Sabrina asked, "Were you born here in Louisiana, Hester?" Sabrina really wanted to ask about her parents, but she wasn't sure that a personal inquiry would be well received.

"No...in Mississippi," Hester replied as she lowered her eyes, but almost immediately they rose again. In a voice that seemed to require much effort she told Sabrina, "My parents still live there." She rose slowly from the white wicker chair, folded one hand over the other and looked around the solarium. "When I was eighteen, Lenore told my father, her brother, that she would be leaving Belleamie to me when she died."

Sabrina saw the turmoil in Hester's face, as though she were going through some inner battle, wanting to speak but uncertain whether she should or not.

As though speaking to herself, Hester continued. "That summer I came here to her home. You see—" she faced Sabrina "—I had never met Lenore Devereaux, and I found it strange that she would want me to have her home, her things. It seemed so personal, so generous of her."

She took slow steps toward a hanging basket that held a wilted achimenes plant and touched its one small lavender flower. "In spite of her illness, Lenore was yet beautiful when I arrived. There was another woman living here who was taking care of her, but she was getting on and decided this house was too much for her. When she left I stayed on."

Turning again, her small voice took on a loving tone, and a peacefulness came upon her features. "I grew to love Lenore Devereaux with all my heart, and I never left, never wanted to."

As Hester spoke, Sabrina realized the strength of the bond that had existed between the two women, that, to some degree, still existed. She thought of the portrait of Lenore that hung in the parlor, and remembered how striking the resemblance was between Hester and her aunt.

"More tea, Sabrina?"

"Please." She really didn't want it, but her client seemed to be at ease unburdening herself at the moment, and Sabrina wanted her to talk, not merely out of curiosity now, but out of genuine concern. Risking it, she asked, "Were the Mansfields more friendly then?"

Hester remained silent as she poured the tea and added ice cubes. She served Sabrina, then sat back in the chair opposite her. A stony expression formed on her face; her voice hardened. "Not one of them ever set foot in this house, nor did they even inquire after Lenore.''

Sabrina recalled that Lenore and David's father had once been engaged. ''She never saw Shelby again?''

''Never.'' Her eyes turned misty as though her memories were painful. ''Lenore often spoke to me about him...always as she had remembered him...young, dashing.'' She leaned forward to punctuate her words. ''It was well that she never did see him again. Shelby changed. He became hard, ruthless in business, cold. His wife's life was not an easy one. She died the same year that Lenore did...ten years ago.'' Tightly grasping the fingers of one hand, her voice turned bitter. ''In those days I sometimes saw Shelby Mansfield in town. He looked much like David does today, but when he saw me, he would look away, making me feel like a leper.''

Sabrina raised one hand slightly in an uncertain gesture. ''Hester, why have you continued to live in this huge house all alone? It can't have been pleasant for you.''

Hester stared down at her palm, which was moist with perspiration. As she wiped it with a napkin, a wry smile accompanied the coldness in her voice. ''To give Shelby's conscience no rest, to be a constant reminder of his sins against Lenore.'' Her stark blue eyes found Sabrina's. ''He jilted her to marry David's mother because she was able to bring more land and money to the Mansfield family. Just like his daughter, today, he had political ambitions then. He used his wife, unsuccessfully, just as he had used Lenore and destroyed a gentle soul.''

Softly Sabrina suggested, ''Aren't you letting him destroy another...yours?''

Hester's mouth spread into a thin-lipped smile. "The man is a devil. He already has." Then, as if realizing she had said too much, she got up and took the tray to the kitchen, leaving behind a perplexed Sabrina.

On the one hand she found herself becoming more sympathetic with the woman's determination to do the best she could to maintain the large mansion, but on the other, she wondered at her client's fanatical dedication to the memory of Lenore Devereaux. And she was uncomfortable with the hatred that Hester had for Shelby Mansfield, although she had begun to understand the woman's reasons. But why would she also blame David and Julie? It was puzzling, to say the least.

Early that afternoon, the maintenance electrician from town arrived, and Sabrina escorted him throughout the house, discussing his recommendations. The attic had never been wired for electricity, and the job was just as extensive as she had known it would be.

Since the original blueprints of the house were not available, Sabrina had prepared a general blueprint for him. His work would have to be done first, as his men would have to rip through walls and floors in order to replace the old wiring system. She made suggestions that would ensure the least amount of damage.

After Sabrina saw him to the door, the phone in the entry hall rang. "Hello," she said in a businesslike tone.

"Sabrina, this is Julie . . . Julie Mansfield."

"Hello!" she responded, surprised by the call. Quickly she dismissed the idea that Julie would be phoning Hester.

"How is the project going?" Julie asked.

Sabrina breathed a smile into the receiver. "Well, it's not exactly going yet. We're still in the planning stages."

Julie's low chuckle resounded in Sabrina's ear. "You've taken on quite a challenge there at Belleamie. Everyone in town's talking about it . . . and you." Her tone changed, became somewhat more formal. "Sabrina, the reason I'm calling is to invite you to dinner tomorrow evening. My father is anxious to meet you."

That took a moment to digest, but she was intrigued at the idea of meeting Shelby Mansfield.

Before she could answer, though, Julie said, "David will be here, of course. I have the feeling he's just as anxious to see you again. You will come, won't you . . . cocktails around six?"

"Yes, Julie, I certainly will, and thank you for the invitation."

"See you tomorrow, then, Sabrina. Bye."

"Bye," Sabrina repeated, and slowly replaced the receiver. For moments she remained by the table, her index finger thoughtfully brushing over her chin. *Why should Shelby Mansfield be anxious to meet me?* she wondered silently. *And why didn't David phone to invite me? What will Hester think of my socializing with the Mansfields?*

She found out the answer to the latter question after dinner that evening as she helped Hester with the dishes in the kitchen.

"Julie Mansfield phoned earlier," Sabrina mentioned casually as she finished drying a plate and set it in the cabinet near the sink.

The lid of a pot that Hester was washing hit the edge of the sink. Her eyes shot over to Sabrina. "To speak to you," she deduced with no doubt or warmth in her tone.

"Yes . . . I've been invited for dinner tomorrow."

"You're going?" Hester began washing the pot lid again—quite energetically. "I said I would. I didn't want to appear rude."

"Humph! You don't know what rudeness is until you become well acquainted with the Mansfields." She glanced up. "Do be careful, Sabrina. There are givers and takers in this life. The Mansfields are takers."

Sabrina was about to try to say something to mollify the woman, but Hester suddenly drew in a deep, painful breath. Without drying her hands she reached up into the cabinet and removed a small plastic container. She quickly swallowed one of the pills inside.

After half filling a glass with water, Sabrina handed it to her, asking, "Are you all right?"

Nodding, Hester took the glass and drank from it. Then she steadied herself by placing a hand on the sink. Looking over at Sabrina, she saw the question in her eyes, then saw her glance at the pill container. She explained, "I have a slight heart problem . . . nothing serious."

From the ashen color of the woman's face and what Sabrina had just witnessed, she wasn't so sure the problem was slight, especially if a mere phone call from one of the Mansfields was enough to bring on the sudden attack. If it was— Well, how could she have even suspected that Hester would react so severely to her having accepted the dinner invitation?

The following evening, a little before six o'clock, Hester knocked on Sabrina's bedroom door, and informed her in a cool voice that David was downstairs, waiting for her.

Sabrina inhaled a surprised breath and opened the door. "David?" One look at Hester's taut lips and she said apologetically, "I didn't expect him to come get me. It's just next door. I don't know why he—"

"I'll tell him you'll be right down," Hester interrupted and walked away.

Annoyed that David's arrival had disturbed the woman, Sabrina fumbled with the clasp of the single strand of pearls until it clicked into place. Rushing, she took a final glance in the mirror, adjusted the belt of her lilac print blouson dress, grabbed her evening bag and went downstairs.

Hester was nowhere in sight, and Sabrina found David standing in the middle of the parlor, staring at the painting of Lenore Devereaux. He turned when Sabrina entered.

"Hello again," he greeted, and his appealing smile almost melted away her annoyance. She felt a sudden warm glow flow through her; it was calming and oddly energizing at the same time. Despite her earlier conversation with Hester regarding the Mansfields, there remained no shadows across her own heart as far as this Mansfield was concerned. How could there be when David looked at her the way he was doing now? He was assessing her intensely, and the slight tilt of his lips indicated obvious approval.

Slowing her steps toward him, she returned his greeting. "Yes...hello again," she half murmured and saw his eyes return to the portrait hanging above the fireplace. Hers followed. "Lovely, wasn't she?"

"Quite," he agreed and moved closer to the painting. He cocked his head a little to the side as he continued to study the face. "It could have been Hester when she first arrived at Belleamie." He turned. "She was a friendly young lady then, so full of fun and high-spirited. I was only twelve at the time, but I thought she was the prettiest girl I'd ever seen." He looked at the painting again. "Just as lovely as Lenore Devereaux."

Friendly? High-spirited? That didn't sound like the Hester she knew, Sabrina thought, and she wondered what had happened to change her so. *Lenore's influence, no doubt,* she decided and thought it a shame.

"Julie and I used to come over here and peek into the house. Sometimes we'd hide and watch Hester and her aunt walk in the gardens." He shook his head slowly. "That Lenore was one odd lady. Never left the place, and after a while no one ever saw her. And we saw very little of Hester."

"Who wanted to?" Hester's wisp of a voice startled both Sabrina and David. They turned to see her standing by the door to the parlor.

David sounded pleasant and sincere when he countered, "I, for one, would have wanted to, Hester."

Sabrina saw Hester's eyes pierce the distance between herself and David, and in that instant she became aware of the similarity of coloration in the blue eyes that stared back to meet each other's. She also had the fleeting impression that perhaps Hester thought she was looking at young Shelby Mansfield and not his son.

His voice interrupted her silent musings. "You're welcome to come with us if you'd like, Hester."

She grimaced. "Would I really be welcomed in the Mansfield home? I hardly think so."

Sabrina was genuinely surprised at the sudden strength in Hester's voice, and when she glanced over at David, she thought she saw only solicitude in his eyes. Forcing an easy smile, she suggested, "Well, I'm ready, David. Shall we go?"

He took her arm gently and they started toward the front door, but, as though on impulse, David turned and looked back at Hester. A brief silence hung over the entry hall, and then he said, "Hester, it's good to see you again."

No response was offered.

As drab and dreary as Belleamie was in its present state of disrepair, the adjoining Mansfield estate was brilliant in every aspect. Its gardens were exquisitely manicured, and the exterior of the Georgian-Colonial house with its antique brick and Ionic columns was spotless. The lights from within glowed through the tall windows that faced the hedge-lined oval driveway in front of it.

Inside, the difference between the two old homes was even more remarkable. There was color everywhere. The expensive-looking furniture was decidedly modern, although there were touches that spoke of tradition, such as the parquet de Versailles floors and the walls of green-and-white veined Italian marble in the salon.

Brian Forestall, Julie's fiancé, had greeted them at the door, and this time Sabrina took a more careful look at him. As she had casually noted when she first met him at the country club, Brian was an attractive man. He was trim with dark blond hair not unlike Todd's and his eyes were an engaging blue-green color. He was not as tall as David, and was a few years older, she imagined. Yet, there was something about him that was oddly unsettling. Perhaps he was just a little too smooth, too ready with the compliments he'd bestowed on her when he had greeted them.

David led Sabrina into the large, formal living room where Julie waited for them. Her face shone with self-confidence, and Sabrina had to admit that David's sister was certainly a striking woman.

Suddenly the biggest dog Sabrina had ever seen came bounding across the long room toward them. Her relief was instant when it headed straight for David and nuzzled his hand.

"Tara," he told her. "She's an Irish Wolfhound."

Looking at the silver-haired hound, Sabrina noted that she was also quite pregnant.

"Cora," Julie said to the maid who was placing another tray of hors d'oeuvres on an ornately carved buffet, "would you please take Tara with you when you leave? My father will be in shortly."

"I'll take her, Cora," David offered, and the dog happily followed him out of the room.

Julie went to Sabrina, extending her hand, "It's good to see you again, Sabrina. I was just telling Brian—"

All heads turned as the double doors leading to another room opened. In came Shelby Mansfield—in a wheelchair. Guiding it was a man in a white jacket.

The first thing she noticed about David's father were the Mansfield blue eyes; his challenged even as they attracted.

Shelby waved the man in the white jacket away and pressed a button on his chair, which sent him wheeling toward Sabrina. "David's damn dog's been in here again. I can smell her," he mumbled and then set his eyes on the auburn-haired woman standing before him. "So," he said in a clipped voice that was a little unsettling, "you're the lady come from New Orleans to fix up Belleamie."

Despite his short-cropped gray hair and the deep lines around the corners of his mouth and at the outer edges of his eyes, Sabrina could see a distinct resemblance between him and David. Before she could respond, Julie said, a tad anxiously, "Father, this is Sabrina Hutchins. Sabrina, my father, Shelby Mansfield."

Approaching him, Sabrina extended her hand. At first he only gaped at her—somewhat rudely, Sabrina thought—but after several awkward moments he raised his hands and took hold of hers. His grasp was firm.

In a tone that was more pleasant, he said, "I was told you were lovely, but—" He stopped abruptly, let go of her hand and pushed the button on the side of his chair.

It glided backward and stopped. His eyes roamed over Sabrina and she desperately wished that someone would say something. She waited in vain, and concluded that in the Mansfield house, everyone waited for direction from Shelby.

"Good evening, Shelby." It was David's voice, and she turned, relieved that he was back. "I see you've already met Hester's guest."

"Guest?" Shelby repeated. "I thought she worked for Hester." Before anyone could soften his words, he barked at his son. "Don't just stand there. Get her a drink!" He lowered his voice again. "What can we offer you, Miss Hutchins?"

"Mrs. Hutchins," she corrected.

"I was told you were divorced," Shelby continued. "Why are you advertising to the world that you're not available? You are, aren't you?"

Her eyes sought David's. He smiled and asked, "Bourbon and water?" remembering what she had ordered at the country club.

Still taken aback by Shelby's abruptness, she quietly replied, "Please."

"A tall glass," he added.

Brian asked, "Why on earth is Hester spending all that money on that wreck of a house? Seems to me it's a little oversized for one woman."

Sabrina didn't at all care for his tone. "I'm sure Hester has her own reasons, personal reasons."

"Living alone like she does isn't healthy," Julie commented. "We all believe Hester would be better off if she sold the property and moved back to Mississippi. I believe she still has family there, doesn't she, Father?"

His shoulders stiffened slightly, and his features took on a troubled expression. "Everyone has family somewhere."

"Do you think Hester should sell and move away, Mr. Mansfield?" Sabrina asked.

He leaned forward in his wheelchair, resting his arms on it and clasping his hands. "Hester's a grown woman. She can do whatever she likes, but as my daughter says, it's not normal for her to live the way she does. She's well on the way to becoming the recluse that Lenore was."

David handed Sabrina a small linen napkin and her drink. The glow in his eyes told her he was right there if needed. "Thank you," she whispered, and he returned to the highly polished mahogany bar in the corner of the room.

Brian followed him, saying, "Word was that half the time Lenore Devereaux didn't even know what day it was. Hester wasn't only her niece...she was her keeper.''

Sabrina noted the pained expression on Shelby's face, and it deepened when Julie said, ''Sometimes Hester strikes me as being a little strange herself. I've tried being civil to her the few times I see her in town, but she just ignores me. Perhaps it's something that runs in the Devereaux line.''

Sabrina's tone was relatively polite in spite of the anger she felt as she listened to the remarks about Hester. ''I find it difficult to believe we're talking about the same woman. Having known Hester Devereaux for only a short while, I've found her to be a very sensitive and friendly woman.''

Shelby guided his wheelchair a little in Sabrina's direction and stopped, never taking his eyes from hers. ''It appears our Hester has one good friend in this town...finally.''

David asked, ''A drink, Shelby?''

Still studying Sabrina, he answered, ''Julie will get it for me.''

The cut the man gave his own son was not lost on Sabrina, and she suffered inside for David.

''Naturally,'' he said, the hurt in his tone clear to Sabrina, but apparently not to the others. As his sister approached him at the bar, David asked, ''How's the campaign coming along?'' Then he handed her the drink he had already fixed for his father.

''I've been getting a lot of flack from the opposition ever since the EPA chemists determined that the chemical endrin was responsible for that fish kill north of here,'' she replied, handing the drink to her father and then going back to the bar to sit down.

''Endrin?'' Sabrina asked.

Brian explained, "It's a chlorinated hydrocarbon insecticide, one of the chemicals produced by our plant."

"By *my* plant," Shelby corrected.

Brian smiled an unctuous smile. "*Your* plant, Shelby." He faced Sabrina again. "Several of the plants in this area produce endrin. Any one of them could be responsible for the illegal dumping in that lake. In fact, every plant in Louisiana should be under suspicion."

The attorney in Julie came forth with, "There's a big difference between allegations and proof. Right now it's convenient for my opponent to lay anything that's wrong in Greensboro at my doorstep, but Brian assures me that Mansfield Chemicals is operating under the guidelines set down by the Clean Water Act and all state, county and town agencies."

David gestured toward a high-back chair near him for Sabrina to sit on. Then he set his eyes on Brian. "And since you're functioning as acting president at the plant, you should know."

Shelby's glare toward David was obvious to all. "He wouldn't be acting president if you'd take over at the plant as I've always wanted you to. No," he spit out, "the Mansfields now have to go to outsiders. You'd think a son would—"

A sudden coughing spell cut him off. Julie rose immediately and rushed over to him. As he took several deep breaths, she rubbed his shoulders gently. "Let's not drag all that up again, Father. You know that David is much happier with his own company."

"Computronics," Shelby snarled and handed her his empty glass. "Best mind to your own business, daughter. Even the possibility of my plant dumping hazardous waste illegally could ruin your chances of becoming mayor. Scandal has destroyed many a promising political career, including my own when I was your age. This town thrives on scandal…gives the nobodies a false sense of being superior.''

Brian leaned back against the fireplace and rested an elbow on the low mantel. ''I can't understand why Julie is looking for all the problems that will come with her campaigning. If there are any skeletons in the Mansfield closet, you can be sure they'll be dragged out before the election in the spring.''

Sabrina took note of the glower that etched Shelby's face as he turned his attention to Brian; it was such that she decided Brian's acting presidency at Shelby's plant was probably a matter of necessity rather than trust and goodwill.

Shelby confirmed her suspicion. ''Don't talk Mansfield skeletons, boy. Your daddy was the noisiest town drunk Greensboro ever had or ever will have.''

Brian seemed unfazed by the remark. ''All I'm saying, Shelby, is that I think being an attorney *and* a mother should be enough excitement for any woman.''

Julie handed her father the refill, looked over at Sabrina and smiled. ''Brian means after we're married.''

After taking a long swallow, Shelby leaned back in his wheelchair. He sounded tired now. ''You're old-fashioned, Brian. If Julie wants to be mayor, you should be there right behind her, cheering her on, not trying to pull her back at every opportunity.'' His eyes drifted to Sabrina. ''What do you think, Mrs. Hutchins? Do women belong in politics?''

She replied pleasantly, ''A woman should be wherever she wants to be if she's capable and has the guts to buck traditional systems.''

Shelby's smile grew as he slowly nodded. He aimed his eyes sharply up to David's. "You listening, boy? That's the kind of woman you should marry. She'd bring intelligence and spunk to my grandchildren—" he straightened up and eyed Julie "—which neither of you two Mansfields is doing anything about." To Sabrina, he added, "You like children, don't you?"

She was caught off guard by his frankness again. "Well . . . yes, I do. In fact, I have a son."

"You can have more, can't you?"

Straightening up in her chair, Sabrina looked up at David.

He set his glass down on the table next to hers. "That's really no concern of yours, Shelby." He took hold of Sabrina's arm forcefully and pulled her up from the chair. "Time for some fresh air, Sabrina. The Mansfields have to be taken in small doses."

CHAPTER SEVEN

IN THE COURTYARD at the side of the house were several groupings of patio tables and chairs, all cushioned in cheerful colors. The walkways were aged brick, and a three-tiered cast iron fountain in the center spouted water, creating natural music. With its high brick walls, lush banana trees, hanging flower baskets and large clay pots full of multicolored chrysanthemums, it was a mini-oasis.

Sabrina took a deep breath of the cool air and moved slowly to the fountain. Leaning over its edge, she ran her fingers lackadaisically through the cool water, watching as the ripples spread across the watery image of her hair cascading about her face. Soon another image appeared in the water.

The reflection of David's smile as he met her own filled her with a sense of contentment. His very closeness enveloped her in warmth. She felt him touch her shoulders and begin to caress her back and arms.

He whispered, "I hope my father's comments didn't embarrass you. He's a man used to saying anything he feels."

Speaking to his reflection, she admitted quietly, "I was thrown, but only for a moment." Then she felt his body touch hers.

She moved instinctively to the other side of the fountain, putting distance between them. Again she stared down at the water in the pool, listening to the soothing, rhythmic splashing. The night was clear and comfortably cool. An expanse of stars shimmered high above in the vast velvety backdrop of night. A balmy autumn breeze wafted through the tall plants in the courtyard.

David's eyes filled themselves with the picture of her leaning over the edge of the fountain. He watched the pale light from the arc-shaped moon play golden tricks with her hair, all the while feeling desperately jealous of the breeze that pushed against the silky material of her dress.

Sabrina looked over at him, and for long moments she tried to comprehend the silent communication of their eyes. When understanding of their unspoken intimacy finally registered, she felt her cheeks flush and a rush of adrenaline shot through her body. She tried to force her eyes away from his, but couldn't.

What was it that he saw in her expression, she wondered as his disarming smile slowly dissipated. She saw a muscle flick uneasily at the corner of his mouth. It was as if he had seen something in her eyes he had not been prepared to see.

Still caught in the strength of his gaze, she managed to say, "This is a charming courtyard."

As though her words had shaken him from some private reverie, David responded tentatively. "Uh, yes, it is." Then he removed his suit jacket and laid it across the back of a chair.

He faced her again and walked slowly but authoritatively toward her, the moonlight accentuating his broad shoulders. His chest and arm muscles made for graceful curves underneath his fitted white dress shirt. His eyes were intense, and focused solely on her.

A stronger breeze streamed across her face; she hoped it would cool the rising heat that warmed her cheeks. It didn't, and when David rested his palm on the fountain's ledge, Sabrina exhaled an inconspicuous, slow breath.

Again speaking of Shelby's comments, he said, "I'm sorry for even your momentary embarrassment. My father has become even more outspoken since his last heart attack. He's not a well man. Being confined to that wheelchair upsets him greatly." He looked directly at her. "He has cardiomyopathy, a disease affecting his heart. He often needs bed rest now."

"I'm sorry," she said sincerely, seeing the concern in David's face.

He crossed his arms and stared across the courtyard. "I think it's particularly hard on him because he was such a vibrant young man. When I was just a kid, he'd take me on week-long hunting trips to teach me how to rough it, how to survive in the wilderness. He tried hard to hammer into me that the world was a place where one had to be strong to survive. I was to learn to get the other guy before he got me."

David's sigh was deep. "I hated those trips. Shooting animals for food is one thing, but to kill them to prove my manliness to my father sickened me. It all seemed so cruel, so pointless."

"Did you ever tell him how you felt about it?"

His answer was a dismayed nod. "That was the first of the many times I disappointed him. Not intentionally," he added.

"But surely he's proud of the success you've made of your firm."

"No, that's just another disappointment. I used to think that if I worked hard at it, he would come around, acknowledge that I'd done it on my own, built it up...but he hasn't. I don't think he ever will."

Softly, almost to herself and thinking of her own father, she said, "And it's important to you, isn't it?"

Then she thought of Todd, also, and realized how much she had wanted to hear him acknowledge her efforts to achieve her dreams for a career. He never had—just the reverse. He'd managed to make her life miserable every time he thought she had gotten out of line as far as his conception of what her life should have been like.

"Enough about me," David suggested, going over to a chair. He sat down and draped his arm over the back of it. Looking up at her, he broke into an open, warm smile. "Tell me about Michael. Does he have any hobbies? How's he doing in school? Any girlfriends?" He corrected himself with a quiet laugh. "At seven, I guess not."

The mention of her son's name caused a surge of happiness to well up within her. Tilting her head back a little, she smiled. "No, I've got a few years grace before having to worry about that." She joined him, sitting down in the chair opposite his. Leaning back, she brought the fingers of her right hand to the side of her neck, and after a pensive moment, she told him, "Michael has been the most wonderful thing to ever happen to me. He's healthy, and he's bright...curious about everything." Her eyes met David's and they twinkled. "Right now he's decided he's going to be an astronaut. He and his friend Eddie are heavily into rocket models."

David experienced a warmth as Sabrina spoke about her son, as she told him how fast the boy was shooting up right before her eyes, how he'd live on peanut butter and jelly sandwiches and cheeseburgers if she'd let him and how much she missed him now.

"Todd and I have a shared custody agreement, six months with me, six with him," she told him, her voice more subdued.

"Is that where Michael is now?"

"Yes," she said, and when she lifted her eyes, David saw the longing that lingered there.

"I'd like to meet Michael someday." Standing, he straightened his shoulders, slipped his hands into his pockets and looked toward the house. He spoke in an odd but gentle tone. "Families...they're so important to children. Why is it there are so few really successful ones?"

Sabrina's thoughts burned with the memories of all the difficult adjustments Michael had already had to make in life, and a feeling of guilt accompanied the instant replay. Looking at David again she saw the grown man who felt he had only been a disappointment to his father.

She was tempted to go to him, to touch him—hold him and reassure him of his real worth. Yet, she felt something else building within her, and it had nothing to do with nurturing.

The realization of her own driving need shocked her. It had touched her that first day when he'd had car trouble; it had taunted her that evening in the country club; and now it loomed up before her, daring her to deny it. She had known there was something special about David Mansfield from the very beginning, but to find that her entire body now ached with undisguised desire, that at this moment it was focused totally on him—

No! she screamed inwardly. There was no room for these dangerous feelings in her busy life. It was complicated enough right now.

Energetically she pushed herself to a standing position. David's head swung toward her, wistfulness in his expression.

"My father was right about one thing," he admitted in a voice that was soft and musical, a voice that almost melted her determination not to become further involved. "You are just what we Mansfields need. You'd bring us caring with your kind of strength and perhaps even...love." His eyes clung to hers as he tried to analyze her reaction to his words. "You're a very special lady, Sabrina Hutchins."

Her pulse began to throb in reaction to his words. Torn by conflicting emotions—wanting to hear more and not wanting to—she forced a glint of humor to mask her troubled thoughts. In an equally pretending tone, she said, "You and your father both seem to be at ease speaking your minds... you, charmingly so. Wait until you catch me on one of my bad days."

He sent her an intimate, arresting smile. "I doubt if you—" He stopped abruptly and turned toward the house.

Sabrina did, too, and saw that Shelby had wheeled himself through the open French doors. He was just sitting there with his hands clasped in his lap. She wondered how long he had been observing them.

David's father propelled himself toward them, saying, "You're to be congratulated, Sabrina...may I call you Sabrina?"

His tone was almost charming, she decided. "Let's make it 'Sabrina' and 'Shelby,' shall we?" she suggested in a gesture of friendship, then asked, "Congratulated? Why?"

He snapped his head toward David without looking at him. "For getting my son to think of something other than that toy business of his."

David grabbed his jacket from the chair it was on. "It's hardly a toy, Shelby. It's my life's blood, and you know it."

The older man's head wagged in disgust. "Listen to him...his life's blood," he repeated mockingly. "Mansfield blood is supposed to be pumping through your heart, and the family needs you now. The plant needs you, and instead I've got to rely on that pencil pusher in there to run it."

He leaned back in his wheelchair and stared up at David. "And your sister needs you. How's she supposed to fight this illegal dumping business all alone? It's only going to get worse. You think Brian's going to help her?"

David shrugged into his jacket and leaned against the fountain ledge. He crossed his arms, his face drained of any expression. "Julie is strong. She takes after you."

"And you take after your mother." Shelby's eyes narrowed sullenly. "Dreamers, the two of you."

Sabrina tried to read David's emotions at this moment, but all she saw in his face was a controlled demeanor. She felt sure that he and his father had gone through this scene many times before, and David had grown used to Shelby's scathing digs.

"Sabrina," the man in the wheelchair said, and she turned in response, "maybe you're the one who'll be able to shake some sense into his head, get him to divorce himself from that company of his." His eyes shot back to David. "Yes, you might as well be married to it. It's all you think about."

Turning toward the fountain and resting his hands on the edge, David's lips twisted into a cynical smile. "Since when is adhering to the work ethic a put-down? Seems to me you spent your life building Mansfield Chemicals."

Shelby banged the arm of his chair with his fist, and Sabrina jumped. "I took time to have a family, didn't I? Where are my grandchildren?"

And again she felt uncomfortable when David looked directly at her. Without taking his eyes from hers, he said, "Julie will take care of that for you, Shelby."

"They'll be Forestalls, not Mansfields."

With those words, Shelby found himself pushed rapidly back toward the house by his son. Sabrina followed at a distance, thinking that her meeting with Shelby Mansfield had not been quite what she had expected. And the father-son relationship that she'd seen firsthand seemed very shaky, indeed.

Inside, Julie and Brian were at the buffet. Brian was chewing on an hors d'oeuvre and holding another one in his hand. With his mouth still busy he said, "Julie and I were just talking about the prospect of having tourists wandering about next door. I'm trying to get her to check the zoning laws, see if we can't put a stop to this idea Hester has."

"Let the woman be," Shelby ordered firmly. "This place isn't your property yet."

Julie said, "It wouldn't hurt for me to check, Father."

Sabrina was surprised by Shelby's show of concern for Hester, but she was also annoyed by the general uncaring attitude that seemed to exist toward the woman. "I've already checked. There's nothing to stop Hester from opening up a guest house."

"I agree with Shelby," David added. "What Hester does on her own land shouldn't concern us. It's not as though we live in some small subdivision and we can see and hear everything that goes on."

Brian washed down another appetizer with straight Scotch. In a voice that sounded as if he'd had enough already, he gave a halting snicker. "I guess a close-down would put your lady friend out of a job, wouldn't it, David?"

Sabrina saw David's set face, his clamped mouth, his eyes fixed on Brian. She also noted Julie's obvious embarrassment and Shelby's attention riveted on his son. Firmly she said, "A job that I have every intention of completing, Mr. Forestall."

At that moment, Cora, the maid, announced that dinner was ready.

Taking Sabrina's arm, David whispered, "As I said . . . in small doses."

AFTER DINNER, while David drove Sabrina back to Belleamie, he glanced over at her as she sat silently. "You didn't have a very good time, did you?"

Jauntily she cocked her head to one side. "It was an experience, to be sure."

"I'm sorry," he apologized. "When Julie told me she'd invited you and you had accepted, I had misgivings." An uneasy sigh escaped from his lips as he nodded to himself. "And I was right. I shouldn't have let you come."

"It wasn't all that bad," she said, trying to put him at ease.

"It wasn't all that good. Shelby is a bitter man, an unhappy man. It eats at him that I'm independent of him and his money. He'd like to have me right under his thumb, just as he does Brian. That man would suck eggs if my father told him to."

He turned the car onto the driveway leading up to Belleamie. "I don't understand what Julie sees in Brian. Sometimes I think she's going to marry him just to get Shelby off her back." He smiled mischievously and brought the car to a standing position in front of the house. "Maybe even to unconsciously get back at him."

Sabrina was saddened by his remarks. "Both would be poor reasons to marry, wouldn't they?"

"I guess," he said quietly. He switched off the ignition and moved his hands slowly over the steering wheel. "Marriage today is a risky business any way you look at it. You have to go into it knowing you only have a fifty-fifty chance of success." Realizing that what he had just said might have upset her, he turned to her. "Sabrina, I didn't mean to—"

"I know you didn't. And thanks for sticking up for Hester tonight. Apparently she needs all the friends she can get."

His expression mellowed. "I don't know what it is about Hester. I've always liked her, but she keeps everyone at arm's length, won't let anyone get near her. It's as though she's afraid of everyone."

Sabrina took hold of the evening bag she had set beside her. "I think she is."

He saw her movement. "I'll see you to the door."

"No need, but thanks for the offer." She wanted to ask when she would see him again, but decided against it. "Good night, David." She opened the car door.

"'Night, Sabrina," he said softly.

She was just about to ease herself from the car seat, but something held her back. Glancing over her shoulder, she looked at David sitting there, his eyes set intimately on hers, and in that moment she realized he was the source of that restraining force.

Duplicating his tenuous smile, she took the hand he extended. "I did enjoy seeing you again, David."

"That makes me happy." He leaned toward her a little.

The force strengthened as she gazed into his blue eyes that now shimmered with silver lightning. She felt her own eyes being drawn to his sensuous mouth, felt that dizzying power pull her as though she were caught up in some magnetic tow. Unable to fight it, she moved closer until she could feel his breath on her lips. Mindlessly she kissed him softly and lingeringly, surrendering to the desire welling up in her body.

Drawing back from him, her heart racing, she saw a surprised look of delight in his eyes, a delight tempered with raw need.

Quickly she alighted from the car and went into the house.

CHAPTER EIGHT

IN THE DAYS THAT FOLLOWED, Sabrina threw herself into her work with even more energy than usual, trying not to think about the parting kiss she had given David. The impact of that kiss had been so vibrant that it had forced her to recognize just how vulnerable she was where he was concerned and just how tempted she was to ignore the warnings of her inner voice. Work, she hoped, would blur the unsettling memory of that kiss.

Under her guidance Belleamie became a beehive of activity. The electricians and plumbers created a cacophony of sound that echoed loudly in every room of the house.

At first Sabrina was afraid that Hester was going to have a nervous breakdown; the constant onslaught of workers would have been enough to unnerve even a more outgoing woman. But Hester endured, and Sabrina began to believe that although this experience was difficult for the woman who was fast becoming a friend, it just might prove to be what Hester needed to get out of the shell she had created for herself.

Quite intriguing, also, was the attention Sabrina observed Hester giving to Mr. Fundy as he and his crew worked on the grounds. Several times Sabrina had noticed her peering out through one of the parlor windows, watching Mr. Fundy at work in the garden. This afternoon she was at it again.

"It's coming along, isn't it, Hester?" Sabrina commented casually.

Timidly she turned from the window. "Oh...yes, it is." She chanced a glance back as Mr. Fundy finished planting a camellia bush near the window. "But then, he is the man who created the botanical gardens in Greensboro."

Sabrina smiled at Hester's exuberance and the pride she seemed to feel in the man's accomplishments.

A tapping on the window startled Hester. When she turned, she saw Mr. Fundy gesturing for her to open it. She did.

"How's that, Hester? Camellia *saluenensis*. I planted it here especially for you. Got a pretty little pink flower, nice glossy foliage. I think you'll like it."

She leaned out the window and eyed the bush. "Oh, I will, Mr. Fundy, I will."

"Plan to put some red and white camellias along this side of the house, but I wanted this one by the window to be special."

Sabrina had come up behind Hester and saw the excitement in her face.

Mr. Fundy did, also. "It'll have a blush just as pretty as your cheeks."

As Hester raised her fingers to touch her face, Sabrina suggested, "Maybe Mr. Fundy would like a cool drink."

"Would you, Mr. Fundy?" Hester asked tentatively.

"Why I believe I would."

"Well...come on into the kitchen." She paused a moment and asked, "Is iced tea all right? Or I could make some limeade in no time if you'd prefer."

"Tea'll be just fine," he told her with a wink and started toward the other end of the house.

Sabrina could see that Hester was nervous, and she sympathized with her, knowing how empty her life had been all these years. It still was, but from the way Mr. Fundy seemed to enjoy teasing her, it might not always have to be so.

After Hester had left the room, Sabrina looked out over the gardens, thinking that romance must be in the air. She hoped Hester was being affected by it; she knew Ina was. She had returned to the apartment after her first date with Eugene all but floating on cloud nine. Sabrina smiled as she recalled Ina's report of that date and the first kiss Eugene had given her outside the apartment door. Now they were seeing each other on a steady basis.

"Must be *something* in the air," she said out loud as a fleeting image of David crossed her mind. "Well, Sabrina, to work," she ordered herself.

During the next hour, she talked with the foreman overseeing the work of the electricians and then with the plumbing supervisor, and decided she was quite pleased with the progress being made. Later, she sought out Hester and found her in the attic, selecting and cataloging the items Sabrina would be taking to Rudy. She had already told Hester that he was particularly interested in the swan centerpiece, and the possibility of a windfall of income had greatly put the woman's mind at ease.

"The electric lights help, don't they, Hester?"

She looked up. "It certainly does make a difference. Now that I can see up here, I'll have to take a broom to the place."

She actually laughed, and that pleased Sabrina.

"Sabrina, you're sure taking these things won't be too much trouble?"

"As long as they fit in the Bronco, there's no problem at all. Rudy will do all the lifting."

Going to the long table on the other side of the attic, Hester said, "Well, I thought maybe we might start with these horse statuettes. They're bronze, you said."

Sabrina picked one up and examined it again. "I'm no authority on oriental works, but this looks authentic to me. Rudy will know."

Hester frowned. "I don't really like them. They look so...so mean."

Sabrina smiled at Hester's reaction. "That's what makes me think they're the real thing."

"I also thought we'd get rid of some of these silver teapots. A person can use only so many...and this thing, whatever it is." She handed it to Sabrina.

"It's a silver tea caddy." She turned it upside down. "Says Chippendale as do the tea pots. The dealer will polish them up for us." She glanced down at the other end of the table and spotted a group of figurines. "Those are good porcelain, Hester." She picked up a figurine of a medieval young woman and a young man leaning against a marble column wrapped in a vine of colored leaves and grapes. "I thought we could set one on the fireplace mantel in each of the bedrooms."

"They would look nice there, wouldn't they?"

As the two women boxed the selected items for Sabrina to take with her on Friday, Sabrina turned the conversation to Mr. Fundy.

"He's quite an attractive man, don't you think, Hester?"

The flush bloomed again on her face. "Why, yes, I imagine you could say that."

"Well, I think he likes you."

Hester's hand poised in midair, holding one of the bronze statuettes. "Mr. Fundy and I have known each other for quite some time. We're just friends, that's all."

Sabrina's interest deepened. "How long have you known him?"

As though calculating, Hester hesitated. Then, as she began to tie a string around the cardboard box they had just filled, she replied, "Well, it's been a little more than twenty years now. I met Mr. Fundy soon after I first came to Belleamie."

"Twenty years!" Sabrina repeated, somewhat surprised. "Did he ever marry?"

As Hester raised one hand to brush back a loose tendril of hair, Sabrina noticed again what lovely hands she had. It was almost as if they refused to age prematurely, as the rest of her had. Sabrina had already decided that Hester was basically an attractive woman, but she did nothing to build upon that attractiveness. She wore no makeup, and usually the clothes she wore were rather drab. And there was much that Hester could do with her hair if she had a notion to. Sabrina remembered seeing it down that night when the library door had blown open. It had appeared to be naturally wavy and had hung past her shoulders.

Answering Sabrina's question, Hester said, "No... he never has married."

She ran her finger along the edge of a cardboard box, then moved slowly to the window at the end of the attic. As she stared out, her voice took on a sweet tone. "He used to come here to do work on the gardens for Lenore. His father was living then. He had started the nursery and landscaping business that Mr. Fundy now operates. Mr. Fundy...Ernest," she said in a whisper, "sometimes brought me cut flowers from the shop they had."

She faced Sabrina. "Greensboro wasn't so big then. Life was much slower, and people took the time to talk to one another." Her voice softened even more; her blue eyes glistened. "On my twenty-first birthday, Ernest gave me a present." Her fingers dipped under the collar of the gray dress she wore. "This locket."

Sabrina stepped closer and watched as Hester carefully opened the little heart-shaped locket. On one side she saw the yellowed picture of a young man who had to be Mr. Fundy years ago. His hair was dark brown then, but Sabrina recognized the same eyes and smiling face. The other side of the locket held no picture, but behind the plastic she saw what looked to be a dried flower petal.

"It's a lovely gift, Hester. What happened? Did Ernest continue to visit you here?"

"For a while he did, but as Lenore grew sicker, and when I found out that—" She snapped the locket shut and put it back under her collar.

"Found out what, Hester?"

She shook her head. "Nothing." Returning to the table, she told Sabrina, "It's getting late. I'd best finish in here and I know you'll be wanting to check on the workers."

Sabrina didn't want to push her any further, but she was determined that if there was still some chance for Hester and Ernest, she was going to do all she could to foster a rebirth of the relationship that, as Hester had intimated, had at one time been akin to love.

She took a moment to glance around the attic filled with cloaked treasures and thought how like Belleamie

Hester was. Just as the house had beauties that were presently veiled to the eye, so Hester appeared to her. While she was speaking about Ernest, Sabrina had sensed the depth and beauty of Hester's soul, and her vulnerability; and although saddened by her confidence, Sabrina strongly believed that Hester—like the house—had great potential for renewal.

Preceding her out of the attic, Sabrina waited as Hester locked the door, and then, arm in arm, the two women went downstairs.

Hester went into the kitchen, and Sabrina conferred with the foreman, whose electricians were now working in what would be the guests' bedrooms. Then she went to the workroom to update her master schedule, pleased that work was progressing ahead of schedule. But, she allowed for loss of time due to problems that inevitably arose. So far at Belleamie, unforeseen problems had been minimal.

Unforeseen problems, she mused, and again David came to mind. Why hadn't he called? she asked herself, although he hadn't said he would. She really hadn't given him the opportunity to say anything that night she had kissed him and rushed from the car. She could phone him, she supposed. And say what? Her self-discipline took charge again, and she returned her thoughts to the job at hand.

It was while she was examining the installation of the new piping to the solarium that she saw the delivery boy from the nearby market pass outside the glass-enclosed room. *Wednesday already,* she thought, knowing that this was the day he delivered the groceries Hester ordered by phone. Although her car, an antique Chevy, was in good working order, Sabrina had observed that she rarely used it, and then only when absolutely necessary.

Sabrina had already chalked Hester's problem up to a slight case of agoraphobia. She recalled an article she'd read about agoraphobics, how it was necessary for them to take one step at a time when attempting to conquer their fear of being in public places. Sabrina imagined Hester's fear was probably centered on the people she might meet in those places.

One step at a time, she repeated to herself as her mind clicked away. She remembered seeing a beauty salon in the mall. She had to visit a fabric store there the next morning. If she could only devise a plan to get Hester into that salon. A styling would do wonders for her appearance—and perhaps her disposition, as well. Sabrina knew it worked for her. But she realized that getting Hester to go would be like pulling teeth. She would approach her later, after she had thought of a strategy for persuading her. "Where there's a will, there's a way," she mumbled as she left the solarium and went to the kitchen.

Hester was writing out a check for the delivery boy, and after he left, Sabrina told her that she had signed the foremen's work sheets for the day and that they had gone. "Can I give you a hand, Hester?" she inquired politely.

"Not tonight," she replied, mystery coloring her words. "I'm planning something special for dinner, and I don't want you around to spoil the surprise. Why don't you work on those books of yours now?" she suggested. "That will give you more time to relax later."

"Sounds good to me," Sabrina agreed amicably.

"I'll call you down when it's ready."

Upstairs in the sitting room, Sabrina immersed herself in the paper she was writing on Structural Theory. While she was checking her bibliographical entries on the books Professor Rawlins had assigned her, she found herself having to go back and recheck them as her concentration was interrupted by thoughts of Michael.

In her last phone conversation with him at Todd's house in New Orleans, her son had bubbled with reports of all the things he and his father had been doing after school. Wracked by a sense of guilt for not having done similar things with Michael in the past, she slapped her pen down on the table and blurted out, "It's not fair!"

She told herself again that Todd had much more free time than she did. Ann was there to take care of all the household chores during the day, and when Michael came home from school, he had the full attention of two fairly rested adults. Reminding herself of that fact and her own hectic schedule did little to alleviate the guilty feelings.

"All right, Sabrina," she told herself, "so it's not fair. Where is it written that life's fair?" She went back to checking her commas, periods, semicolons and colons in the bibliography and was quite happy when Hester called her, announcing that dinner was ready.

When she entered the formal dining room, Sabrina's eyes brightened. The large room had taken on a warmth previously missing. Two places had been set together at one end of the long table. The silver candelabra shone, as did the sparkling crystal wine and water goblets. A large tureen that Sabrina had earlier recognized to be Limoges—delicately beautiful, gilded and edged in green-leaved moss roses—matched the dishes in the place settings. All rested on a soft yellow and intricately laced cloth.

"The table looks lovely, Hester," she praised, "and something smells delicious."

"*Crevettes à la Nouvelle-Orléans*, a favorite of Lenore's."

"I love shrimp. What would creole cooking be without it?" Sabrina left the chair at the head of the table for Hester and sat down in the one adjacent to it. As Hester poured the white wine, Sabrina asked, "What are we celebrating?"

Her smile was replete with an unusual happiness. "I'm not sure myself." She stopped pouring and looked down at Sabrina. "But this is the first time in many years that I've felt like sprucing things up a little. Maybe it's all the work being done on the house." She finished pouring wine in her own glass.

Something to do with Ernest? Sabrina wondered hopefully, and then she noticed the dress that Hester was wearing. Sabrina had been so engrossed in eyeing the table, she hadn't noticed that Hester sported a lovely, full-skirted aqua-colored dress. Its cut was quite ordinary, and a closer inspection determined that it wasn't new, but it was more feminine and cheerful than anything Sabrina had seen Hester wear to date.

Things could be looking up, she decided as she watched Hester return the wine bottle to its silver holder and then spoon a careful ring of fluffy rice onto two plates. As she lifted the cover to the tureen, a steaming, tangy aroma wafted across the table, a delightful emanation of spices, some that Sabrina couldn't readily identify. Hester spooned the mixture onto the plates inside the ring of rice, served the warm, crusty French bread she had baked, and then sat down to eat.

Sabrina rolled a piece of shrimp around in her mouth, savoring the delicious, spicy sauce. "Mmmmmm . . . fabulous! Hester, you could open up a restaurant here, also. What is it that gives it such a unique flavor? I can't place the seasoning."

"Madeira. Lenore loved Madeira, before dinner and sometimes afterward." Her eyes softened in remembrance, and she laughed softly. "She used to say that it reminded her of balmy island breezes."

After taking a sip of the white wine, Sabrina remarked, "You loved her very much, didn't you?"

"More than my own life. It pained me to watch her rapid decline. It came so quickly, but lasted so long."

"What was her illness?"

Hester stared at her wineglass. "It was more an illness of spirit and the mind." Her fingers eased over the delicate crystal pedestal. "Her heart was broken when Shelby married Dolores Escobar, and then when Dolores bore him children, first David and then Julie, Lenore sank into a deeper depression. Her life became an intensely private one. Soon, even her friends stopped coming."

"Is that why Ernest no longer came here?" Sabrina saw Hester's fingers tremble, watched her sip the wine and return the glass to the table.

"No, Sabrina," she answered, her voice fragile and shaking, "I sent Ernest away."

"But why? From what you told me earlier, I assumed that you and he . . . that you both felt something for each other."

Hester's blue eyes looked deeply into Sabrina's inquiring hazel ones. In that moment, Sabrina thought her companion was thinking about telling her some deep, dark secret, but she only said, "Sometimes in life there are things we must do even if they bring us a great deal of unhappiness. Sending Ernest away was just such an instance."

Sabrina concluded that Hester was not yet ready to confide in her further regarding Mr. Fundy. Returning her attention to the dinner before her, she guided her fork under the rice and pungent sauce, tasted it again and said, "Don't let it get cold, Hester."

During the remainder of their dinner, Sabrina brought the conversation around to Belleamie, bringing smiles of delight to Hester's face as she told her how fine the house would look in just a few months. Then, after they had finished the dishes, they went into the parlor, where Hester served coffee.

Sabrina spoke of the work to be done in the parlor, but the portrait of Lenore Devereaux that hung over the fireplace soon brought the subject to the Mansfields.

Hester placed her coffee cup back down on the table next to the settee where she sat. "Are you going to see David again, Sabrina?"

From the wing chair across from her, she answered, "I really haven't given it much thought." That was not exactly true. But Sabrina felt trapped by the tension that she knew existed between Hester and her neighbors. On the one hand she was more than fascinated by David; on the other, she didn't want to bring Hester added grief as long as she was a guest in her home. "I've been so busy that I'd be hard-pressed to find the time." Unhappy, though, at the prospect of not seeing him again, she asked, "Would it bother you if I did?"

Standing, Hester gazed up at the painting. "It would worry me, Sabrina." She turned. "The Mansfields are opportunists. Shelby used Lenore and then deserted her when he thought it would be politically advantageous to marry an Escobar, but that same decision caused a scandal in this small town, a scandal that caused him the mayoralty he so badly wanted."

"Scandal?" Sabrina asked, wanting clarification.

Hester moved closer to the portrait, clenching her fingers so tightly her knuckles whitened. "People here love gossip. They said that the reason Lenore's father sent her to Mississippi, to my parents' home, was because Lenore had been pregnant with Shelby's child, not because she was so upset about his upcoming marriage. The voters seemed to think that if they couldn't trust a man to behave well with a woman, they couldn't trust him to behave well with them."

Sabrina's lips moved to ask the inevitable question, but before she could, Hester faced her again. "And just as Shelby used her, his son will use you," she warned. "Don't become involved with David, Sabrina. He may be charming, but over the years he's been involved with several young women. The society column was full of his activities. But he never married any of them."

Stepping back to the settee, Hester reached down and grasped the back of it. "David's a driven man. I've watched him grow up in Shelby's house, a house that has been shadowed by unhappiness and friction. It's true, people do talk here, and I've heard stories I'd never repeat of how Shelby treated his wife and alienated David."

She lifted her hands and curved one around the other. "I've even felt sorry for David at times. Over the years I've followed his career, read about him, seen how hard he worked to build that company of his. I've had the feeling that the man is trying awfully hard to prove himself to his father, that he's engaged in some sort of rivalry to best him, to show him he can be even more successful than Shelby has become." Her eyes pleaded with Sabrina's. "But at what cost? No, you'd be wise not to become involved with David Mansfield, for your own sake."

As Sabrina listened, she remembered Shelby's having accused David of being married to his business. And now Hester was telling her to be cautious or she would be just another woman who caught his interest—as others had done. *A word to the wise,* she thought.

Yet, she realized she would be living right next door to David for some time to come. Would she be able to help getting involved with him? That is, if he wanted an involvement. It had been more than a week since she had seen or heard from him.

She was mulling that one over when Hester said she was tired and was going to turn in. After thanking her again for the wonderful dinner, Sabrina remembered the plan she had thought of to try to get Hester to the mall in the morning.

"Hester, after I check on the workmen tomorrow, I have an appointment to meet with Mr. Frazer at the fabric store in the mall. He has some samples of materials I'd like your opinion on." She saw that Hester was about to object. "Also," she continued quickly, "remember when we talked about using a fabric wallpaper in the dining room? Well, Mr. Frazer says he has a Toile de Jouy fabric in stock, a wine print on a cream background. If you approve of it, maybe he could order the same toile to be used for the upholstery in the dining room. Would you mind driving into town with me?''

''Couldn't he bring the samples out here?''

''Yes, but it would be much simpler if we went to the store ... and quicker. We may not be happy with the ones he'd bring to show us.''

''The sooner the better, I guess,'' Hester said as though weighing the idea.

''Good.'' Sabrina took the empty coffee cups Hester had picked up. ''You go on to bed. I'll take care of these.'' As Sabrina exited the parlor, she smiled, thinking, *So far so good. Next stop, the mall.*

IN THE MORNING, as the two women rode toward town in the Bronco, Hester told Sabrina how much Greensboro had changed since she first arrived as a young girl. Nearing the hub of the town, she pointed out the areas that were then vast fields of rice and corn. They were now new subdivisions with rows of small homes, one looking much like the other.

''It used to be,'' Hester said, ''that I could give you the names of all the businessmen in town, but now with all the new companies coming in, making things like transistors and electronic equipment, things I've no need for, driving through here is like being in a strange city.''

To get to the matter of her shady project regarding Hester and the hair salon, Sabrina said, ''I think Ernest did a beautiful job landscaping at the mall. I remember thinking how professional it looked when I first saw it, particularly the placement of the magnolia trees.''

Hester smiled. ''The magnolia is the state flower.''

"The gardens at the house are coming along nicely, too, don't you think?"

"Oh, I knew he'd do exemplary work."

Now, Sabrina, she decided. "Hester, after we finish at the fabric store, would you mind if we stopped at the hair salon. I really need a quick shampoo and set. I just don't have the time or energy at night to do it myself. It won't take long." She felt rather than saw Hester's eyes shoot over to her. "Depending, of course, on how busy they might be. I didn't make an appointment. The idea just occurred to me."

Silence.

"We needn't worry about the workers," Sabrina assured her. "I mentioned to Ernest that we'd be gone a few hours. He said he'd keep a close eye on things inside. He's probably parading the halls like a school monitor right now," she said jokingly as she turned the Bronco into the mall parking lot.

Still, Hester didn't agree or disagree.

"Well, we'll see how it goes at Mr. Frazer's. I can always stop at the salon another day."

Their meeting with the owner of the fabric store went quite well. Hester liked the Toile de Jouy fabric wallpaper, and Mr. Frazer said he could order the upholstery fabric to match. Sabrina also got the sample swatches she'd wanted, materials she planned to use in the guest bedrooms.

As the two women made their way through the high-ceilinged mall, Sabrina purposefully found reasons to slow their pace, window-shopping as they neared the salon. Little by little she felt Hester's interest grow as they discussed the autumn skirt-and-sweater display in one window, casual separates and fashionable coordinates in the next, each time getting Hester to visualize herself in one outfit and then another.

While they were examining mannequins in print dresses, Sabrina commented on how attractive one yellow and beige outfit would look on Hester. Her response was less than hopeful.

"I have more clothes than I could possibly wear in a lifetime, Sabrina. No sense wasting money."

"Rudy, the antique dealer I talked to, is waiting enthusiastically for the first shipment I'll drop off this weekend—" she guided Hester to the next window, the hair salon "—particularly the swan centerpiece. He thinks that alone could bring you four or five hundred dollars...more if it turns out to have collector's value."

"That much?"

"At least." Sabrina pointed to one of the hairstyle posters in the window. The woman pictured was not much younger than Hester and her hair color was similar to hers. But her hair was much shorter and softer looking, loosely framing the woman's face. "Now that would be wonderful for you, Hester...and wouldn't Ernest be surprised!"

Then began a verbal tug-of-war as Sabrina cajoled, teased, dared and reiterated how pleasantly surprised their Mr. Fundy would be.

It worked!

CHAPTER NINE

SABRINA THANKED FATE that the salon was almost empty. She had all but dragged Hester into the fashionable shop, and experienced a pang of regret when she saw the young beautician attack Hester's hair with a pair of snapping scissors. Before they left, her friend's hair was shampooed, cut and styled.

Even Sabrina was amazed at the change in Hester's appearance. Her hair, now shiny, fell in soft waves to just under her ears, and if she had had a single strand of pearls to adorn the simple gray dress she wore, she would have looked almost stylish.

Their conversation became more animated as they walked through the mall toward the exit, but as they turned into one section, the one by David's office complex, Hester froze. Ahead, Sabrina saw Julie in the middle of a crowd of shoppers, campaigning. She recalled David's saying that he was letting his sister use one of his offices as her campaign headquarters.

They watched in silence as Julie shook hands with the passersby while campaign workers handed out leaflets. Sabrina recognized Laura Tyson, whom David had pointed out to her the evening they were at the country club. Laura was talking on the bullhorn, telling the shoppers of Julie's plans for creating a Downtown Development Board to assure shoppers there would be additional malls in the area if she were elected mayor.

Hester had started to turn to leave, and Sabrina was just about to, when Julie spotted her.

"Sabrina!" she called and approached them, her eyes widening when she noticed the woman with her. "Hester?" she asked as though not certain it really was. Without waiting for confirmation, she said, "My, but you're looking well, quite different from the last time I saw you. At the pharmacy, wasn't it? But that was some time ago."

"Yes, Miss Mansfield, it was."

Sabrina heard the coolness in Hester's tone, and it seemed to her that Julie was trying to be pleasant, just as David always had been. For the first time she wondered if Hester overestimated the Mansfields' animosity. To break the tension she felt rising, she said to Julie, "I see you're hard at work trying to obtain the electorate's favor."

Julie's eyes rose toward the ceiling. "If I could just do it in slippers. These floors are murder!" She placed a friendly hand on Sabrina's arm and her eyes went to Hester, but the woman was staring down at the handbag she carried. Looking back at Sabrina, she asked, "Are you going to stop in and see David? I'm sure he'd want you to." She laughed lightly. "Then you can tell me how he is. I hardly see him anymore. Doing this and trying to take care of my law practice keeps me busy, and David...well, he'd be miserable if he weren't busy. Now he's working on getting a government contract . . . something to do with the space program."

Sensing that Hester was about to bolt, Sabrina told Julie, "Not today. We've got to get back to the house. There are workers everywhere."

"So, Hester," Julie said casually, "you're going into business. I wish you luck."

"Forced into business is more like it, Miss Mansfield," she corrected and started toward the exit, her low heels striking hard on the floor of the mall.

"I'll see you, Julie," Sabrina said quickly and went after Hester.

During the drive back to Belleamie, Hester was stony silent, in spite of Sabrina's attempts at small talk. Sabrina hoped Ernest would be able to snap the woman out of the dark mood she had succumbed to. But once they arrived at the house, Hester charged up the staircase, went to her room and closed the door. Sabrina decided the wisest course of action would be to take none, to let Hester be.

After the workmen left for the day, Sabrina debated about whether or not to knock on Hester's door to make certain she was all right. She decided to let some more time pass, and set to work on making swatch boards with the material samples she and Hester had picked up earlier at Mr. Frazer's. The boards would be handy color charts, one for each of the guest bedrooms.

She had suggested, and Hester had agreed, that each room would be decorated according to a color name: the red room, the yellow room, and so on. Sabrina had decided to use closely blended colors in each, that the red room would be done in red, red-orange and red-violet; the yellow room in yellow, yellow-orange and yellow-green. And she would use similar combinations for the blue, violet and green rooms.

In the workroom, she began to staple bits of material onto stiff pieces of cardboard, but as she worked, thoughts of David continued to be insistent. *At least he could have called,* she complained silently. Maybe he was waiting for her to call him. Should she? If she could take the initiative and kiss him the way she did, she could certainly phone him!

Reaching for another piece of cardboard, she let loose a smiling "Humph!" and thought *He probably thinks I'm too liberated.* She placed a swatch of green material over a yellow-green piece, and her thoughts tumbled on. *Well, if working my tail off makes me a liberated woman, I'm as free as I can get.*

The piece of blue-green material she was about to staple to the cardboard remained in her fingers as she realized that tomorrow was Friday and that she would be returning to New Orleans. The feeling of longing for David intruded without warning. Maybe he'll phone on Monday, she thought—hoped.

Then she began to vacillate, wanting to phone him, yet telling herself that she didn't want their relationship to develop into anything serious because of Michael. The boy was confused enough as it was.

Or did she want it to?

She set the cardboard she was working on down on the table and leaned back in her chair. She'd been doing so well before meeting David, but now she had to face the fact that she was missing something very important in her life: love.

It had been so long since she had felt a loving man's arms around her. Yes, she wanted to feel that intimate excitement. Again she reminded herself that her life was already too hectic to even think of anything so personally gratifying. But then, maybe she drove herself so hard just to avoid coming to terms with thoughts like the ones that were now nagging at her.

The image of David sitting in the car as she leaned toward him repeated in her mind's eye, and she rose quickly and went to the phone in the entry hall. Her hand reached out to pick up the receiver. She paused. Again her hand inched toward the phone. She could almost hear his voice saying, "Hello." But then she pulled her hand back, thinking, *Don't start anything you don't want to finish, Sabrina.*

Determined not to, she returned to the workroom, completed the swatch boards and checked tomorrow's work schedule. That done, she went upstairs and knocked on the one closed door.

"Hester, are you all right?"

"Yes . . . I'm fine."

"Would you like me to fix you something to eat? You haven't had a thing since breakfast."

Hester's response seemed to come nearer to the door. "I'm not hungry, Sabrina. I'm just very tired."

Feeling somewhat responsible for having rushed her into the situation in the mall, one that she obviously wasn't fully prepared for, Sabrina asked gently, "Hester, would you like to talk for a while?"

The door opened a crack, and Sabrina saw that she had been crying. "No, Sabrina, but thank you. I''ll be fine in the morning. You get some rest, too." Then she closed the door.

Earlier in the day, Sabrina had fixed herself a sandwich, and right now she had no appetite, so she went to her room, deciding to skip the books and call it a day.

Sometime during the night she was awakened again by the creaking sound of the floorboards in the hallway outside her door. She made a mental note to see to it that they would be taken care of when the carpenters arrived. Then, realizing it must be Hester wandering about again, she donned her robe and went downstairs.

She found her in the parlor, standing before Lenore's portrait with only the moonlight tempering the darkness in the room.

"Hester," Sabrina said softly, but the woman didn't respond, so she switched on the light. "Are you having trouble sleeping again?"

Hester turned toward her, and Sabrina noted her distraught features and red eyes. She also saw that she was holding a small blue velvet book in her hands.

"Is something wrong, Hester?"

The woman's chest heaved and she emitted a deep sigh. "Too much is happening too quickly, Sabrina. It has me confused."

"The house," Sabrina guessed. "Yes, it has been nerve-wracking around here lately."

Looking down at the book she held, Hester admitted, "Not just that."

"Then what?"

Without raising her eyes, Hester replied, "Yesterday morning, Ernest asked me to have dinner with him one night."

Sabrina's laugh came without thought, but she stifled it when she saw how seriously upset Hester was. Not understanding, she asked, "But that's wonderful, isn't it?"

She shook her head slowly. "I can't. I really want to, so very much."

Perplexed, Sabrina asked, "What's to keep you from trying to enjoy yourself a little? Ernest is a fine man, and it's obvious he cares for you. What in the world could possibly—"

Hester suddenly raised the velvet-covered book, and Sabrina stopped midsentence. She saw Hester open the book to a page that was marked with a faded blue ribbon attached to the binder. ''This, Sabrina.'' She handed her the book, walked over to the settee and slowly sat down.

Sabrina glanced at the book, then at Hester. She hesitated a moment and then she, too, sat down, in the chair opposite the settee. Her first impression was that the book seemed to be a diary: on the top of the page was a date: May 3, 1947. The handwriting was beautiful, that of a woman's, she thought.

As she started to read, her brow wrinkled. A minute later the line of her mouth tightened, and she looked up from the book to see Hester's head tilted downward. Then she turned the page and read on, taking in deep, concerned breaths as she did.

What she was reading, she discovered, was indeed a diary—Lenore Devereaux's diary. The woman Hester had called ''aunt'' had been, in actuality, her mother. Lenore Devereaux had been unwed and her child unwanted by Hester's father: Shelby Mansfield.

The pieces slowly came together in Sabrina's mind as she quietly sat there, stunned and shaken. Lenore had been pregnant when her father had sent her to Mississippi, to her brother's home, where Lenore had given birth to Hester. Her brother had then raised the baby as his own. Hester had already told her the rest, how Lenore had decided to leave Belleamie to her ''niece,'' how Hester had arrived, an eighteen-year-old girl, to take on the burden of this house and an ailing aunt. And David had supplied the added comment that when Hester had first arrived, she had been a lovely girl, friendly and full of the joy of life.

Sabrina closed the book and sat pensively, thinking that Shelby's heart condition and Hester's were probably the same. What of David and Julie? Had the congenital illness been passed on to them? Sabrina had heard or seen nothing to indicate that, but then, perhaps in the genetic pool Dolores Escobar's genes had been dominant. Hester was Sabrina's main concern now, though. She looked over at her.

"Hester—" She was about to tell her she was sorry, but that didn't seem appropriate. Instead, she asked, "How long have you known about this?"

With eyes still lowered, she told her, "Since just after my twenty-first birthday. My mother was becoming more disturbed mentally. One day she called me 'daughter,' and when I corrected her, she gave me that book to read."

With a heavy heart, Sabrina glanced down at the diary she was holding. "Is that why you sent Ernest away?"

Hester nodded and then raised a trembling hand to brush away the tear that had started to roll over her cheek. "How could I expect him to love a woman who had no right to a name, a woman whose father wouldn't even acknowledge her? And Ernest's parents? Would they have wanted anything to do with me if they knew the truth? I doubt it. Anyway, how could I have burdened them with my shame, with the cutting talk that surely would have started." Her moistened eyes rose to meet Sabrina's. "No, I loved Ernest too much to bring such trouble to him and his family."

What a waste of two people's lives! Sabrina thought, realizing that when Hester had been born, illegitimacy had carried much more of a social stigma. And she was struck with the emotional pain her friend had lived with: caring for her ill mother for so many years, while being unacknowledged by her own father who lived so close by, and then living alone in the deteriorating house.

"Hester," Sabrina said softly, waiting for her to look up again. When she did, Sabrina saw the Mansfield blue eyes staring back at her. "Does Shelby know that you're his daughter?"

Her response came slowly and sounded tortured. "I believe he does, and his silence has only fueled my hatred of him... but not as much as for what he did to my mother."

After setting the diary on the table next to her, Sabrina rose and began a slow pacing. She stopped and faced Hester. "Do you think David and Julie suspect?"

"I doubt it, but their father's coldness toward me and this house is bound to have had its effect on the way they think of me. I do know that the Mansfields wish I would disappear from the face of the earth. It would free Shelby of the guilt he carries... if he's able to feel any. He's been buying up the land little by little, and if I had sold out to him, I'm sure he would have had the house razed to the ground."

Sabrina felt a strong surge of protectiveness for Hester develop within. She also found herself angry with the position the Mansfields had taken toward her friend. Yet she had other strong feelings—feelings for David—and the two opposing emotions clashed inside her.

She sat down next to Hester on the settee and tenderly placed her hand on the woman's shoulder. She felt Hester give a sudden, nervous jolt. Gently, in an attempt to comfort her, Sabrina stroked her shoulder.

"Hester, why haven't you ever approached Shelby with Lenore's diary? Maybe if the matter were brought out into the open, it would make a difference."

Hester's eyes rose to meet Sabrina's, and in them was a shimmering plea. "I can't ask my father to love me, Sabrina. He either does or he doesn't."

What kind of man is Shelby Mansfield? Sabrina wondered. She couldn't blame Hester for saying what she just had, and she remembered the way he had treated David. She eased her arm around Hester, drew her closer and felt her tremble as the tears came.

IN THE MORNING Ernest asked Sabrina what was wrong with Hester. He had tried to talk with her, but she refused to engage even in conversation about the gardens. Sabrina explained that Hester wasn't feeling well, that it was nothing serious, and she asked him to be patient with her, assuring him that Hester did consider him a close friend. He'd gone about his work, but Sabrina realized that he, too, was troubled. The morning passed, and as was the habit now, the workmen left at noon on Friday, just as Sabrina did.

When she turned the Bronco onto the road outside of Hester's property she felt a weight lift from her shoulders. At least she could pretend to leave the knowledge of Hester's dilemma behind for the time being. As she drove by the Mansfield estate, though, she thought of David and the implications of what Hester had told her the night before: he was Hester's half brother. She tried to force the ramifications of that from her thoughts and headed toward New Orleans, a little faster than usual, wanting to catch Ralph Sadler at the office before he left for the weekend.

She did, and as he studied her recent figures and schedule on the Devereaux project, she watched the bobbing of his head and saw the little twitch of his nose that she knew occurred just before he was going to say something he wasn't certain he wanted to.

"Good...very good." His eyes bore into hers. "Now you see why I knew you were the right person for this job. You maintain this schedule and there'll be a bonus coming for you."

Just like a man, Sabrina thought. Once you had one pegged, he'd do something that would surprise you. But she didn't want to thank him; she knew she'd earned it.

"You know," he continued, "we should be able to get some darn good publicity out of that place when it's finished...might even open the door to further expansion for Delta Associates. I've been toying with the idea of opening an office in Shreveport. It'd be near enough to pick up some of the business from Texas and Arkansas."

"Never hurts to think big, Ralph." She started to replace the papers he'd been studying back into her attaché case. "How's the Cosgrove project coming along?"

He let loose with a sound that was somewhere between a snort and a chuckle. "You were right—he wanted the satin stainless steel pedestals for the loft. Wouldn't let Jack change anything you worked up."

Sabrina felt a sly sense of vindication at that bit of information. "So, maybe I'm more than just a nice decoration around here."

"Touché—" again his nose twitched "—but we really have missed you," he said sincerely. He went to the conference table in the middle of his large office and opened a file folder. "While you're here, take a look at the drawings Jack has come up with for the furniture in the reception area."

This day was going to be one of her better ones, she decided when she saw the note Jack Myers had penciled in on the margin: Check with Sabrina, per Cosgrove. She scanned the drawing of a semicircular reception desk, with modernistic chairs placed around it for waiting clients. "Looks fine. Just one thing, though. I think I'd add floor-to-ceiling low-gloss slats at this end of the desk: the receptionist's computer could be set behind it. It would still be convenient for the employee, but wouldn't scream high-tech business to clients walking in the door. I'd also place a three-tiered hanging basket in front of the slats... it would give the room a softness and a more creative ambience."

He picked up the drawing. "Yeah... Cosgrove will like that."

Again Sabrina felt a glow of satisfaction, but she was also surprised that Ralph had actually let her see Jack's marginal note. Maybe all the hard work she'd put into her career was finally beginning to pay off.

Ralph handed her a manila envelope. "Finally got the adjusted contracts typed up for the Devereaux lady to sign. What's she like?"

"Just like you said, Ralph... she's a lady."

WHEN SHE DID REACH HER APARTMENT, it was quiet, and its silence cheated her of the usual contentment she felt whenever she returned to the more familiar surroundings in New Orleans.

After setting the celebratory white pastry box down on the dinette table, she placed her briefcase on the sideboard and kicked off her pumps, letting them remain where they fell. Then she hit the radio's On button, and it sent forth somber strains of orchestral music that she recognized as Mahler. It was a little too depressing for her mood, so she changed the station, quickly bypassing the sounds of hard rock, until she located some nondescript background music.

Sabrina felt a heavy sadness as she looked around the empty apartment, but she told herself she'd feel more "up" when she saw Michael tomorrow. And she was sorry that she'd missed Ina, who had probably left for symphony rehearsal earlier than usual.

Recalling Ina's philosophy—if one took life seriously at all, one would be taking it too seriously—she opened the pastry box, mumbling, "Wait until you have children, Ina. Life gets pretty serious whether you like it or not." She opened wide and sank her teeth into the chocolate covered creamy éclair. As she rolled the velvety sweetness around in her mouth, her brain momentarily forgot all else but the instant gratification of the sugary delight. Then she stared down at the exposed rich filling, asking, "When did I begin using you for a crutch?" Continuing to converse with the French pastry, she told it, "Well, better you than smoking again."

She took another bite, and as she swallowed, Sabrina wondered if Ina and Eugene were having dinner together. She thought about how wonderfully uncomplicated that relationship was. They were two young people without real cares, as far as she knew. So unlike Hester and Ernest. For that matter, so unlike herself and David.

At the intrusion of the door buzzer, Sabrina guessed that Ina had forgotten her key again. The girl was brilliant on the cello but not too swift when it came to mundane things like keeping track of apartment keys.

One finger after another received a quick lick as she made her way to the door, oblivious to the fact that much of her lipstick and the corners of her mouth were covered with dark chocolate.

As she opened the door, surprise brought fire to the green that flecked her hazel eyes. "David!" she blurted out and found herself looking up at the wide grin on his face that grew right before her.

In her stockinged feet, Sabrina appeared quite petite to David as he stared back down at her. The chocolate mustache also added to the little-girl look that took him totally by surprise. Was this really the more-than-competent, beautiful architect who had been on his mind so much lately?

Impulsively he raised his hand, and in one quick motion, wiped a smidgen of chocolate from her upper lip and stuck his finger in his mouth. "Mmmmm," he said, his eyes aglow, "you taste good."

Sabrina's palm flew over her mouth, and she glanced down at her hand. Then her eyes shot back up to his. "What are you doing here?" Having not yet recovered from the unexpectedness of his arrival, she tried to control the intense rhythm of her heartbeat.

"Having dessert before dinner, I think." He paused. "Do I get to come in?" he asked gently.

Moving backward, she opened the door a little more. "Of course." Her eyes followed his slow stride into the apartment, and she closed the door.

"Nice," he commented as he looked around. "Comfortable, homey." His eyes settled on the pastry box. "Hope you haven't spoiled your appetite." He glanced back. "Or were you having dessert?"

Feeling as though she'd been caught doing some-thing socially unspeakable, Sabrina charged over to the table, slapped the lid down on the box and headed for the kitchen. "No, just snacking."

David's voice rose. "You are hungry, aren't you?" He heard the refrigerator door close, and when she appeared in the doorway, he glanced down at her feet.

Sabrina's eyes followed his. She moaned silently and scanned the floor, trying to remember where she had kicked off her shoes. Seeing them by the sideboard, she hurried and stepped back into them.

Now she felt reasonably in control again—that is, until she saw that grin widen his mouth once more. The damned chocolate! Back into the kitchen she went.

While the water in the sink ran, David moved to the bookcase on this side of the kitchen wall, noting, among others, the titles *Frank Lloyd Wright* and *Mies van der Rohe*.

A poised Sabrina reentered the living room, smil-ing. "You caught me by surprise."

Blue eyes twinkled in his suntanned face. "I know. You can find out a lot about a person when you do that."

Why didn't that sit so well? she wondered. "A habit of yours?"

He shook his head and took in the appealing con-tours under her apricot colored dress, thinking that the color made her skin look even more creamy than he had remembered.

Realizing that he was assessing her, Sabrina felt a mixture of pleasure and concern. "How did you find out where I lived?" Before he could answer, she guessed. "The phone book."

"Clever of me, wasn't it?" He slipped his hands into his pants pockets. "I had some business that had to be taken care of here in New Orleans this afternoon. I thought maybe we could have dinner together."

There came that quickening in her heartbeat again, but this time it was accompanied by a hollow feeling in her empty stomach. "I'd love to...but it's my treat this time," she told him, wondering if the excitement she felt was obvious in her voice. "Give me a few minutes to change." She started toward her bedroom door, then turned. "Make yourself comfortable. I won't be long."

A renewal of the dating-again nervousness caused Sabrina's hands to bypass one dress and then another. She finally decided on a sleeveless tan linen sundress with a matching jacket, since she planned to take David to the Court of Two Sisters in the French Quarter, and she knew it might be cool in the patio restaurant.

Sabrina had been right in her judgment. As she and David sat at their table on the plant-studded patio, she felt a cool but pleasant breeze blow. Suddenly she felt incredibly relaxed. As she sipped on her cocktail, her eyes settled on the wishing well at the center of the patio and then on the lush foliage lit by flickering gas lamps. It all reminded her of the courtyard adjacent to the Mansfield house.

David was watching her intently, intrigued by the way the soft light from the hurricane lamp on the table was playing across her face. "Do you come here often?" he asked.

Returning her attention to him, she replied, "Usually with clients. I like the atmosphere...relaxed yet filled with that magic everyone expects from New Orleans. I find that clients open up quicker here, and I get to know them faster. It makes my job decisions easier.''

A red-jacketed waiter served them: tasty Rock Cornish game hens with mustard lemon butter, hearty pan-roasted potatoes and succulent brussel sprouts. As they dined, David asked after Michael, and then his inquiries centered on Todd. Sabrina found herself opening up to David, much in the way that her clients opened up to her at the restaurant.

''We married young, too young, probably. I had just turned twenty-two, and Todd was only a year older. After Michael was born, I found that instead of a husband and a child, I had two children on my hands. To my way of thinking, at least, Todd has never really grown up emotionally.'' Her quiet chuckle was a self-reproach. ''Don't ask me why I hadn't figured that out before marrying him. I have, many times.''

David wiped his lips with a napkin before sipping the Asti Spumante Sabrina had said she liked. He was very content to let her talk it out, imagining that she might not have done so before. That thought made him feel special.

''Divorce is never any one person's fault,'' she continued, ''but Todd was no happier than I was. The little boy in him made him want to argue whenever anything didn't go exactly his way.'' She glanced at David thoughtfully. ''Brian reminds me a lot of Todd, the way he seems to be jealous of Julie's career ambitions.''

''I take it Todd was unsympathetic to yours.'' He couldn't help but study her face again. *God, she's beautiful.*

''Unsympathetic?'' Her brows raised for emphasis. ''He was impossible. Like Brian, Todd was determined that being a mother and his wife should have been enough for me. Granted, for some women it would have been, but I'm sure happy that I do have a career to fall back on now. I feel sorry for divorced women who don't.''

"You said he married again."

Sabrina nodded. "Ann, his wife, is a homemaker, just the type Todd wants. But he's already curtailed some of the charity work she used to do. Perhaps Ann can take that. I wasn't able to."

Over café brûlot, a strong coffee mixed with brandy and spices, Sabrina turned the conversation toward her dinner companion. Smiling, she said, "People seem to think you're bordering on being a workaholic."

"People? As in whom?"

She stirred her coffee with the little silver spoon. "I got that impression from your father, for one."

"And who else?" he asked, his tone indicating interest.

Still glancing down, she fingered the handle on the ornate cup. "Hester mentioned it." The instant she said the name, Sabrina's thoughts were flooded with recollections of the conversation she'd had with David's half sister last night. Again she had to wonder if he suspected the truth.

"Hester? Why would she be concerned with my work habits?"

Sabrina's eyes rose and met David's. In them she saw only a sincere questioning, no indication that he was afraid Hester's secret might have been shared. She felt a great sense of relief; David was obviously not a party to hiding that secret.

She tried to answer casually. "She's apparently followed your success via newspaper and local TV news."

A leisurely smile softened her expression. "We both noticed the article written about Mantek in last week's newspaper. You have to admit that you are one of Greensboro's most eligible bachelors." Her eyes narrowed and with a glint of humor in them she added, "The reporter said so." She raised her cup to her lips, watching for his response over the rim, enjoying the amusement that played in the blue eyes that scrutinized hers.

"Maybe Shelby and Hester are both right," he admitted. "I've put my heart and soul into developing Mantek. I felt I had to make it a success. Shelby has nagged me to take over the chemical plant ever since I finished college. That's a lot of nagging." His voice took on an edge. "He's been waiting for me to fall on my face, to fail—" determination hardened his expression "—but I'm not going to, Sabrina. If I have to work twenty-five hours a day, that man is not going to best me."

Perhaps this was her evening to feel uneasy about things, she thought, but from the way David looked when he had just made that pronouncement, she had the feeling that devils were goading him on. Shrugging to hide her confusion at his statement, she said, "Competition like that between father and son seems somewhat odd, David. Sibling rivalry, yes, but between you and your father? I'm not sure I understand that."

Leaning back in his chair, he rested his forearms on the edge of the table and placed his palms around the brûlot cup. His thumb moved slowly across the top of the handle. "I'm not even sure I do...not totally." He looked directly at her and his voice became more troubled. "Shelby's already getting some vicarious kick from Julie's running for mayor, but I'm not going to let him use me to get his business kicks in that plant of his. I can't even stand the smell of the place. Besides, I'm my own man. I needed to build something of my own, needed to prove that I could ... and I have. I'm proud of that.''

Sabrina felt a similar pride in David's having done so, and she had to admire his independence and the ability he obviously had. She had learned that Mantek was a very successful computronics firm, and in that field things were changing every day. It took a good mind to keep up with the changes, let alone be a leader in the field. Yet, she wondered about this animosity between him and Shelby, and she also wondered what his obsession for work would cost him.

Lightly she commented, ''Working as you do can't leave time for much else, can it?''

He leaned forward. The muscles in his jaw relaxed, and a smile stimulated the corners of his mouth and then took full charge, softening his expression. In a voice that reached out to her and all but caressed her, he said, ''I really haven't seriously thought about much else ... not until recently, not until you came along. Since then I've been doing a lot of thinking ... about you, Sabrina.''

The choking sensation she experienced in her throat was sudden and intense. She wondered if he had any idea how sensuous his voice sounded, or if he knew what those blue eyes of his were doing to her. They were opening a door and beckoning her to enter. But what lay behind that door? she asked herself. Happiness? Pain? Temporary satisfaction? She couldn't be certain, but she was sure of one thing: David was extending an invitation to her, an invitation that—God help her—she wanted to grab.

Wanted to, yes. But she had to remind herself that what she wanted was not of primary importance right now. What would be best for her son had to take precedence.

Time seemed to stop as she felt herself being drawn into David's intimate gaze, and she admitted to herself that it would be so easy to fall in love with him. Not only easy, but delightfully so. Each time she was in close proximity to him, she felt his aura envelop her entire body and tantalize her with sensual promise, tease her with ardent temptation. Did he know what he was doing to her?

Michael. She must think of Michael! It would be her only salvation.

Forcing her eyes from David's, she reached for her napkin and signaled their waiter for the check, anxious to leave the restaurant.

CHAPTER TEN

OUTSIDE ON ROYAL STREET, Sabrina searched for a taxi. Experience had taught her that driving to the French Quarter was a definite no-no: parking places were nonexistent. Suddenly, though, she felt David tug on her arm, and she found herself being guided toward the corner.

"David, there's a better chance of finding a cab here on Royal."

"We're not looking for one."

"We're not?"

He glanced her way, and she saw the mischievous glow in his eyes. "Uh-uh. It's early yet."

They rounded a corner. "But I've got a lot of work to do. There's the—"

"It's Friday."

"That doesn't mean I—"

"It means we should both take a breather from our jobs."

That was surprising, coming from Mr. Workaholic, she thought as they turned onto Bourbon Street. Through her linen jacket, Sabrina could feel the strength of his hold on her—and the warmth of it. She didn't want to enjoy the feeling as much as she did, but he was right: she needed a break, some time off just for herself. And if she were to spend it with anyone, she would choose David.

Her attention was suddenly drawn to the glare of neon lights. The blare of jazz assaulted her ears as David led her deeper into the night world of the French Quarter. As usual it was packed with tourists, soaking up the atmosphere of primitive abandonment that made the Quarter famous. Her nose tingled with the pungent smells of beer, seafood and rich spices. Bourbon Street had always seemed to her to be a place where anything could happen, a place where above everything else people wanted and expected a holiday mood. At night particularly, it glowed with a unique carnival atmosphere, a gaiety that promised laughter and maybe even romance to all who entered the Quarter.

She felt David's arm slip around her shoulder and cup it tightly. Her own eased around his waist, and she looked up at his smiling face that was golden in the muted lamplight. For her, tonight, Bourbon Street seemed almost unreal, an illusion created by the vitality of the man next to her, by the music, by the parade of people seemingly lost in the sensual aura of the "city that care forgot."

As quickly as Bourbon Street had engulfed her, it disappeared as David led her into a dimly lit lounge. It was so dark that it took a while for her eyes to make the necessary adjustment. She had left the blare of jazz outside; now she was immersed in a sea of intimate whispers.

Holding her hand, David led her to a small table in a dark corner, and Sabrina eased herself onto the wall seat, feeling his solid thigh settle insistently against hers when he sat down. Her reaction was immediate and intense, exciting and alarming.

"Two Sazeracs," David ordered.

When the waiter left she eyed David playfully. "The martini of New Orleans."

"They make for easy conversation."

Sabrina watched David watching her, his face swathed in shadows from the flickering candle on their table. His smooth complexion glistened and tantalized, and in the soft light his long, dark lashes accentuated the beauty of his azure-blue eyes.

Sitting here with him now, she totally forgot her earlier concerns. She was just enjoying being with him. It was a feeling that boded danger, a kind of overpowering surrender to desire, a relishing of the idea that something wild in her was being released.

Again she caught that look in his eyes, that provocative inquiry that was so intimate as to be almost embarrassing. Feeling a disturbing mixture of excitement and vulnerability, she forced herself to quietly ask, "Do you come here often?"

"I used to." He glanced around the room, its only light coming from the candles set on each small table. "Actually I haven't been in here for several years." Finding Sabrina's eyes again, he added, "I was wondering what it would be like to be here with you."

She felt his hand go to the back of her neck and begin a slow toying with the soft hairs at her nape. The easy pressure of his warm fingers began to have a soothing, hypnotic effect on her. Arching her head backward slightly, she wondered if this particular lounge held some important significance for him.

Just then the young man who had taken their order brought the Sazeracs. David raised his glass to hers, and looking at her with eyes that seemed to be undressing her, he said, "Here's to what follows friendship.'' He touched his glass to hers and enjoyed the mild look of shock in her eyes.

She sipped the drink that tasted something like an old-fashioned but with a licorice flavor. After setting it down on the napkin, she thought about David's toast. Moving her finger over the cold glass, she asked, ''What does follow friendship, David?''

He took another swallow, his eyes not leaving her lovely profile. ''Sometimes love does.''

Without looking at him, she sipped her drink again, thinking she was getting quite warm. She started to remove her jacket, and David assisted as she shrugged out of it. In an attempt to make light of his response, she asked, ''Do you find yourself falling in love often?''

''Not really, but I've read that men do fall in love quicker than women.''

She smiled—a little nervously. ''And out—I've read.''

In answer she felt his hand slip slowly down her back to her waist, leaving quicksilver shivers dancing along her spine.

With one hand still caressing her, David propped his other elbow on the little table, rested his chin on curved fingers and gazed into her eyes. Softly he told her, ''Not with the right woman, they don't. Take you, for instance. You're a lovely lady, Sabrina. I could sit here and look at you forever.''

''Forever is a long time.'' She felt the back of his fingers move up and down her bare arm slowly. It was getting even warmer now, she decided as she watched his eyes following the gentle motion of his fingers. After a quick sip of the potent Sazerac, she asked, ''Tell me, David . . . have you really ever been in love?''

His hand stopped moving, and he rested it on the edge of the table and studied his glass. "I guess I thought I was . . . a few times, but they weren't love affairs." He turned to face her. "They were more like sexual affairs, not the real thing."

"All starting with friendships," she suggested. "Like ours."

"No," he said quickly, "not like ours. With you, Sabrina, I feel different. I'm not sure I can explain it, but I feel wonderful when I'm with you and miserable when I'm not. I don't confuse love and sex anymore."

He leaned toward her and moved his lips softly over her cheek before leaving a gentle kiss there.

Feeling the surge of warmth his kiss brought to her cheek, she asked in a whisper, "And what is it you're after right now, David?"

"Both."

"Both?"

"Yes." His lips touched her cheek again. "With you, one without the other would be no good."

After a few moments of silence, he straightened up in the seat and cupped his glass with his hands, taking a moment to digest what he'd just admitted to her. He turned the glass slowly, then looked at her in a questioning sideways glance. "How long does it take to fall in love, Sabrina? One year? One month? One week? Can it happen in one day?"

What had started as playful banter, now seemed quite serious. Yes, she was wonderfully attracted to David. Yes, she had told herself it would be easy to fall in love with him. Yes, she knew she would if she wasn't extremely careful. Instantly she was afraid to encourage him, more for her own sake than his. With her mind totally cleared, she said, "I guess that depends on the people involved."

"You don't find me attractive," he suggested.

No! she screamed silently. "Uh, yes, I do but—"

"But you're just not attracted to me. Is that it?"

She felt her eyes being drawn to his. Why couldn't she shape the words? What words? She didn't know whether to say yes or no.

But in the depth of her hazel eyes, eyes now shimmering with gold from the candlelight, David saw her response; and Sabrina knew he had read the truth in her eyes, because his waiting expression gave way to a soft smile as his lips parted and a sensuous flame shone in his eyes.

His face moved closer to hers, and her senses registered his soft breath just above her lips and the sweet odor of licorice blended with a more potent and pleasant masculine aroma. Then came the fragile touch of his mouth on hers, moving ever so gently, so sweetly. His soft "Sabrina" was more of an agonized moan of desire that crossed from his lips to hers, only to be followed by their joining and a deep kiss.

When his tongue eased against hers and began its lovely probings, she felt her body tense, react with an immediate yearning for more of him, for everything he would offer her. Her breathing became deeper and more difficult and her lightheadedness gave her no control over her arms. They eased around his neck as his tongue danced more wildly with hers—now darting, cajoling and caressing.

She felt a weak murmur leave her mouth and flow into his as she began to yield to his sensual force. With his warm, possessive lips on hers and his arms around her, she suddenly welcomed the giddiness that spread rapidly throughout her body, playing havoc with her reason.

It seemed to her that David held her for an age, that his mouth was on hers for eons. She felt she had not a breath left in her when he finally withdrew his lips from hers. Tilting her head backward, she inhaled deeply in the darkness of the lounge. Her words came slowly and breathlessly. "Obviously I...am attracted to you, David." To herself she added, *too much so*.

Knowing that she should immediately put some distance between the two of them, Sabrina affably suggested they depart the lounge, enumerating the many things that lay ahead of her to do this weekend. Somewhat shaken himself, David agreed, and outside he hailed a passing cab.

The ride was a quiet one, as both of them struggled with private thoughts. Sabrina's struggle was more of a war, however.

In the past hour, David had made her aware of her female sexuality in a way Todd never had. The implications were tremendous. Ahead of her lay the possibility of experiencing what she had never known she could. The door David had opened for her now seemed like the entrance to heaven. She had never thought of herself as a particularly sensual woman, but then, no man had ever brought her to the pitch of excitement with just a kiss. What would it be like to know him more intimately? To have him know her? What would be so terribly wrong if she were to live for Sabrina for just a short while?

David, also, was lost in a tumble of emotions. He had never felt like this before. What he had previously named love had been insignificant compared to the way he felt about the woman sitting so quietly next to him.

But why was she acting this way now? So withdrawn, so reticent? Had he come on too strong? Had he said something to upset her? Should he apologize? For what?

His body was a mass of nerve ends, and he ached with the need for her. Stealing a glance in her direction, he saw the street lights flick over her somber expression. What had he done wrong? The way she had reacted to his kiss must have meant something. Maybe he shouldn't have mentioned the word "love" so soon. Maybe it had frightened her, he told himself.

The taxi pulled up in front of the apartment building, and when they were upstairs and she was getting her key, he leaned back against the corridor wall and shoved his hands into his pockets. "You had another great evening with me, didn't you? First my father tells you to bear my children, and then I blow it."

"Wha—" she started. Then, she attempted a smile, understanding that he thought she'd had a lousy evening. "David... I had a wonderful time."

He looked at her dubiously. "You did?"

"Yes."

He took the key from her, unlocked the door and nudged it open, letting her go inside first.

As Sabrina entered she thought, *He's going to leave now.* Glancing back, she saw him still standing in the hallway, an expectant expression on his features. "Would you like to come in?"

His face lit up, and he quickly closed the door behind him.

As she set her purse down on the dinette table, Sabrina asked, "Are you staying in town tonight?"

"No, I'm driving back to Greensboro . . . staff meeting in the morning. I've just taken on a new client, the Lawton corporation."

"Oh," she said quietly, "it's a long drive."

"Depends on your mood," he suggested, wanting desperately to take her in his arms and smother her with kisses. A silence hovered over them. "Well, I guess I'd better get started."

Sabrina's pulse raced and she took a step toward him. "Would you like some coffee first? It might help keep you awake." *Stay a little while longer,* she pleaded silently.

David tugged at his tie, wondering if she'd kiss him goodbye like she did in the car. He wasn't going to risk doing it again. "Thanks, but I usually stop in Alexandria . . . it breaks up the trip."

Sabrina inched closer. "Well, I guess it's good night, then."

He merely nodded, keeping his expression deceptively composed, trying to keep his mind off the urgent sensation he felt whenever he was near her.

"I really did have a wonderful time," she said again, and in the next step she took, she was directly in front of him, looking up into his eyes, trying to decipher his thoughts.

Her own wonderful fragrance drifted up into David's nostrils, and he thought he could actually feel the warmth of her body surrounding his. The memory of the taste of her in the cocktail lounge returned with full force. In a swift motion, he pulled her up against his emotionally charged body and kissed her with a fevered intensity.

Sabrina gasped as her body was pressed up against his, and she felt a searing heat pass through her. Her arms flew out to the sides and then they instinctively reached for his shoulders.

Instantly she was lost in his torrid embrace, and she gave herself up to him, concentrating on the easy undulations his body was making against hers as his mouth worked feverishly, capturing her staccato breaths. As her trembling fingers spread through his soft hair, she lost all sense of control and became the initiator, moving her tongue over his teeth, attempting to fully cover his lips with hers, propelling her own body against the growing excitement of his. She wanted him. She wanted all of him there was to have—now!

But in the next instant she felt cold space rush between them. David slumped back against the closed door, holding Sabrina at arm's length, his own dizzied eyes staring at hers. "Lady," he mumbled, trying to catch his breath, "when you say good night...you say good night!"

Sabrina's fingers went to her tingling lips, and she emitted a little cough as she tried to steady herself. When David let go of her shoulders, she took a step backward and ran unsteady fingers through the side of her hair, attempting nonchalance.

Straightening, David raised his own unsure hand, saying, "I...I'd better go now...right now, or I'm going to carry you to the nearest bedroom and make love to you until we both pass out." Staring at her, he reached behind him, searched for the doorknob and pulled it.

Finally letting go of her gaze, he turned and stepped into the hallway. He gave her a salute with two outstretched fingers toward his brow. "We'll do this again, Sabrina...soon." He closed the door quickly.

For long moments Sabrina just stood there, wondering what had happened, and wondering how soon "soon" would be.

CHAPTER ELEVEN

SATURDAY AFTERNOON at the apartment Sabrina tossed the towels into the dryer, mumbling what an idiot Todd had become.

The day had started off well, in spite of the intermittent sleep she'd had during the night. Her waking moments had been given over—quite pleasantly—to reexperiencing her evening with David, particularly their parting kiss. Each time she had returned to consciousness during the dark hours, her body, which had been fine-tuned to an elevated pitch by the man, ached with wanting him. Her need was too real, too great to be ignored.

Even her trip to Rudy's antique shop early that morning had been gratifying. When he had his first look at the pieces she had described to him, he was extremely impressed and eager to receive more.

Yes, the day had gone well—up to the time she met Todd and Michael for lunch. She had listened as her son peeled off all the activities he had shared with his father: the roller-skating, the trip to the marine laboratory where Todd worked, the personally escorted trip to the zoo at feeding time by Todd's friend who worked there—and on and on, each event causing deeper guilt feelings to strike at Sabrina.

The last straw came when Michael announced that after lunch his father was going to take him shopping for a pair of cowboy boots. Todd told her he was thinking of taking Michael to Houston one weekend, that the boy would enjoy seeing Todd's parents again and the Shetland ponies they raised.

She had tried to calm herself, had tried to be thankful that Todd, when the mood struck him, was extremely attentive to Michael. She wanted them to be close, and she certainly wanted her son to be happy, but several things bothered her, and outside the restaurant after lunch, while Michael was distracted at the window of the neighboring pet shop, she said to him, "Listen, Todd, I don't want Michael to be the victim of your on-and-off attentions. I don't want him disappointed when the off time comes."

"You're jealous."

"Jealousy has nothing to do with it."

His gray-green eyes narrowed. "You're just afraid he's going to have a better time with me than he does with you. Admit it."

Trying to check her emotions, she replied, "You're partly right there. I don't think it's good that whenever he goes to live with you, he expects it to be one big holiday. I certainly don't want him experiencing a letdown whenever he returns to me. Do you think that's fair?"

"Fair? What's fair got to do with it? Have you always played fair?"

Disbelief altered her expression. "*What* are you talking about now?"

He stared out across the street. In a low voice he rasped, "You know damn well. You've always tried to magnify my weaknesses in front of the boy."

Sabrina sighed and told herself she didn't need this. But she forced herself to say calmly, "Well, I'm glad you finally figured out you do have one or two 'weaknesses.'" Then she saw the boyish pout he always manufactured whenever he felt he wasn't getting his way. "Todd, if I did do that, I never did it on purpose. But if I was strong, it was because one of us had to be. You never were much on preplanning . . . anything."

"Did it ever occur to you that just maybe you carried what you call 'preplanning' to an extreme? In fact, you were damn compulsive about it . . . drove me bananas. You want to make everything just perfect for everyone in the entire world, but just because you think faster than most people doesn't make you special."

Sabrina thought about that for a second, but she convinced herself that Todd's view of reality was very much affected by what he wanted to see. What did really surprise her was his next remark.

"Ann's starting to do the same thing now." He studied the top of his wing-tip shoes. "For a while everything was really good between us."

As long as she did everything your way, Sabrina thought, but she didn't want to hear about his problems with Ann. "Todd," she said calmly, "let's not fight. I'm only asking you to take a look at things from my point of view."

SABRINA PUNCHED THE DRYER to On and the sound of the drum tossing the towels around proved louder than the rehash of her earlier conversation with Todd. Then she went into the kitchen and started a grocery list. She was halfway through when Ina stuck her head in the doorway.

"Kiddo, can I borrow your pearls?"

"Sure . . . the single or double strand?"

"Single. I want to look elegant in Memphis."

Sabrina turned and gaped at the lacy bodysuit Ina was wearing.

"Like it?"

"What there is of it."

"It has an underwire demi bra." Ina's palms slithered over her hips. "The saleslady said this would hug and define my every curve. Does it?"

"Well . . . it beats the cotton slips you usually wear."

"I think Eugene will like this better. I don't want him thinking I'm square."

"Believe me, he won't. What time are you meeting him at the airport?"

"At seven." She looked up at the kitchen clock. "I'd better get a move on. Don't forget the pearls, okay?"

"I'll bring them right in."

When Sabrina went into Ina's bedroom with the pearls, she commented on the smart-looking black and white linen-weave suit. "Nice. Have you robbed a bank or something?"

Ina shut her suitcase, saying, "It'd be a lot easier than what I think I'll be doing tonight." She looked across the bed to Sabrina. "I'm a nervous wreck. He's going to know it'll be my first time."

Moving behind her, Sabrina placed the pearls around her neck and snapped the clasp. "You're right about that. You remembered to pack your pills, didn't you?"

Ina patted the suitcase. "Right next to my handkerchiefs . . . in case I decide to cry instead."

Sabrina didn't want to give Ina any advice, feeling this decision was one she should make on her own. She went to the dresser and leaned back against it. "Maybe you two could just go to the symposium in Memphis tonight and listen to the music."

Ina picked up her handbag and suitcase. "My brain might decide that, Sabrina, but I know my heart would override it. I love the guy."

"And he loves you?"

"He says he does." She smiled. "And I believe him." She paused for a moment, then said, "I gotta go." At the apartment door she turned. "Wish me luck."

Again Sabrina found herself in an empty apartment. She wasn't used to the peace and quiet. Other than Michael, there was only one person she'd rather be with. He was in Greensboro.

The dryer buzzed, but she didn't care. She curled up on the sofa, realizing how difficult it would be for her and David to have any kind of a permanent relationship. So much was against that ever happening.

For one thing, what if he were ever to find out that she knew Hester was his half sister and hadn't shared that information with him? Would he really understand why she hadn't? And would Michael ever understand that she was able to love a man without endangering the love she felt for him? And what about her own future? She was working so hard now trying to maintain a home, trying to outperform fellow workers in her career—and the night courses. How much of her nonexistent free time would David demand? Would she be jumping out of the proverbial pan into the fire? It was all so bewildering.

Yet, she told herself as she finally got up to fold the towels, she didn't have to decide anything just this second. Time was a great manager; it usually ended up arranging things well. A little bumpily, maybe, but well.

TIME PASSED. September drifted into October. Ina returned from Memphis with stars in her eyes. Work at Belleamie progressed according to schedule, and Hester, with much support from Sabrina and Ernest, emerged from the period of withdrawal her meeting with Julie had triggered.

Although Sabrina was a little taller than Hester, they wore the same dress size. On one occasion Sabrina had coaxed her into wearing one of her stylish wraparound numbers and trying just a touch of makeup. And once Ernest had generously praised her new hairstyle, it hadn't been at all difficult to get Hester involved in a minor shopping spree in town.

But Sabrina still worried about her. She knew in her heart that Hester would not ever be whole until she could shed the bitterness she felt toward the Mansfields.

And David. He was another matter altogether. As long as she didn't think of the future, he brought her only joy and excitement. He had phoned her in Greensboro shortly after the evening they had spent together in the French Quarter to suggest that she meet him at the mall. To her surprise, he had arranged for lunch in his private office. But it was Sabrina who had been the one to kiss him first during that lunch, a tender kiss on his cheek.

"You're a brazen woman, Sabrina Hutchins, did you know that?" he joked as he reached for her.

She drew back and eyed the table near the wall. "And a hungry one. I smell Chinese food."

"Pepper steak from the restaurant in the mall. Have a seat. I'll serve."

Sabrina opened a paper napkin and spread it over her lap. Then she filled her eyes with David as he dished out their pepper steak from the carry-out containers. She knew she was playing with fire, but the flame was so lovely, so enchanting. And she had to admit that ever since that evening in her apartment when he had kissed her, her heart had belonged to him. She hadn't offered it to him; her heart had chosen him.

"Soy sauce?" he asked, holding up the small bottle.

"Please."

After sprinkling both their plates liberally, he started to sit down across from her, but shot back up. "The tea . . . almost forgot." He picked up two covered containers and took quick strides toward the wall unit where he opened a carved wooden door, revealing a small microwave unit. He inserted them and punched some buttons. "It'll just take a minute."

"You have all the makings of an apartment here," she told him, looking over at the large sofa against the other wall.

"Tell me about it. I usually have lunch in here and have fallen asleep on that sofa many a night."

"I'm flattered that you're giving up a working lunch today."

The microwave beeper went off and he joined her at the table again. "I'm not giving up anything. I'm getting the pleasure of your company."

"The feeling is mutual," she said quietly as she lifted the cover from the steaming black tea.

"Chopsticks or fork?"

"Fork . . . unless your entire afternoon is cleared for lunch. I never quite got the hang of chopsticks."

"Fork, definitely," he decided and handed her one.

While they had lunch, David inquired about the progress at Belleamie, and Sabrina learned more about

his work and that he was starting a branch of Mantek
in Atlanta. She had to admire his drive; it was much
like her own. Yet in her heart she wished they could
have more time together.

After lunch she offered to clear the table, but he told
her an employee from the restaurant would take care
of it. Then his secretary called, and he got involved in
a lengthy conversation. Sabrina was just about to motion a goodbye at the door when he got off the phone,
strode toward her, and put his hand over hers on the
knob.

"Don't go yet . . . please."

She looked into his pleading eyes. This was what she
wanted, but also what she feared. "You have work to
do, David, and so do I."

He raised his hand, and with gentle fingers he
stroked her soft hair. "You know what they say . . . all
work and no play."

Quietly she asked, "Now who's being brazen?"

"I am." He kissed her forehead and then each closed
eye. "And it's all your fault."

"How did you arrive at that conclusion?"

"You're too beautiful, too tantalizing and far too
desirable." He lifted her chin with a gentle finger and
looked into her eyes. "I want us to make love, Sabrina, but not here. I want it to be right for us when we
do. I want it to be slow and pleasurable for you."

She felt his warm palms caress her face and she
closed her eyes as his lips lowered to hers. That same
dizziness she had experienced with him in her apartment returned with added intoxication, and the taste of
him urged her on, increasing her desire for him. She
held his shoulders tightly, feeling her knees would col-
lapse if she didn't. And when his arms encircled her,

forcing their bodies together, she knew he was yearning for her just as she was for him.

But it frightened her to realize that he had only to touch her like this and she felt powerless to refuse him.

Thankfulness tinged with sadness overcame her when he drew back from her. He attempted a smile. "I don't know how much time I have left before I go stark raving crazy. I want you, Sabrina, so very much. I need to get as close to you as I can, lose myself in you."

Softly, she replied, "I want the same thing, David. Honestly, I do, but . . . I need time."

She was glad to hear him respond, "It's all right. We have time. It's on our side."

Before she left, Sabrina asked if she might see him again when she came into town on business. His face brightened at the prospect, but he suggested that for the time being they not meet in his office—the couch was too much of a temptation.

They met often during the following two weeks. With David, even the everyday things—lunch in the mall, brief window shopping tours, ice cream on the outdoor patio—became shining occasions.

She knew it was useless to fight it any longer. She was falling hopelessly in love with him. Maybe it was the way he would throw back his head and let out a great peal of healthy laughter when she would tell of an incident at the house. Maybe it was the way he would suddenly place a gentle hand to her face with a bemused smile on his lips, making her realize how desperately she wanted to share his thoughts. Or perhaps it was just the way he'd walk beside her, his entire body an exercise in grace and casualness. Perhaps it was just that he was David.

Her meetings with him became a secret part of her life. She didn't want to cause Hester added turmoil, and she feared Michael wouldn't understand her need to love and be loved. Besides, Sabrina, always one to plan for the future—had to prepare herself for the unavoidable: when her work was finished in Greensboro, she would have to return to New Orleans for good, taking with her only a beautiful memory.

During one early-morning drive from New Orleans, Sabrina retuned her car radio when the music started to fade out. The woman's voice she heard sounded familiar.

"...a problem that has to be dealt with and firmly."

"Miss Mansfield," a man's voice said, "the EPA seems to feel that local governments should be doing more to prevent this illegal dumping of hazardous liquids and solids. As you know, the drums found recently had their identification numbers filed off. What could you do as mayor that's not being done now?"

"I would work to update existing laws and propose new ones if necessary to guarantee public safety. I personally believe that stronger controls and inspections of all firms in Greensboro dealing with large amounts of chemicals are warranted."

"Even your father's plant?" the interviewer asked.

"Especially my father's. The voters have every right to expect that I would."

As Sabrina listened to Julie, her reaction was one of admiration, and she had to smile, thinking that there was no doubt Brian had gotten more than he'd bargained for in so competent a woman. Again she was reminded that Brian's attitude toward Julie was much the same as Todd's had been toward her. She decided that Julie would get very little support—if any—from her husband-to-be in the years to come.

When she parked the car in front of Belleamie, Sabrina looked out over the gardens. Ernest Fundy certainly knew his job. The once unkempt hodgepodge of greenery now meandered gracefully, but not formally, in an expanse of care. With pride, Hester had told her that in due season the long walks would be bordered by scarlet amaryllis and snowy yucca, by azaleas, camellias, cannas and roses.

Then she spotted Hester coming from around the side of the house, walking with Ernest. Sabrina was pleased to observe the physical changes that had taken place in her. Slowly she had become more vibrant and attractive. Even her complexion, which had formerly been so pale, had taken on a healthy color. But although the physical changes were apparent, Sabrina knew that the psychological ones would take much more time. She silently blessed Ernest. If anyone could help Hester, Sabrina knew he could.

She reached for her attaché case and got out of the Bronco. When she closed the door, Hester turned, waved and started toward the driveway.

Approaching Sabrina, she said, "You're early. It's not even ten o'clock yet."

"I wanted to check on the cleaning solution Ed's men are going to use on the carved ceiling in the parlor. We don't want them taking off anything other than the grime that's accumulated."

That was half the truth. The other half had to do with the comforting feeling that came over Sabrina when she was close to David. When in New Orleans, it seemed to her that he was on the other side of the world.

She looked up at the men working on the gallery and then scanned the outside of the mansion and smiled, deciding that the face-lift was coming along nicely. With its newly painted exterior, the house just about seemed to smile back at her.

Inside, the place was also just as busy: the comings and goings of busy workmen made it sound like Grand Central Station during rush hour.

As they passed the library, Hester glanced in the room. "Be careful with that standing desk. It's a valuable antique."

Sabrina smiled, enjoying the fact that Hester was beginning to take a more active part in the restoration.

"You have to watch them every minute," Hester complained as they entered the workroom. "How would you like some fresh coffee?"

"Sounds wonderful. I'll talk with Ed and meet you back here."

She did and then stopped in the dining room to check on the progress of the worker who was restoring the gilding on the giant frames holding the mirrors. That conversation was interrupted when the man from Mr. Frazer's fabric store arrived with the Toile de Jouy wallpaper.

As she tried to carry on the two conversations at one time, Sabrina noted, from the corner of her eye, a tall figure standing in the doorway. Turning, she saw it was David. He gave her a smile that sent her pulse racing and warmed her from across the long room. Quickly she concluded her talk with the two men and started toward the door.

"Hi," he said in the intimate way he had of greeting her whenever she returned to Greensboro, and in her heart Sabrina hoped that he had missed her half as much as she had missed him.

"Hi," she said back to him, but then the smile deserted her face as Hester loomed up in back of David. She was carrying a tray with coffee and two cups.

The instant change in Sabrina's expression was more than obvious, and David turned. Cheerfully he said, "Morning, Hester." He noted the tray. "Let me take that for you."

The woman's eyes went from Sabrina's to David's. Begrudgingly she let him have the tray. "I'll get another cup," she mumbled and took off back to the kitchen.

"Where to?" David asked, pleasantness still shining in his eyes.

"Uh, the solarium is about the quietest place right now."

"Lead on."

The room had yet to be worked on. It was to be Mr. Fundy's next project. As David set the tray down on the white wicker table, Sabrina wondered how Hester would take his unexpected arrival. At least this time she hadn't disappeared from sight. And she was the one who offered to get him a coffee cup.

Over her shoulder she heard David say, "I can't meet you in town today, but I had to see you." Then she felt his tender kiss on the side of her cheek. "Hope you don't mind my stopping by uninvited."

Her heart skipped a beat, and she wanted so much to hold him, to return his kiss, to feel the touch of him under her fingers, but she knew Hester would return any minute. Quietly she told him, "I'm glad you did."

Hester entered with another cup, and Sabrina began to pour coffee for them, waiting for an indication of

Hester's mood. She handed her a cup, checking her expression. It was taut, to say the least.

"Thanks," David said when Sabrina handed him a cup. To Hester he remarked, "I'm impressed with what you've done to the house. You're to be congratulated. It's really going to be a showplace when it's finished."

"Sabrina's the one to be congratulated," she said stiffly.

At least they're talking, Sabrina thought.

"Yes," David agreed, his eyes set on the auburn-haired woman across from him, "she is special, isn't she?"

"How is your father?" Sabrina asked and then wished lightning would strike her. What would ordinarily be a polite question had backfired on her. The look on Hester's face confirmed that.

"Shelby's all right. Still gets tired very easily. The work you two are having done here is the talk of the town. In fact, when Julie was telling Shelby about it last week, he said he'd like to stop by to see it when the work's completed. Said it would remind him of the old days when Belleamie was the fanciest place in these parts."

Hester's cup hit the table with a thud, spilling a little coffee onto the saucer. "It surprises me," she ground out, "that Shelby Mansfield can even think of the 'old days' without cringing." With that said, she left the room.

David stared at Sabrina. "What did I say?" he asked, confused by Hester's parting shot.

Knowing there was no way she could explain it without betraying her friend's confidence, Sabrina set her coffee down and took David's cup from him. "I think it might be best if you left. All the disorder around here has Hester upset.''

She walked him to his car, which was parked next to the Bronco. But before opening the door he said, ''I have to go to Atlanta for a few days. I'm leaving on Wednesday. Will you have dinner with me before I go? We need to talk. How about tonight?''

Sabrina glanced back at the house and then told David, ''Not tonight,'' thinking she had troubled Hester enough for one day. ''Tomorrow, all right?''

He smiled and nodded.

Then, considering the situation, she suggested, ''I'll drive to your house and meet you there.''

Understanding, he told her, ''That might be best. I seem to set Hester on edge, but I'll be damned if I know why.''

The explanation was on the tip of Sabrina's tongue, but she wouldn't permit the words to come out. How she hated this business of not being honest with him!

''See you tomorrow evening, then.''

Sabrina touched his arm lightly, asking, ''What time should I meet you?''

''About seven-thirty would be good. I've got to get the data ready for—'' he saw the sunlight sparkling in her eyes ''—the hell with work. Let's say six o'clock. That will give us more time together.''

A playful smile settled on her lips. ''Is that David Mansfield saying 'to hell with work'?''

''See what you're doing to me, lady, making me forget my responsibilities.''

Her hand moved to cover his. ''I don't know. You said you're usually in the office by seven in the morning. One ten-hour day won't make you totally irresponsible.''

Seriousness darkened his blue eyes. "No, but you could...if you wanted to," he confessed and ran his fingers along her flushed face. "Tomorrow...at six," he repeated, his quiet voice seething with barely checked need. "Oh," he added, "and bring along that brazen Sabrina Hutchins with you."

She smiled again. "Tomorrow," she said just as quietly, hating it when his fingers left her cheek, feeling bereft as she watched him get into his car and drive off.

CHAPTER TWELVE

DAVID'S ARMS ENCIRCLED SABRINA as they danced after dinner on the steamboat that was now permanently moored alongside the Mississippi River, having been transformed into a charming nineteenth-century restaurant. Its intimate dining rooms had thick carpets, heavy chandeliers that glittered, gigantic oil paintings and massive carved and gilded furniture.

When the music stopped, David suggested a walk on deck. Sabrina leaned on the ship's railing and looked out across the dark, shimmering water. Overhead a canopy of stars sprinkled the night with jewellike dots, while below, the Mississippi lapped rhythmically against the side of the ship. A cool breeze off the water rippled Sabrina's soft white dress.

"Cold?" David asked. "Want me to get your wrap?"

"No, but thanks." Facing him as he stood next to her at the railing, she reminded him, "I'm used to the Connecticut winters. They get cold. This feels like early spring to me."

He leaned an arm on the railing as he continued to enjoy the moonlight streaming over her face. "Do you miss Connecticut?"

"Sometimes. Particularly in the autumn. The colors are so vibrant, so magnificent."

"How is it you didn't return after the divorce?"

"Lots of reasons, really. The main one, of course, is that Michael would have to be in New Orleans with his father half the year." She shook her head slowly. "I couldn't take being separated from him for that long a period. It's bad enough as it is."

David looked out over the water. "When am I going to get to meet Michael? I'm anxious to."

Sabrina leaned back against the tall post that connected the sections of railings. "Right now I just about have to make an appointment to see him myself, but I would like you to meet him . . . and I want him to meet you."

"Let's walk a little." He put his arm around her shoulder as they casually strolled on deck. "Are your parents in Connecticut?"

"My father is. He's a foreign-exchange trader for a bank in Hartford." David's hand slipped down over her bare arm, and she covered it with hers. "My mother died when I was sixteen. She went into the hospital for an ordinary appendectomy, and they found a malignant tumor. She never came out. It was all so quick and so unreal."

"That's rough," he sympathized. "My mother died when I was twenty-three. I know it must have been much harder for you at sixteen."

"It was difficult, but my father and I were very close then. We helped each other through it."

As they walked around the prow of the ship, he asked, "You're not close now?"

"I'm afraid not. He changed so after my mother died. I think a little of him died with her. And matters only became worse after the divorce. He blames me, although I've talked myself blue trying to explain the situation to him. I guess he honestly feels I should have stuck with Todd no matter what."

She stopped at the railing again, and David stood next to her, setting his arm about her waist, telling her, "Parents do have a way of surprising us, don't they? Because they're older, they tell us they're much wiser, but I'm not sure that's always the case."

Sabrina leaned against him to be closer. "You don't get along very well with your father, do you, David?"

He moved his chin lightly over her hair, enjoying the silky feel of it. "He's not the easiest man to get along with. I don't know what it is, but I've got the feeling that he must have suffered some deep disappointment early in his life, one that he's never really gotten over."

Sabrina felt a tightening in the pit of her stomach as she recalled the things Hester had told her about Shelby and Lenore.

Continuing, David said, "Shelby has always been a cold man. I never even remember seeing much affection between him and my mother. He's done well by the family, though. He saw that chemical plant of his built from the ground up, guided its operation to the money-making success it is today."

As she turned in his arms, Sabrina looked up into his eyes. "Reminds me of another Mansfield I know. He's done pretty well on his own, too. Maybe you're more like your father than you'd care to admit."

"A little hard-headed when it comes to business, maybe, but I'd never want to be a carbon copy of the man. There's a hollowness about him…as though he's turned off all emotion. Everything seems so cut and dried to him. Sometimes I think he doesn't have any feelings."

Sabrina placed a palm on David's face. "Everyone has feelings, whether or not they're acknowledged."

Taking her hand, he moved it to his lips and kissed her palm. "I'll admit to mine, Sabrina. I think I've fallen in love with you." Before she could respond, he gently cupped the nape of her neck and drew her head to his shoulder. "But if you don't feel as strongly about me, I'll try to forget thinking about you in that way."

She placed her arms around him and could feel the warmth of him penetrate her fingers. "Would it be so easy?"

"No," he breathed out and kissed her head, "I don't think I really could forget. Just tell me that you do care a little."

Snuggling closer, she told him, "I do care, David. I care very much."

His eyelids flicked a few times before he asked, "Enough for us to make love together?" He felt her stiffen in his arms, but he held her firmly and pressed her closer. "I need to make love to you, Sabrina. God! how I need to. I haven't really been able to concentrate on anything I've been doing lately. I can't even sleep at night for thinking what it would be like to have you lying there next to me." He felt his breathing catch at just the thought of it. "Sometimes, with my eyes closed, I lie in bed and pretend you are there, but when I reach over to you and you're not—"

Her fingers eased up to the side of his neck, and she could feel his throbbing pulse.

"Sabrina, I want to—"

Now her fingertips pressed against his lips. "Hush," she said in a whisper. Then she drew back from him and looked at him with eyes full of love. "David, I do care enough."

The drive back to Greensboro was a quiet one. Many times David stole a glance toward Sabrina, but he was actually afraid to speak, afraid she would change her mind. Sabrina's own thoughts were not so simple. Like David, though, she had felt the sexual tension mounting between them; like him, she had yearned for deeper intimacies, but unlike him, she had to be concerned for another—for her son. She had tried to avoid a time such as this with David. She didn't want him to be hurt, and she didn't want to be hurt herself. But it had been impossible to avoid. With all her heart she now knew it was meant to be.

When David drove up the long driveway to his home, he passed Sabrina's Bronco, which she had driven over earlier, and steered the car to a small cottage that was set off to the side at the rear of the house, privacy ensured by the tall box hedges that curtained it from the main dwelling.

He parked the car and told her, "A guest house." Then they alighted from the Jaguar.

While he was unlocking the Dutch door, a breeze struck the wind chimes that hung to the right, creating a silvery tinkling. David saw that Sabrina's attention was drawn to it. "Nice, isn't it? The sound, I mean." He tapped the chimes with his finger, causing a renewed musical jingling. "I hung it there years ago when I first started to spend time here in the guest house working late at night. I used to leave the door open so I could hear it."

"It has a sweet sound," she agreed.

He took hold of her hand. "So very sweet," he said in a whisper and led her inside.

David went to the draped window at the side of the room and pulled the cord. As the material parted in a flourish, a wide beam of moonlight scattered its rays over the comfortable colonial furnishings.

Sabrina remained quite still in the center of the room as David approached her, took her wrap and purse and set them aside on the nearby sofa. Then he held out an arm to her. She moved to him and took the offered hand, feeling the now familiar warmth and pressure of his fingers as he pulled her to him. Willingly she entered his embrace and guided her arms over his shoulders.

At once she was lost in the feel of his lips gently brushing hers and in the comfort of his hands that soothed her back. Then she felt the tenderness of his kiss at the corners of her mouth, on her cheeks and closed eyes. Covering his warm ears with her palms, she let herself become wonderfully attuned to the pleasurable molding of their bodies as they held onto one another.

After inhaling deeply and letting his breath flow over her hair, David whispered, "I can't believe this is happening, that we're here together, alone." Holding both of her hands, he stepped back as if to prove that fact to himself. The sight of her standing there bathed in the soft blue-silver light was almost too much to bear. He felt his heart pound against his chest and sensed vibrations echoing in his ears. "Oh, Sabrina," he murmured.

Still holding one of her hands, he led her to the adjacent bedroom where he again opened drapes to let in the soft, natural light. Sabrina watched as he tossed his jacket and tie onto a chair, and the import of the moment became all too real. Hesitation tore through her thoughts, clamoring for a last-second decision. Go forward or retreat? The struggle was decided for her when David slowly moved toward her and began to unbutton his shirt. Even in the semidarkness, she saw the blatant need shining in his eyes, and his need ignited her own, sending a burning desire shooting through her body.

She let go of all hesitation. All risk was forgotten; only the man coming to her was real, and she acknowledged the truth. This was her own special time, the time for Sabrina, the time she had not allowed herself. And she determined to grab at it with all her will and strength.

Stopping in front of her, David's words were a plea. "Finish for me, love."

Her breath caught as she watched him ease the shirttail from under the rim of his pants. Then he stood there in the silence, waiting. With trembling fingers she started on the remaining buttons and parted his shirt, exposing the muscled contours of his chest and firm stomach. Her pulse quickened, and she guided her hands over his warm body, her sensitive fingertips registering the softness of his dark hair, and the hardness of his body. Her hands pushed aside the shirt until it slipped from his shoulders and fell downward, revealing the power of the arms that hung at his sides. Then she leaned to him and kissed his bare chest.

David gasped for air, fighting the urge to take her quickly, to satisfy his own desperate torment that increased with every movement of her hands. His body tingled with her every exploratory motion, and now he ached desperately, wanting to touch her. His hands moved slowly but surely, as he started on her clothing, and finally he dropped the last of it onto the carpet by his shirt and drew her to him, dizzied by the feel of her body pressed against his own.

Sabrina, too, felt the pleasurable light-headedness as their body heat mingled, as his encircling arms forced her breasts against his. Her stomach quivered when she sensed his hot breath at the side of her throat and felt his lips begin a trail of kisses that ended on her mouth. "Sabrina," he murmured and she accepted the full force of his tongue as it sought her own.

Her knees weakened. David sensed it, and she found herself being swept up by his strong arms and carried to the bed, where he set her down in a pool of moonlight. The coolness of the sheets under her agitated body felt wonderful. Her heart was racing already, and began to beat even faster as David removed the remainder of his clothing and stood for moments, looking down at her.

"You are so beautiful, Sabrina, even more lovely than I had imagined." He leaned down and gently took one of her small feet in his large hands and kissed it. His lips slowly drifted up her leg and farther, leaving her skin dotted with tender kisses.

For Sabrina, his bed became a silken cocoon of pleasure as David sent her spiraling with his hands and mouth. His lips covered every inch of her, tormenting her, caressing her, loving her with his ecstatic probings, slowly bringing her to the point where her senses registered a totally new experience.

With closed eyes, she sighed deeply and felt the bed give as David lay down next to her. Propping himself up on his elbow, he gazed down at her. When he did speak, his voice was quiet and breathy.

"This is how I pictured you lying next to me, love." His fingers moved ever so slowly over her cheek. "Just like this . . . in the moonlight."

Sabrina felt his warm hand slip around her neck, ease across her shoulder and caress her arm. And when he began a soothing motion over her thigh, her body became alive again. Reaching up to him, she whispered, "Kiss me, David."

He cupped her face with one hand and pressed his lips to hers once more. When he moved closer to her, Sabrina took hold of him. His tortured groan filled her mouth, and he drew his face up from hers. "Love, I don't think I can hold on much longer. God knows I didn't want this to be rushed."

"Now, then, David. Make love to me now...please."

He raised himself over her. "Oh, Sabrina," he murmured and thrust into her, feeling her surround him with her moist warmth as he penetrated deeper.

Her own response was immediate and intense. She encircled his body with her arms to bring him closer, loving the weight of him against her breasts and the feeling of ultimate closeness in their union. She gasped at his continued upward intrusion, and her ear tingled from his rush of hot breath against it. Then came his slow undulations against and within her.

"Sabrina, love, you feel so wonderful...so good. I don't want this to ever stop. Tell me what you want...anything...everything." The undulations became surer and faster. She couldn't respond to his request; she could hardly breathe. Now David's thrusts were coming fast and hard, carrying her again to a feverish pitch. She wrapped her legs around him and they soared together. She heard her name being cried out and then his. All became glorious sensation....

When Sabrina opened her eyes, David's moist body was still heavy on hers. She didn't care. His shallow, hot breaths were like sweet music, and the feel of him yet within her body increased that wondrous experience of oneness that was overwhelming. She slowly moved her fingers over his smooth back in gentle caresses, and felt his heart pound under her hands.

"Dear God, woman," he mumbled close to her ear, "you're not only brazen, you're dangerous." He raised his head a little and gazed down at her lying under him.

And Sabrina looked up, seeing the brilliance that glittered in his blue eyes—and the happiness. "Dangerous?" she asked.

"Add sexy to that." He touched his lips to hers tenderly and kissed the tip of her nose and eyes. "Definitely sexy." He raised himself up, eased out of her and rolled over onto his back. His sigh was deep and satisfied. Extending his right arm, he whispered, "C'mere," and she snuggled against him, loving the feel of his arm when he folded it around her.

Sabrina was content, filled with a peacefulness she had never experienced before, a peacefulness that seemed bottomless, almost euphoric. She basked in the knowledge that she had pleased David and that he had been so caring as to make certain that she had been pleasured before satisfying his own need. And even as her fingertips now dallied in the fine hairs on his chest, his soothing caresses on her shoulder and back were most reassuring.

She enjoyed touching his body; she could tell he enjoyed it, and now her hand moved in soft, feathery strokes over the curve of his hip. His murmur, "That feels so good, love," caused her lips to part in a lazy smile. Never had she thought that intimacies between a man and a woman could be so reciprocal, so free. Now she completely understood that "magic" other women had talked about.

Cuddling her and ever so lightly moving his fingers over one nipple, his voice was quiet and dreamy when he inhaled a deep breath and said, "Sabrina, we have something special together, you and I. We've got to protect it, not let anything ruin it for us." His eyes opened slowly. "I hate having to go to Atlanta now, hate the thought of leaving you."

His head turned toward hers, but his eyes took in only her auburn hair shimmering in the moonlight. "Will you miss me?"

She tilted her head up. "Yes...I will miss you. How long will you be gone?"

He gazed toward the ceiling. "I'll try to get back on Friday."

As though speaking to herself she said, "And I'll be back in New Orleans."

David was quiet for a while. Then he asked, "Do you have to go back? Isn't Michael with his father now?"

"Yes." Her finger formed an imaginary circle on his thigh. "But Saturdays are the only time I get to see Michael now."

"Oh." He took another deep breath and put his hand over hers. "Sabrina, it's important that Michael and I get to know each other. The sooner the better...right?"

She felt a disturbing fear replace her serenity. What if her son didn't take to David? But how could he not? Yet, there was no way of knowing if Michael would accept another man in their lives—a stranger. She knew the boy was too young to understand her need to love and be loved by a man—like this. She had approached the subject once, and now recalled Michael saying he wanted things to stay just as they were. He'd told her he was happy with just her and Ina.

And Sabrina understood why Michael felt that way. He'd had to make so many adjustments in his young life already, and now he perceived change as a threat. Sabrina had had to remind herself that she was the adult in the situation, and she would have to be the one to so act.

Finally, with some reservations, she answered David's question. "Yes, it is important that Michael get to know you."

"When?" he asked, deliberately.

Sabrina sat up slowly and raised her knees. With her arms around them, she looked across the semidarkness. "I . . . I don't know. Your weekends are so busy, and even if you could arrange to come to New Orleans, I'm not sure it would be the best thing for you just to show up to have lunch with Michael and me." She glanced at him over her shoulder. "It would be better if I prepared him first, told him about you."

David raised himself up onto his elbow. "You think he might not want me moving in on his mother?"

Eyes on her tightly clasped hands, she admitted, "That's the problem. I'm not sure what he'll think."

There was an intensity in his lowered voice when he said, "And that will make a difference in any plans we might want for the future."

"Yes," she told him over her choking, beating heart. Sheer black tension swept through her as she watched him raise himself up further and sit on the opposite side of the bed, his back to her. The silence that hung over them was almost deafening as he extended his arms and grasped the edge of the mattress.

What was he thinking now? she wondered. Didn't he realize the position she was in? How could she choose between her son and him, if it did come to that?

Just the thought shattered her, and her stomach clenched tightly when David got up from the bed and started to dress. In her heart she had dreaded this moment, and now that it was upon her, she wasn't sure what to do or say, but she had to do something—say something.

"David," she asked hesitantly, "you do understand, don't you...that I have to think of Michael?"

As he picked up her garments from the floor and laid them on the bed, he looked down at her sitting there so forlornly, and his heart went out to her. His smile was sincere but somewhat forced.

"Sure I do, and we're going to work this thing out together. Patience is not one of my strong points, but remember, you're very special to me. I will be patient." He thought a moment and suggested, "Maybe you could bring Michael up here for a weekend to stay at the cottage." His smile broadened. "It would give him a chance to look me over, see if I measure up."

The idea burned itself in Sabrina's memory, leaving her with a feeling of hope. "That would be wonderful, David. How could Michael help but like you?"

He leaned down and kissed her softly. "You'd better get dressed now. Hester will have the Sheriff's Department out looking for you."

Outside the cottage, a dark cloud cut off the light of the moon; the wind chimes were still. Inside, the room darkened as Sabrina sat very quietly, wondering if David really did understand.

CHAPTER THIRTEEN

"MANSFIELD CHEMICALS?" Hester asked Ernest as she poured him another cup of coffee. Having gathered all of her nerve yesterday, she had invited him to come to the house early this morning to have breakfast with her and Sabrina.

"Yup, your neighbor. That Shelby's in hot water."

Concerned, Sabrina said, "But I thought several plants were under suspicion, that any of them could have illegally dumped those drums the EPA found."

"They were," he told them as he reached for another blueberry muffin Hester had baked, "but only three of them are being investigated. Something to do with the chemicals they analyzed. Only three plants hereabouts produce that kind."

As she sat down at the kitchen table, Hester's expression was troubled. "Shelby Mansfield may be a lot of things, but killing fish and poisoning water—" She shook her head in disbelief.

"I agree," Sabrina commented in such a way as to indicate the idea was preposterous, but she was concerned, knowing that Shelby's heart problem had worsened, or so David had told her. She wondered how both men were taking this development.

She hadn't seen David since last Tuesday night when he'd taken her to the cottage. In fact, she hadn't heard from him, either. True, he had left for Atlanta the following day on business, but she had expected he would have phoned by now.

She knew that David had felt disappointed, hurt, even, after the talk they'd had about Michael. What man would have taken what she had told him any other way? Even Todd, Michael's own father, had found her attention to him threatening. Sabrina had chalked it up to Todd's self-centered personality. But David? Whenever she thought about his reaction, she quickly justified it in her own mind, telling herself that probably all men were like that where the woman they loved was concerned.

But, she had to remind herself, David had never actually said he loved her; he had told her he *thought* he was falling in love with her. That wasn't exactly the same thing. He had, though, alluded to plans he and she might think of making for the future....

"Sabrina," Hester repeated, bringing her back to the present, "more coffee?"

"No, thanks," she said, smiling at her, "the workers will be here soon, and I've got a bone to pick with Ed. If he thinks those wall sconces in the library have been reinstalled properly, he's got another think coming."

"That's it, Sabrina," Ernest agreed, "give 'em hell or they'll walk right over a woman boss."

"No one, Mr. Fundy," Hester corrected from the chair next to him, "is going to walk over Sabrina. Just let them try."

He leaned sideways in his chair and touched her shoulder. "When are you going to stop calling me that, Hester? You know my Christian name, or at least you used to."

Sabrina saw the blood rise to Hester's cheeks and decided to leave the two of them alone. "I've got to get to work." She raised a hand. "No need for you two to rush, though."

That afternoon, when Sabrina and Hester were watching who Hester now called "Ernest" at work in the solarium, Sabrina, knowing they were out of ear-shot, asked, "I wonder how serious this business of Shelby's plant being investigated is?"

Hester, as was often her habit when she was going to be adamant about something or the other, clasped her hands in front of her. "It's really no worry of mine."

Sabrina saw the woman's lashes move nervously, and then Hester eyed her, her voice taking on a more sympathetic tone. "If he's done nothing wrong, there won't be any problems."

Not sure if it was wise to go on with the conversation, Sabrina hesitated but then decided that Hester might just be more concerned than she was letting on. If she were, talking about it might help. "It's his heart condition I'm worried about. David said Shelby was having difficulties lately. This business of investigations could put an added strain on him."

Hester's eyes followed Ernest as he worked on a bamboo palm; her voice faded to a hushed tone. "I'm not certain the man has a heart."

Placing her hand over her friend's, Sabrina said softly, "He *is* your father, Hester. If anything should happen to him, you might be sorry you didn't risk telling him you knew that."

The expression in Hester's moist blue eyes—eyes so much like David's—seemed to plead for understanding. "You met Shelby, Sabrina. Do you really think he would welcome me with open arms? If he does know

I'm his daughter, he decided long ago he wished I weren't, and if he doesn't know, finding out could be a shock for him.''

Sabrina said no more about Shelby, but she regretted the animosity Hester felt toward him. It also troubled her that David's relationship with his father wasn't as good as might be hoped for. Perhaps Shelby wasn't the most loving parent in the world; indeed he seemed to be a man driven by something unknown to all involved. Still, he had fathered both David and Hester... surely there was some feeling he had for both of them. She couldn't help but wonder if Shelby did realize Hester was his daughter.

Father and child, Sabrina mused. A bond that could be nurtured or destroyed. Right then she decided that she was going to find some way to repair the bond that had once existed between her and her father. She needed to reach out to him and tell him that she did love him. And she determined that Michael's relationship with Todd would also be nurtured, that neither son nor father should ever forget that bond.

The next day in New Orleans, however, Sabrina had to bite her tongue to keep from snipping at that bond. She had met Todd and Michael at the petting zoo for children in Audubon Park and Zoological Gardens. Sabrina knew Todd was trying to get the boy's mind off the stars and down to earth, where he himself was more at ease. While her son was busy petting the animals, she lashed into Todd.

''You know I've made every one of the Halloween costumes Michael has ever worn, and you know that I've enjoyed doing that. This business of your buying him a space suit that must have cost God knows what—''

"It's what he wanted, Sabrina. What the hell's wrong with that?"

She tried to calm herself. "Todd, no seven-year-old needs a costume that expensive. This business of a headgear with a digital attachment that indicates the amount of CO_2 and the time elapsed in a supposed space walk . . . well it's just damn stupid."

"Michael doesn't think so." He eyed the white slacks and maroon sweater she wore. "You're looking good lately. Been getting some rest?"

From the way he was examining her, she wondered just how badly things were going for him and Ann. She wanted to tell him he looked like hell, but he didn't. He was just as handsome as ever. "Let's get back to Michael, Todd. If you really want to make him happy, for God's sake don't overwhelm him with gifts and then drop him all of a sudden. Even when he's with me, you could consider taking him for a weekend every now and then. That way he'd believe you really cared about him."

Todd tugged at the rim of his pants. "That's what I want to talk to you about. Thanksgiving. How would you like to have him with you for the week?"

Sabrina's heart skipped a beat, and her eyes lit up. "You mean it?"

"Sure, I know how much you miss him."

She looked over to see how Michael and the kid goat he was petting were doing. Then she looked directly at Todd, a little suspiciously. "What are your plans for Thanksgiving?"

He didn't hedge. "Ann wants to go to the Bahamas, thinks turkey would taste better down there."

Sabrina didn't mince words. "She's not too thrilled with having Michael around, is she?"

Leaning back against a railing, he made an awkward face. "Well, a boy Michael's age is a responsibility. I can't say I blame her. He's not her son."

"Still shy on helping out, aren't you, Todd?"

"Look, Sabrina, I bring in the money. Isn't that enough?"

She wasn't going to rehash this all over again. "The Thanksgiving plan is wonderful, Todd. Thanks."

Afterward, on her way back to the apartment, Sabrina's mind clicked away rapidly. She wondered if she should take Michael out of school a day or two early. She could take him to Greensboro with her. David had already offered them the use of the cottage, and it would give him the chance to get acquainted with Michael without him knowing that was the purpose for the visit. With Hester's house all torn up, he'd see why the use of a neighbor's house would be reasonable. Suddenly things were looking up, she decided.

No sooner had Sabrina gotten her shoes off when the door buzzer sounded. This time she knew it wasn't Ina. She and Eugene were off on another weekend together. The buzzer sounded again as she stepped back into her pumps.

She opened the door to a courier. After signing for a package from Atlanta, she rushed to the table and tore into it, finding a small package wrapped in gold paper with a gold velvet ribbon around it. With more care she opened it. It contained a delicate gold charm bracelet with a single gold heart on it inscribed, "Love."

Joy bubbled in her heart, and tears formed in her eyes. David *was* thinking of her, just as she was almost constantly thinking of him. "How sweet," she breathed as she held the bracelet in her palm and examined it. Slowly she ran a slender finger over the inscription. Then she carefully clasped the bracelet around her wrist. There was a letter, also.

Removing it from the envelope, she started walking toward the window at the rear of the room.

My darling Sabrina,
It's only been three nights since we were at the cottage, but how I've missed you! Have you missed me?

She stopped at the window and leaned back against the frame, answering his question in a voice that was low and loving. "Oh, I have missed you, David, so much." She read on.

The work here is going to keep me in Atlanta for several more days, I'm afraid. Charles, who's in charge of the branch of Mantek that is supposed to start operations here next month, is having an ongoing feud with the supervisor of the converter operators, who in turn aren't getting along with the console people. This, too, will pass, I tell myself.

"Poor darling," Sabrina whispered and turned the page.

What will never pass are my memories of that night at the cottage, Sabrina. Believe me when I say that I've never felt so alive before, never suspected the joy that I could feel. And when I do get back to you, love...well, be rested! Until then, think of me.

Love and sweet kisses,
David

Sabrina refolded the pages and held the letter to her breast as she gazed out the window. It was still light out, but in her mind's eye she saw a moonlit filled room and a dark-haired man looking down at her. She could almost feel the warm touch of his hands, taste him as he kissed her. Her eyelids closed slowly, and her lips moved slightly. In a voice echoing her longings, she said softly, "Come back to me soon, David."

During the following week, work continued at a hectic pace at Belleamie, and now, each time Sabrina would ride up the long driveway toward the house, she thought the stately mansion was all but smiling at her. It was almost as if it had a personality all its own. Sabrina would laugh at her speculation, reminding herself that a house was not a person. Still, she would continue to think of Belleamie the way she thought of Hester: as a phoenix rising from the ashes to begin a new life.

Sabrina didn't want to do anything to spoil Hester's new-found happiness. One morning, though, when Hester asked how Michael was, Sabrina found herself between a rock and a hard place.

"He's doing just fine. We're both looking forward to the Thanksgiving holiday.... He'll be spending it with me. In fact, I'm thinking about taking him out of school a little early so we can spend more time together."

Hester's expression showed her delight. "Wonderful! You will be bringing him to Greensboro, won't you?"

"Uh...yes...I was thinking about that." She decided it was going to be more difficult than she thought to tell Hester David had suggested they stay at his cottage.

Hester clapped her hands and held them up, exclaiming, "Sabrina, that is just what this house needs...the sound of a child's laughter. Oh! it will make my Thanksgiving so much more wonderful. I haven't cooked for guests in so long—" she paused and smiled at her "—besides you, of course."

Sabrina hated her own weakness for not being able to get the words out, but her friend was so happy. Instead, she told her. "Well, it's not really settled yet, but I do want him to meet you. I've already told him a lot about you and your home here."

"Nonsense, it is settled. Michael is more than welcome here."

For the remainder of the morning, Sabrina walked around heavy with guilt. She was somewhat relieved when Hester accepted Ernest's invitation to drive into town so he could show her how his business, Fundy's Landscaping and Nursery, had grown since she had last seen it so many years ago. And she was pleased, too, that Hester would be seeing Ernest's mother again, whom she hadn't seen for almost two decades.

Sabrina supposed that Ernest had never lost the feelings he'd had for Hester. What with his attentions and the money that was coming in from the antique dealer in New Orleans, Hester was feeling more secure emotionally and financially, although Sabrina had become aware that with her land holdings, the house and the furnishings, the woman was financially well off anyway.

Even more hurtful was the realization that she was still being pulled in two directions: toward David and toward her son. It was a feeling she didn't welcome at all, but how could she make the pain go away, ease the tugging that promised to rip her apart? The answer was simple, she realized—she would have to go in one direction only. That would be toward Michael, of course. He would always come first. *Simple?* she asked herself silently, feeling a melancholy frown reshape her features.

The following afternoon, Sabrina received yet another overnight delivery from Atlanta. It was a plane ticket from New Orleans to Atlanta, accompanied by a brief plea from David: *Please try to come. I'll be waiting for you at the airport. I miss you and need to be with you.*

So much for the simple stopping of the tug-of-war!

After taking the plane ticket and David's note to her bedroom, Sabrina went up to the cupola and looked toward the Mansfield estate. She tried to see the cottage where she and David had made love together, but it wasn't visible. The tall box hedges and old oaks hid it from view. Was she losing her mind, she wondered, or could she actually hear the delicate tinkling of the wind chimes?

She took a deep breath, trying to decrease the terrible tenseness she felt in her neck and shoulders, but she was less than successful. She felt David reaching out to her and knew that she would be rejecting his gesture—and him—by not going. Her heart didn't want to hear what her mind was shouting, but she had to listen. There was no way she could disappoint Michael. She had promised him she would see him every weekend.

No matter what her own yearnings would be, she would hold fast to that promise.

The slamming of a car door below seized Sabrina's attention. Looking down from the cupola she saw Ernest opening the passenger door of his pickup truck for Hester. She was carrying a small bouquet of cut flowers. Sabrina rushed downstairs to find out how Hester's visit with Ernest's mother had gone.

She found her friend in the kitchen, getting a vase from the storage room adjacent to it. Ernest, apparently, had returned to work in the solarium. One look at Hester's face convinced Sabrina that all had gone well. The woman was actually glowing.

"So, Ernest is giving you flowers now."

"Aren't they lovely?" Hester set to arranging the mixed bouquet in the same crystal vase that had held David's roses.

"How is his mother?"

"Getting on, but I was surprised at how active she still is. Lucille must be in her late seventies, but she was repotting orchids when we arrived, and she worked in the greenhouse the whole time I visited."

"Did she remember you, Hester?"

"Yes." Sabrina noted the blush that appeared. "Lucille told me that I had grown to be a beautiful woman and she hoped I wouldn't be stranger." Her eyes found Sabrina's. "Can you imagine...me...a beautiful woman! Her eyes must be failing her, the sweet soul. She invited me to dinner this Sunday."

Sabrina moved closer. "You're going, aren't you?"

"Ernest insisted."

Sabrina sighed with relief. At least relationships were working out for some people, she told herself and had a fleeting thought of Ina and Eugene.

"Ernest told his mother that your son would be spending Thanksgiving here. She said she'd love to see him." Wiping her hands with a towel, she added, "He also told her what wonders you were doing here at the house, and she made me promise she could be the first one to see it when it was all done over."

Sabrina's inner voice urged her on. *No time like the present.* "Hester... would you feel bad if Michael and I stayed at the Mansfields' while he's here? They have a guest cottage, and with all the work going on here, I just thought that—" The cold look in Hester's eyes stopped her dead.

"You've become quite friendly with them, haven't you?" she asked, her voice shaking.

Sabrina's throat became thick; she felt a throbbing at her temples. "Yes, I have...with David, at least. I've been seeing him quite often."

Hester set the towel down slowly and turned away from her.

The thickness in Sabrina's throat became a lump as she watched Hester turn her back on her. She had known she would be disappointed at her request, but she hadn't thought it would cause her so much distress. She was sorry that it did, but she also felt an irritation at Hester's lack of understanding.

Or maybe, Sabrina thought, as they both remained silent, Hester's reaction only epitomized the many obstacles that stood in the way of any lasting relationship she might have with David. Damn it! When would her turn come for a little happiness?

"Hester," she said finally, trying to sound considerate and calm, "I'm sorry that you don't like David, but I can't help that. It's important to me that Michael has a chance to get to know him. He needs that chance and so do I. And I need David, just as you need Ernest.''

Facing her, Hester said quietly, ''Ernest and David Mansfield are totally different men. Ernest is dependable and considerate.''

''David is, too.''

''Ernest is trustworthy.''

''And David isn't?''

Hester stepped closer, but stopped at the table and flattened her palms on the top of it. ''He's had affairs with several women already. I told you that, and he's tossed them aside, just as his father did! Shelby was never faithful to his wife. Like father, like son. Are you satisfied to only be added to his list?''

The distraught woman's words struck Sabrina like a knife to the heart, not because she believed what Hester was trying to warn her of. David was not a youth; there was no reason to believe he had been celibate all his life. No, the words hurt because she realized the damage Hester's hatred had done to the woman herself, the bitterness that it had fostered.

With a great deal of effort, Sabrina successfully convinced herself that Hester spoke out of friendship and not maliciously, and it was because they had become friends that she didn't want them to argue.

Feeling her head ache, Sabrina raised tense fingers to her brow. ''I love David, Hester. Nothing can change that now. Be happy for me…please, just as I'm happy for you and Ernest.''

Hester's vacant stare roamed the large kitchen. ''Perhaps it's this house, but I've come to expect very little happiness in it.'' Her forced smile was etched in sorrow. ''Happiness…it frightens me. It's always been a prelude to pain.'' The sigh that followed was more of a shudder. "Stay with the Mansfields if you want. Take the boy to them. Maybe the two of you will be more fortunate than I have been."

Sabrina shook her head slowly. "I'm sorry for that, Hester, but I can't remake the past. I can only hope for the future." She left the room quietly.

The cool November air felt good on Sabrina's face as she walked in the gardens at the side of the house and made her way to the newly painted gazebo. For minutes she stood there, trying not to think of anything, trying to fill her consciousness with the natural surroundings of the woods behind the gazebo. Then she sat down on one of the seats next to the railing, leaned her arm on it and let the tears come.

She saw Ed go to his truck in the parking area and realized she hadn't signed his work sheet for the day. Maybe Hester had. Sabrina didn't care. The heaviness she felt in her heart wouldn't let her care about anything but her own sorrow. And she knew the only person who could lift that load from her was in Atlanta.

How she wanted to go to him . . . have him hold her and tell her everything would be all right. But then that warning voice took over, triggered by Hester's words, perhaps. The voice demanded that she think seriously about what she was rushing into, insisted that she realize just how vulnerable she was where David was concerned, how hurt she could get if she were misreading his feelings for her.

As she listened, though, her fingers toyed with the heart-shaped charm, and her eyes lowered to read the inscription. "Love," she whispered, and the word itself caused a renewed courage to well up in her heart.

"Sabrina!"

Her head shot up and she saw Hester waving to her.

"Mr. Hutchins is on the phone!"

"Oh my God," she murmured as she rushed toward the house. Todd had never called before, but she'd given him this number in the event of any emergency concerning Michael. That was all she could think of when she grabbed for the receiver.

"Todd! What's happened?"

"Happened? Nothing's happened. I just wanted you to know I'm taking Michael to visit my parents in Houston this weekend."

She flattened a palm over her chest. "Oh, I thought something had happened to him."

"Lord, you're a worrywart. I swear, Sabrina, I think you enjoy it."

"Todd, let me talk to Michael."

"He's not here."

"Not there? Where is he?"

"There you go again. The kid's gone to the movies."

"Alone?"

"No, not alone! Ann took him. One of those *Star Trek* things. I can't stand that stuff myself."

"Well," Sabrina said, talking more to herself, "I guess he'll enjoy the trip."

"Sure he will, and it'll give you a break." He snickered. "You'll have a whole weekend with nothing to do."

That registered. "Yes," she said, again to herself. "I will."

"Not necessary to thank me, Sabrina."

"All right, Todd, I won't."

"Take care."

As she replaced the receiver, Sabrina's face shone with a steadfast and serene determination. Ina had told her that she had organized her life so that there was little time for what Sabrina wanted. And she wanted David with all her heart. "This weekend," she said, voicing her thoughts, "will be for you, Sabrina!"

FRIDAY EVENING, as the jet began its descent to Atlanta International Airport, Sabrina was filled with joyful anticipation at the thought of seeing David again. It increased as she walked through the sheltered walkway from the plane to the terminal building. She felt it in her quickening heartbeat and in the almost frenetic searching of her eyes.

He said he'd be waiting, she told herself as she scanned the crowds that milled around in the vast terminal, the blaring voice announcing arrivals and departures filling her ears.

"Sabrina!"

She turned. His tall figure was pushing its way through travelers heading in the opposite direction. His handsome face was alive with a dazzling smile that increased the pounding in her chest.

Reaching her, he stopped and exhaled a deep breath. "You came. God, I didn't know if you would or not."

Gathering her into his arms, he held her close. Sabrina felt his warm breath against her ear and heard his deep voice whisper, "Oh, I've missed you so."

Clasped in his embrace, all was suddenly peace and contentment. The noise of the busy terminal dissipated. All that existed was the elation she felt at this moment and the knowledge that what she was doing was so right.

After collecting her luggage, they took a cab to the elegant seventy-story Peachtree Plaza Hotel, where David had already registered them. The room was large and comfortable, beautifully appointed in warm earth tones. By the wide, draped window was a sitting area with easy chairs and a small table.

As she hung up her clothes, Sabrina asked, "Is this how you've been roughing it here in Atlanta?"

Sitting on the rust-colored bedspread, David filled his eyes with her movements. "Uh-uh. Usually when I come to Atlanta, I stay with Charles. Eileen, his wife, invited you, too, but I thought this would be nicer. I didn't want anybody or anything sharing this weekend with us. Well," he admitted, "I do have to go to the office for a few hours in the morning, but other than that this weekend is ours."

Sabrina closed the closet door and went to him, taking his face in her hands. "That's exactly how I feel."

David's hands moved to her waist and he rested his cheek against her stomach. "How I love you," he whispered.

Then Sabrina found herself being pulled down to the bed next to him.

Gazing at her lying there, he smoothed back her silky auburn hair with gentle fingers. "What have you done to me, Sabrina Hutchins?" he asked, his voice velvet-edged and deceptively calm. "All my life the only thing that really mattered was proving to myself that I could be a success."

"You are a success. You would be no matter what you had chosen to do."

"No...success for me is always the next venture, the next challenge." Tenderly he traced the curve of her ear. "Or it used to be...until I met you."

Softly she asked, "And now?"

"Success would be making you fall hopelessly in love with me, so hopelessly you couldn't think of anyone or anything else."

His face moved closer and he kissed her with a hunger that belied his outward calm. The prolonged anticipation of this moment had almost been unbearable for her, but now that his mouth was on hers, now that she could taste him, touch him and feel his warmth permeate her entire body—the waiting had been worth all the torment. They were together again, and she knew he would be hers completely; she would willingly be his.

Raising himself up, David felt a trembling on his lips. A silvery blue light played in his eyes when he warned her, "We had better get out of here right now. If we don't there'll be no dinner." He stood up. "I've made reservations for us." He reached down, took hold of her hands and pulled her up, encircling her waist when she stood before him. "Like Russian food?"

"Better than sushi."

"Sushi?"

"A private joke."

"Oh?" he commented with mock suspicion, "so we're going to have secrets between us." He began tickling her, and she squirmed in his arms. "Private joke with whom, woman?"

"Ina!" she blurted out, trying to make him stop.

"Well, that's okay. How's she doing with Eugene?"

As Sabrina checked her hair in the mirror, she told him, "She left me a note at the apartment. Eugene's taken her to meet his parents in Arkansas."

"Sounds serious."

She looked at his reflection in the mirror and nodded. "I think you're right. Guess I'll be looking for a
new roommate soon."

"We'll see about that."

NIKOLAI'S RESTAURANT boasted a rooftop setting
overlooking the glorious night lights of Atlanta. Even
the weather seemed to be cooperating for their weekend together: the night was clear and sprinkled with
sparkling stars; the air was cool, but pleasantly so. Atlanta was enjoying an Indian summer.

David ordered for the two of them, and they sipped
on vodka and nibbled at Beluga caviar on thin toast.
When dinner arrived, Sabrina's palate tingled with
unfamiliar flavors. First there was borscht, served hot
with sour cream and *pirojok*, a tiny meat pastry. The
entrée was *Karsky shaslik supréme*, a superbly barbe-
cued lamb cutlet. The tea accompanying their dinner
was served in the traditional glass rather than a cup.

While they dined, Sabrina told David of her conversation with Hester regarding Michael's visit and their
staying at the cottage.

"Sabrina," he asked, honest confusion in his voice,
"what's with that lady? I've tried to be nice to her, but
all I get is the cold shoulder. Has she ever told you why
she acts that way?"

She had to conquer her involuntary reaction to the
gentle, loving look she saw in David's eyes. Her lips
had actually parted to tell him the reason, but then she
silently agonized over the consequences. If she did
confide in him, she would be breaking the trust Hester
had placed in her; if she didn't she would be lying to the
man she loved. Worst of all, it would be a lie that af-

fected him personally. Frustrated, she finally decided that the appropriate time would come. This wasn't it.

Grasping her glass of tea, she looked down at it and told him, "Whatever reason Hester has, I'm sure it's quite private."

He shrugged dismissively. "Maybe it's because Shelby's been buying up her land as fast as she's been selling it, but why would that bother her so much?"

Sabrina smiled and said, "I thought we weren't going to let anyone or anything intrude on our weekend."

Leaning forward, he set his forearms on the edge of the table. "Do you have any idea what a captivating picture you make when you smile like that?"

"Uh-huh," she teased. "What are you going to do about it?"

David felt her question send maddening currents through his body. Speaking through the knot that choked his Adam's apple, he lowered his voice. "Let's get dessert over with, and I'll show you."

Feeling her own lurch of excitement, Sabrina's eyes raked boldly over him, then stared directly into his. "I'm too full for dessert."

"Good. Let's get the hell out of here."

CHAPTER FOURTEEN

DAVID LOWERED THE VOLUME on the music center built into the hotel room wall. He had already changed and was now wearing only a short velour robe. There was an expected knock on the door. Taking great strides across the thick carpet in his bare feet, he opened it for room service and signed for the champagne he'd ordered when Sabrina had gone into the bathroom to change. He wanted everything to be just right tonight.

He fumbled as he popped the cork, smiling at himself for feeling as nervous as a bridegroom. His eyes went to the bathroom door, and he raised his palms to smooth back the sides of his hair. God, he'd never been so excited in his life. She had turned his whole world upside down, and he was loving every minute of it! He knew he'd have to calm down eventually; he had to get his mind back on business. But not tonight....

He heard the bathroom door open. Turning, his breath stopped, and his blood rushed as he gazed at the woman who had unlocked his heart and soul. Standing there across the room, Sabrina appeared to be pure elegance, a bewitching figure borne of an enchanting dream. Her hair hung wavy and shiny; her face was that of an angel. The robe she wore was a diaphanous ivory-colored creation without the undergarment he suspected was made to go with it. His eyes took in the hints of flesh, the peaks of her breasts and the alluring curves of her slender body.

He swallowed hard. "Lovely, just lovely," he murmured.

Sabrina enjoyed his obvious approval; it was what she had hoped for, and more. The smoldering flame she saw in David's eyes confirmed the fact that she had pleased him, and that made her happy. Her own inspection took in the way the light from the other side of the room cast his features in a soft semishadow, the way his short robe exposed a vee of dark, silky hairs on his manly chest. He stood there tall, eager and desirable. And he was hers.

Having thought of this moment many times since meeting her at the airport, and having promised himself that their loving would not be rushed this time, David forced his attention to the wine and went to the table where it had been set. "Champagne," he said, again filling his eyes with the beauty of her.

She just about floated across the carpeted floor, her long, slender legs parting the lacy gown as she moved toward him. "How sweet of you, David."

As she came nearer to him, he caught a whiff of her perfume. It reminded him of fragile springtime flowers. He reached for the champagne bottle and hoped she didn't notice his hand shaking a little as he filled the glasses.

Accepting the wineglass from him, Sabrina raised it, and with compelling eyes she toasted, "To us, David."

His own eyes were bold as they lowered to the lacy bodice of her robe, and he had to fight to hold to the promise he had made to himself. His whole being was filled with the mad desire to take her right there where she stood. After biting the inside of his lower lip, he raised his glass, also, and touched it to hers. "To you, love," he managed to get out.

"No," she corrected immediately, "to *us*."

With eyes meeting eyes, they sipped, David quite a bit more than Sabrina. He needed the cool, tingling liquid to temper his hot tongue and parched throat.

"This is nice," she told him, then turned and took a few steps. "The music is nice, the room is nice."

His eyes riveted to her charming derrière, and when she turned again—quickly this time—he had the sinking feeling that his promise had been in vain. His eyes shot up to her face, and he saw that amusement lingered there.

Quickly he drained his glass and poured himself another drink.

After setting hers down on the table between the easy chairs, Sabrina extended her arms. "Dance with me, David."

Now his throat really needed the cooling effect of the champagne he gulped down. He set his glass next to hers and took her into his arms.

In the dim light of the room they moved slowly for a while. Then Sabrina stopped, kicked off her slippers and snuggled up against him. She breathed in the pleasant masculine smell of his body, and decided it was more intoxicating than the champagne. As David rocked her slowly in his embrace, she loosened the belt of his robe with her left hand and slipped her arm inside and around his waist.

His skin was warm and smooth and when she lowered her palm over his buttock, she could feel his muscles tense. Resting her head in the curve at his neck, she eased her other arm around his waist and slowly moved her hands upward and downward, capturing the exciting heat of his body in her palms.

The music was soothing; she felt content. Even more so when David's arms tightened around her. They were barely moving now, merely holding one another in the dimly lit room as though they were the only two people in the world.

David raised one hand and wiped at the perspiration beading over his upper lip. He took in a deep breath and raised his eyes to the ceiling in frustration. His legs were strong and well-muscled, but he could feel his knees turning to jelly, and with each movement of Sabrina's body against his, it got worse.

"Sabrina," he murmured, his voice somewhat higher than usual, "I think it would be a good idea if we didn't dance anymore."

She stopped and tilted her head up. "I imagine you're exhausted. You've been working day and night here."

A promise is a promise, he ordered himself. To her he replied, "Yes...that's it exactly."

Taking his hand in hers, she pulled him to one of the wide easy chairs. "Sit down and relax, David."

Smiling at her thoughtfulness, he did, noting the mischievous light that sparkled in her hazel eyes as she picked up his wineglass and refilled it. Handing it to him, she looked down at his wonderfully attractive face. Sabrina knew she didn't need any more wine; she was already heady with wanting David, and she could tell at a glance that the hot tide of passion was raging through his body, too.

She slid onto his lap and cupped his face with her hands. Softly and slowly she kissed his lips and then began to smooth back the strands of hair that draped over his forehead. "There now... are you relaxed?"

Feeling the wonderful warmth of her body resting on his, he moistened his upper lip and attempted a nod with closed eyes. The torment was delightful as she moved one slender finger over his lips, then guided it down over his chin, throat and onto his bare chest where she traced each of his hardened nipples. He emitted a long, deep sigh. "I take it you are comfortable."

"I'm always comfortable with you, David," she told him in silken tones, her last word smothered on his lips.

Her sensuous tongue sent shivers of hot desire racing through him, knotting his stomach. His arms rushed around her and his thoughts became fragmented when her kiss deepened and became even more tantalizing. He savored every wonderful moment of it, just as he delighted in the way she was taking the lead in their lovemaking.

His delight turned to ecstasy when he felt her lips move over his ear, felt the tip of her tongue delve inside and moisten it seductively. With one powerful movement he rose from the chair. lifting her in his arms as he did.

Smiling, he gazed down at her. 'Brazen, my love... you're wonderfully brazen."

With her arms lovingly around his neck, David carried her into the bedroom, and moments later Sabrina lay cuddled against him, her cheek resting on his chest, her arms across his waist.

"Love," he whispered, his voice soft and playful, "you have some winsome ways about you."

She smiled against his flesh. "I want to please you, David. It's important to me that you be happy."

A languid sigh slipped past his lips, and he tilted her chin up and kissed her forehead. Lowering his head back onto the pillow, he admitted, "I've never been this happy in my entire life. It's all such a new and wonderful feeling."

"It's never been like this for me, either." She began to stroke his arm slowly with her fingers. "You make me feel—" she sought the right word "—well, you make me *feel* again. You've made me realize that for so long I've just been existing, not really living." She touched her lips to his chest. "With you I'm alive, and the feeling is wonderful, David."

In a throaty voice he whispered, "I want you to feel that way all the time." Then, he moved his hand over her stomach and began a slow caressing motion. "You're so soft, so warm and sweet."

Sabrina's fingers tightened around his shoulder when she felt his palm ease downward, his expert touch offering her deeper joy.

"Look at me, love," he whispered, "I want to see your face." He moved his arm a little so she could rest the side of her head on it, all the while continuing to increase the pressure of his palm. "I love the way your eyes change when you become excited. It excites me, too." His hand played gently around her silky triangle, and then he searched for that special place, never taking his gaze from hers. "Those hazel eyes of yours take on little sparks of green—" her gasp told him he had found it "—and your eyes seem to be on fire...like they are now."

"David," she murmured, clutching the back of his neck, "kiss me...I—"

"No, I want to watch you now." He caressed and rubbed more firmly, his own breathing increasing to match hers as he felt her body tense in his arms.

"David! . . . Ohhhhh!"

He held her tightly and smiled radiantly as he absorbed the beauty of her eyes at the moment she cried out, and then he claimed her lips, crushing her to him while he brought her to one searing climax after the other. Her shattered breaths were like manna as he took in as much of her as he could. The feel of her body trembling and jerking as he held her excited him as much as her soul-drenching sighs. Moving over her, he quickly entered her wet softness and sank into her deeply. His love for her filled her like warm honey.

Sweetly drained, they lay closely together afterward, her back to him, his arms around her, his thighs pressed to her buttocks. Sleep was almost upon them when David whispered into her hair. "I love you, Sabrina."

Her lashes flicked in the darkened room, and she felt his breath on her ear as he asked softly, "Are you awake?"

"Yes," she answered quietly.

He moved his knees up a little to touch the back of hers. "I said 'I love you.' Doesn't that get an 'Oh' or a 'That's nice,' even?"

Tightening her hold on his arms, she smiled. "I love you, too."

"Oh," he said lightly, "that's nice." Then his voice took on a seriousness. "What are we going to do about it?"

She rolled over onto her back and looked into his inquiring eyes. "Do?"

He nodded.

"What options do we have?" She tried to put off answering the question she sensed was coming.

He rolled over onto his back and clasped his hands behind his head. "Well...we could take out a full-page ad in the Greensboro Chronicle, or we could have it skywritten over New Orleans, or...we could get married."

For long agonizing moments David stared up at the ceiling, waiting for a response from her. None came. "Or," he suggested glumly, "I could shut up and we could go to sleep."

Why wasn't she shouting for joy? Sabrina demanded of herself. Those were the exact words she had wanted to hear—half in anticipation and half in dread, she had to admit. Why was she lying here, agonizing over them? But she knew why.

Marriage was just too big a step for her right now. She could just picture herself introducing David to her son, saying, "Michael, this is David, your new father," and watching her son's face crumple in confusion.

Still staring up and waiting, David offered, "Those are the only options I can come up with at the moment. You don't seem impressed with any of them."

Sabrina raised herself up and looked down at him. Trying for lightness, she told him, "Pushy, aren't you? Do I have to decide right now?"

His eyes darted to hers. "You mean you have to think about it?"

She fingered some strands of hair back over her ear. "I have to think about how Michael would take my telling him his mother has decided to get married again."

"What am I...an ogre? I'd do my damnedest to make him like me."

"David...I just think it would be better if he grew to like you before I told him we were all moving in together."

He stared up at the ceiling again. "Love, I'm not getting any younger. I'd like to be able to walk to our children's graduation ceremonies, not be wheeled in."

"Children!" She paused to digest that idea.

"You know...we make love...nine months later?"

"David, marriage is a big step. Both our lives would change drastically. Why...there are so many things we haven't even discussed yet. And when you start talking children—"

"So...discuss."

"David, be serious," she told him, raising herself into a sitting position. "That's something we should do in the light of day, not in the...the—"

"Heat of passion?" he suggested.

"Look, I love you and you love me. Why can't we just leave it at that for now?"

He sat up next to her. "Play it by ear, you mean."

"Well...yes."

David raised a hand and with a pointed finger he tapped her breastbone. "You, lady, are weird."

"Who's weird?"

"You." He tapped again, twice and said half-playfully, half-seriously, "You get me all fired up to make what is probably the biggest decision of my life, and now you want to play it by ear?"

"I got *you* fired up?" Sabrina responded, hurt.

"Yes, you!"

"What about the adjustments I've made?" she asked, trying to keep her rising anger under control.

He pursed his lips in frustration and said, "Women are supposed to want to get married!"

"Nuts!" Sabrina announced bluntly, and then she fell back onto the pillow and covered her head with the sheet.

Disconcerted, David crossed his arms and looked across the room, his imagination swimming through a haze of feelings for the woman lying next to him, her face covered with that damn sheet.

He sat there, hating the silence, wondering why she wouldn't sit up and fight. The quiet continued, increasing his frustration. He didn't know how to handle silence. But he knew he didn't like the yelling, either. Slowly he lifted the edge of the sheet and peered down at her.

"Listen," he asked quietly and cautiously, "was it something I said?"

She jerked the sheet from his fingers and recovered her face, mumbling, "Go 'way."

David shook his head and chuckled at her. Then he lay down on his stomach and rested his chin on the back of his crossed hands. "Women," he said aloud, "the confusing sex." The sheet didn't move. "Sabrina...you're going to suffocate." Only silence greeted him. David began to hurt inside. "All I said was that I loved you. I thought you'd be pleased." He heard her deep sigh, then the sheet was lowered, and she looked over at him.

It was impossible for her not to return his disarming grin. "I am pleased, David," she said with a touch of sadness in her voice.

"It's always Michael, isn't it? You're worried about what he'll think." He watched her nod. "Well, we've got to do something about that." Not liking the distance between them, he asked, "Is it chilly in here to you?"

"No."

"It is to me. C'mere...please," he asked and extended his arm.

Sabrina moved to him, and she, too, felt relief when he placed his arm around her.

"I've got a week during Thanksgiving to win him over, huh?" He patted her shoulder as he thought. "I'll take some time off work, and he and I could—"

That registered. "Did I hear right? You'd actually take time off?"

"Watch it," he teased. "You're starting to sound weird again. Sure I would. See what you've done to me, a confirmed workaholic."

"You'll live longer," she told him and snuggled closer.

He was busy thinking again. "Do you suppose there's any chance of Hester joining us for Thanksgiving dinner?"

"I doubt it," she replied.

After a few moments, David asked, "Michael is the only problem we have, right?"

"Yes," she said softly against his chest and held him a little tighter. *If we don't count your half sister.*

CHAPTER FIFTEEN

SABRINA ROLLED OVER onto her back. Lackadaisically she raised her arms straight up and stretched, smiling at the still sensitive parts of her that David had made love to time and again during the wonderful night. Her lips felt slightly bruised, and the stubble of his beard had left her cheeks tender, but gloriously so.

With her eyes yet closed she lowered her hands and reached over to feel the warmth of him, but they shot open when she felt only the bed. She jerked her body up and found herself alone in the quiet hotel room. The bathroom door was ajar, but no sound came from there, either.

Now she was wide awake and hurried to slip on her robe. Then she saw the note David had left. It was propped against the half-full bottle of champagne on the table.

> Love, I'll be back as soon as I can. You looked so beautiful while you slept, I hated to leave. Phone room service or have breakfast in the restaurant downstairs. Love you.
>
> David

Sabrina then remembered his telling her that he would have to go into the office for a few hours this morning. She went to the dresser where she had placed her watch. It was a little after ten o'clock. She wondered how early David had left and hoped he would return before too long so they could have lunch together.

Taking his advice, she phoned room service, but ordered only a pot of coffee. It was delivered shortly and she poured a cup before taking a hot shower, and another while she put on some makeup. She decided to wear a rust and black tweed sweater dress, although she didn't know what David had planned for them today.

It was almost eleven-thirty when she thought of the Do Not Disturb sign David had hung on the outside door knob last night. It was still there. After setting it on the dresser, she took her handbag, left the room and smiled pleasantly at the maid who was rolling her cart of fresh linens down the carpeted hallway.

Downstairs in the lobby she bought a newspaper and sat down to read, giving the maid an opportunity to do her work.

"May I have the sports page?"

Looking up, Sabrina saw David smiling down at her. "Good morning," she said in a silky voice, her hazel eyes filling with love.

His brimmed with tenderness when he asked, "Did you miss me?"

"I did," she said playfully and asked, "Did you have time to miss me?"

"You'd better believe I did, and the rest of the weekend is ours. Did you have breakfast?"

She shook her head.

"Neither did I. How about brunch?"

She agreed and he led her into the hotel dining room, where they ordered omelettes and sausages.

As they ate, David said, "Hope you brought some comfortable walking shoes with you...I plan to give you a scenic tour of Atlanta."

Before sipping her hot coffee, she asked, "Do I have a choice?"

"Sure. What did you have in mind?"

Her eyes bore into his. "What do you think?"

He studied her face and beamed his approval. "Is it what I'm thinking you're thinking?"

She watched his eyes lower to the deep vee of her sweater dress, and they exchanged a subtle look of amused understanding. Chewing her omelette, she nodded slowly.

David began eating a little faster. "You're my kind of woman. I'll show you Atlanta tomorrow."

"Maybe," she told him and took a final swallow of coffee.

With the Do Not Disturb sign in place again, Sabrina and David intimately explored, played and became lost in each other, dipping fully into love's cup and draining it eagerly. Throughout the afternoon, they alternately made love and slept, both of them knowing how much they had to squeeze into this time they had together. During one peaceful interlude, David held Sabrina in his arms, wondering why he had fallen in love with her so quickly, and so deeply.

Sure, the first day he had seen her—the time when she had stopped when he'd had the flat—he had seen how lovely she was and had wondered even then what it would be like to make love to her. But that feeling wasn't at all like the feeling he had for her now. That first response had been only a crazy kind of desire. He had experienced that feeling of walking on air with other women, though it had always evaporated rather quickly.

But with Sabrina that original sexual attraction had only deepened with time, making it impossible to get her out of his mind, forcing him to yearn for the next time he would see her. Then the terrible longing had started, a sort of heart sickness, a fear that she might not feel the same way about him. And when she had kissed him the night he had driven her back to Belleamie, hope had surged high.

Sabrina's lashes brushed against the hairs on his chest, and she felt David kiss the top of her head as she eased her leg between his. She was feeling so comfortable, so warm and cuddly and she wanted the feeling to last forever. In her half sleep she pictured herself married to him. *Mrs. David Mansfield.* It had a ring to it, she thought, smiling at her thoughts. *Michael Hutchins? Michael Mansfield?* Well, she'd cross that bridge when the time came.

Her fingers moved almost imperceptibly over David's stomach. His body smelled so good, so potent. If they were to marry, she pondered, Michael would have a real family again and so would she. At that thought her smile broadened.

"Awake?" he asked softly.

Tilting her head back, she looked over at him with hooded eyes and received his tender kiss.

Placing his other arm over her, he began a soothing stroking of her back. "It's got to be tough being a single parent. How do you deal with it?"

With closed eyes, she moved her fingers around his jawline. "I just do."

"I think it would be good for Michael to have a man around all the time."

She eased her hand down and began stroking his shoulder. "It'd be nice for me, too."

He asked quietly, "Did you and Todd do a lot of this...just lying in bed together?"

The stroking stopped and her eyes were open now. "What makes you ask that?"

"Just curious. Can't blame me for wondering how much you loved the guy, how much he loved you."

She slipped her arm around his waist. "No, it was never like this, never so...relaxed, so natural."

"Good," he said, satisfaction in his tone.

Her eyes opened wide. "David Mansfield, you're jealous."

"I am *not*. I was just wondering, that's all." His hand moved over her belly. "We'll have children, won't we? I mean yours and mine."

"Not now we won't."

"After we're married?"

Anxiety coursed through her suddenly, dissipating the contentment she had been experiencing. Thinking about marriage was safe, easy, but actually planning on it, talking about it as if the decision were a *fait accompli*, was something she wasn't ready to do, not yet.

Her silence disturbed him, as did the pensive expression on her face. He raised himself up. "You're upset."

"No."

"It's me again, isn't it?"

"It's not you. It's me."

His palm went to her cheek. "What's the matter, love? Is it Michael?"

Sabrina lowered his hand and began to stroke it with hers. "It hasn't been easy for him, David. He was uprooted from his friends in Connecticut when he was five because Todd wanted to take a position in New Orleans. Then there was the divorce, and now this business of his being shuttled back and forth every six months from one home to another.''

She looked up at David. "I know he hasn't gotten over the loss he felt when Todd moved out, and now I'm afraid that when he finds out you've come into my life, he'll think he's losing me, too." In anguish, she pleaded, "I can't put him through that...I just can't."

Lying back down, David drew her close to him. There was sympathy and understanding in his voice when he said gently, "We won't rush him, Sabrina, I promise you. Let's not think about it now. Remember, this is our time, our weekend."

And the remainder of it was. That evening David took Sabrina to The Abbey on Piedmont Avenue for dinner—a converted church where the waiters were garbed in monks' robes. Afterward they sat hand in hand, listening to an all-Brahms program by the Atlanta Symphony.

On Sunday they rose early, wanting to squeeze the most out of the last hours they would have together. David rented a car and they toured Stone Mountain, just outside of Atlanta, taking the cable car to the summit. They walked hand in hand through Grant Park and went through the Swan House, an elaborate example of Italian Palladian architecture. They enjoyed the day immensely, but each felt the hours slipping away.

Early that evening they dined in Dante's Down the Hatch, a make-believe sailing ship, and tried to enjoy the wine and the jazz, but the time soon came for David to take Sabrina to the airport.

In the terminal, after Sabrina had checked in, she and David stood by the window in the waiting room. She stared out, watching the squat vehicles carting luggage to waiting planes, and she realized soon she'd be back in Louisiana. Out of the blue, a question invaded her thoughts.

"David," she asked, "just how serious is this business of your father's chemical plant being investigated?"

He turned his attention from the tarmac below to her. "If I can believe Brian, Shelby's got nothing to worry about. Before I left, Brian assured me everything at the plant is being done according to the law. Julie's representing Eiler's plant in the matter—she doesn't want to handle Mansfield Chemicals, and rightly so. It would appear unethical, and she'd be accused of maneuvering a cover-up."

"How is your father taking it? When I heard about the investigation I was concerned for his health." She saw the troubled look in David's eyes and watched him stare out the window again.

As he followed the lights of an ascending jet in the distance, he said, "I'm worried about him, to be honest. He's not a strong man any more, not like he used to be. And the weaker he gets, the worse I feel." There was a touch of irony in his low laugh. "You know, there was a time, a long time ago, when I thought the sun rose and set on that man." His jaw tightened. "I couldn't have been much more than six when he informed me there would be no more good-night hugs. Men didn't do that sort of thing... it wasn't masculine. People would think I was a sissy, and no son of his was going to be that."

He looked back at Sabrina. "At the time, the only thing I knew, the only thing I understood, was that my father, the man I worshipped, was shoving me away, telling me there was something wrong in my loving him. He didn't even want me to touch him anymore. So I didn't. All I did was wonder what I had done. It must have been something bad . . . real bad."

"You don't believe that now, though," she said, feeling David's pain.

He shook his head slowly. "No. Now I realize how confused Shelby has always been about loving. Even when my mother died, Shelby took it *like a man*...and expected the whole world to praise him for it."

Reaching over, Sabrina looped her arm around his. "That's not being a man. It's being unfeeling . . . inhuman."

"It got worse after she died. The only emotions he permitted himself to show me were negative ones like anger. He was good at that." He faced Sabrina. "I'd never be like that with Michael . . . never."

"I know," she said quickly. "You'd be good for Michael, and he'd be good for you. Both of you have so much love to give."

"The three of us do. That's what makes everything so right for us."

The announcement to board her plane echoed in the waiting room. Sabrina felt a huge, painful knot inside her stomach. Her sorrow at having to leave David weighed heavily. To cover it, she forced an uneasy smile. "How much longer do you think you'll be in Atlanta?"

"I'll be back in Greensboro on Wednesday, I promise. Let's have dinner, so we can talk about Thanksgiving plans."

The order to board sounded again.

"This weekend was heaven and more, David."

"The first of many," he told her and kissed her.

Afraid he would see the tears she felt coming, she said, "I'd better go now."

David walked her to the line of passengers waiting to depart. He watched until he could no longer see her and then he waited until her plane was out of sight.....

High in the clouds, Sabrina undid the seat belt and leaned back. As she gazed absentmindedly out at the darkness, she realized just how bad she felt for David. She fairly ached as she thought of how he must have felt as a boy not much younger than her own son when his father refused the love David had offered him, replacing it with a relationship that was formal, stiff and cold. Sabrina remembered having had a glimpse of it that night at Shelby's home.

But she had to admit also that in some ways David was his father's son, whether he would concede it or not—particularly when it came to work. To some degree she now understood that competition David felt between him and Shelby. Perhaps that was the only level left on which the two men could now communicate. And perhaps David's almost compulsive need to succeed was his way of trying to regain Shelby's love. It all seemed very sad to her and such a waste of the affection that could exist between father and son. Sweet David, he had so much affection to give.

Thinking of Hester's relationship with Shelby, Sabrina shook her head sadly, realizing that both she and David would have to come to terms with their feelings toward him—before it was too late.

ON MONDAY EVENING Sabrina and Hester were in the parlor, watching TV on the new color console. At seven o'clock, Hester told her that Julie was to be interviewed at a local station and asked if Sabrina would mind watching. Surprised, she told Hester that she would enjoy it, and she then thought that perhaps her friend's feelings for the Mansfields were not as cut and dried as she'd pretended. She certainly seemed to have an interest in what David and Julie were doing. When Hester switched channels, the interview was already in progress:

"... skyrocketing property values," Julie was saying, "and our population growth rate in Greensboro makes it essential that we control our development and not vice versa. I don't believe it's too early for us to be planning for the kind of community we want to have in the year two thousand."

The interviewer, a young man with glasses, said, "That's admirable thinking, Miss Mansfield, but what exactly will you do if you are elected mayor?"

"The first thing I plan to do is create a Downtown Development Board to decide what can be done with existing properties and what kind of development might occur in the future. Greensboro's leader *must* make judicious decisions that will foster sensible development. More does not necessarily mean better."

As Julie talked, Sabrina stole a glance at Hester, and she would have sworn the older woman's lips threatened a smile of pride that became more of a reality as Julie answered further questions on issues including the school board's banning of Chaucer and Aristophanes from school libraries for moral reasons. Julie made it clear that she was against the censorship of books, particularly the classics.

"Miss Mansfield," the interviewer asked, "the problem of protecting the environment is often discussed nowadays. I ask you to be specific. What is your commitment on the issue?"

Looking directly into Sabrina's and Hester's eyes, via the TV camera, Julie said, "This issue is of particular concern to me. I am committed to protecting the environment first, economics second, unlike my opponent. When I am elected I'll push hard for an improved water treatment plant and a garbage-to-energy plant outside—"

"Excuse me, Miss Mansfield," he interrupted, "but what our viewers really want to hear you address is this problem of illegal hazardous waste dumping, since your father's plant, Mansfield Chemicals, is currently being investigated."

Sabrina saw Hester lean forward in her chair as Julie responded. "Is *one* of the plants being investigated, Mr. Crenshaw." She again directed her words to the camera. "Whichever firm is doing the dumping to avoid the costs of transporting the waste to EPA approved out-of-state landfills will eventually be singled out by the State Attorney's office. As an attorney myself, I am representing Eiler Chemicals, one of the—"

Julie stopped midsentence as a young woman handed her a note. Sabrina and Hester looked at each other, then turned back toward the TV. They saw Julie's face blanch. She looked up into the camera. "I ask your indulgence. I must leave. My father has just had a serious heart attack." She rose and left the set.

As the station went to a quick commercial, Hester got up and switched off the TV; her face was as pale as Julie's had become. She stared at Sabrina. "He's going to die, Sabrina. I can feel it."

Sabrina rose. "I'm sorry, Hester, so very sorry." She attempted to reassure her, adding, "Shelby has had several attacks, and he's survived them."

Hester remained silent, clasping her hands in front of her, her face filled with ambivalence.

"We could call," Sabrina suggested, "find out if he's at the house or has been taken to the hospital."

The response she received was only a slow shaking of Hester's head.

Sabrina tried again. "If it is serious, you might consider going to him."

The woman's eyes lifted, and Sabrina saw the sheen of tears in them as Hester said, "He has to send for me, Sabrina. I have to know he wants to see me." Then she hurriedly left the room and went upstairs.

PHONES HAD BEEN INSTALLED in all of the bedrooms, and it was a little after two a.m. when Sabrina was awakened by the sound of hers.

"Uh . . . yes?" she responded, sleep still possessing her faculties.

"Sabrina . . . David."

She sat up. "David? Where are you? In Atlanta?"

"No, I'm here at the Greensboro Memorial Hospital. Have you heard about Shelby?"

"Yes, Hester and I learned about it earlier this evening." She glanced at the clock next to the phone. "Last evening, I mean. How is he?"

"Not good. It's been touch and go ever since I got here an hour ago." He paused. Then: "Sabrina, he wants to see you and Hester. Can you both come to the hospital?"

"Now?"

"Please. I know it's the middle of the night, but he said he had to talk to both of you. About what, I'll be damned if I know, but if it will pacify him—"

"Of course we'll come," Sabrina told him, not at all certain what Hester's response would be.

"Good. I'll see you in a while, then."

Sabrina had not quite been prepared for Hester's reaction of sheer terror upon being told of Shelby's request, but she could well understand it. After half a lifetime of hating the man, the woman was now expected to go to his bedside and converse with him. And Sabrina knew that there could be but one topic of mutual interest between them. But why had Shelby included her in their meeting?

David was waiting for them near the entrance. Sabrina's heart sank when she saw his face; he looked so tired, so worried. She was surprised to see that Julie wasn't with him.

He saw them and embraced Sabrina. "They think he's going to make it." He heard Hester's audible sigh and glanced at her quizzically. "Thank you both for coming, particularly you, Hester. I don't know what's going on in his mind, but I'd like us all to humor him right now. Julie and Brian are in the cafeteria having coffee. She's been here since last evening. I don't see how she's even staying on her feet."

Quietly Sabrina asked, "Is he conscious, David?"

"On and off. He's just been moved to a private room in the cardiac care wing down the hall. They've been monitoring his condition constantly." He raked his fingers through his hair. "Damn! Why does it take something like this for people to get in touch with their true feelings?"

Seeing the question in Sabrina's eyes, he told her, "Shelby and I talked for a while when I first arrived. He said he wanted to make peace with me before he died. We were both a real mess. He was apologizing for being so blasted ornery, and I was apologizing for being so damned independent." He took hold of Sabrina's hand. "He actually told me he loved me and was proud of me; asked me to be patient with him for just a while longer."

Sabrina saw the shimmer of tears that had begun to form in his eyes, and she placed a gentle palm on his cheek. "It was time for that, David. You both needed to get rid of the barrier between you." She looked over at Hester as though to suggest it was time for her to do the same.

"Let's go in now," David said. "He's waiting for both of you."

David led the way and stepped inside Shelby's room first, holding the door open for them. The lights in the room were dim, and Sabrina had to hold back a gasp when she saw Shelby. The man had not been well when she had last seen him, but now his face was ashen, his cheeks sunken. An intravenous needle was in his arm; a plastic oxygen tube was inserted in his nostrils. He lay on the bed quite still, but she could tell from his shallow breaths that he was alive.

David approached the bed quietly. For a moment he just looked down at the man lying there, and Sabrina saw years of lost love fill David's eyes. She watched as he gently stroked Shelby's gray hair, and then she heard him whisper, "Father." It was the first time she had heard David call him that. "Father," he said again, and the man's eyelids twitched.

"David." His response was as feeble as the smile he attempted.

"Hester and Sabrina are here."

With effort Shelby opened his eyes a little more. "Hester...I must talk to Hester."

David stepped back, and Hester went to the side of the bed.

"Where's Sabrina?" Shelby asked. "I want her here and you, too, Son...to witness what's being said."

Sabrina and David moved nearer. As they did, she looked at Hester, who seemed to have complete control of herself as she stared down at the man in the bed.

"Lean closer, Hester." She did, and he peered up at her. Slowly Shelby raised an unsteady hand and touched Hester's cheek. His words came falteringly, but there was a softness in his eyes and voice when he said, "You have her face...but they're my eyes, aren't they?"

Sabrina's eyes darted to David's, and in them she saw confusion mixed with concern.

In a voice that was seemingly devoid of emotion, Hester quietly said, "So, you *have* known all along, all these many years."

"No, Daughter, I've only suspected."

David's lips parted to say something, but Sabrina quickly shook her head.

Then Shelby's hand fell back onto the white sheet, and his eyes closed. "But you've known, haven't you, Hester?" He struggled to reopen his eyes. "Did she tell you?"

Hester responded in a choked voice. "My mother had a name."

During the quiet moments that followed, all listened to the man's tortured breathing, but then Shelby's face took on a sudden peaceful look and he whispered, "Lenore."

David stared at Hester, then took a faltering step backward, away from his father's bedside. He dug his fingers into the back of his neck, his thoughts in whirling disorder as he slowly made sense of what had just been said. After another glance toward the others in the room, he went to the nearby window and looked out at the darkness.

Sabrina was about to go to him when Shelby said, "Sabrina," and she returned her attention to him. "You're the one person I know whom Hester trusts. I want you to witness that I acknowledge Hester as my daughter. Do you understand?"

"Yes, Shelby, I do."

Shifting his watery eyes to Hester, he asked, "Why didn't you ever come to me?"

She asked, "Why didn't you ever send for me?"

"Because I've been a stubborn old fool, too proud, too afraid."

"Of me?" Hester asked in a thin voice.

Shelby's head wavered from side to side. "No. I was afraid to face the man I had become." He gasped several painful breaths. "Hester... I loved your mother, but I was young then and that wasn't enough. I didn't realize I... I would be destroying her... and myself." He gazed up at her. "How you must hate me."

Sabrina gently touched Hester's arm, and she glanced at her momentarily. Then Hester told Shelby, "No, Father, I don't hate you now. I did when I first read Lenore's diary years ago and when she told me what had happened. And, yes, I did hate you when I watched how she suffered. But now—" her voice nearly broke "—no, I don't hate you."

"David!" Shelby said with a sudden urgency.

As he neared the bed, David's eyes looked deeply into Hester's, then he softly said, "Yes, Father. I'm here."

"In the drawer there, the top one. There's an envelope I had Julie bring me. Get it for me...please."

David retrieved the sealed envelope. It bore the return address of the law firm that handled Shelby's legal matters.

"Open it," he told David. "I kept it in the safe at the house."

He did and saw that it was a predated check made out to Hester. "It's for you, Hester," he said and extended the sizable check to her.

After a quick glance, Hester said, "I don't need your money, Father. That's not why I'm here."

Shelby's voice came with a little more force. "It belongs to you. You're a Mansfield." He lifted a weak hand. "And your land that I bought...it's all been reverted back to you."

"Why?" she asked. "You said you weren't sure I was your daughter."

He rested his hand on hers. "I think that in my heart I knew...those eyes of yours, and when you first came to Belleamie, I saw Lenore in you, and it hurt, Hester. Every time—" A fit of coughing overtook him.

"Father," David pleaded, "don't tire yourself. You've got to rest."

"There'll be plenty of time for that soon enough." With effort he opened his eyes again and looked up at David and Sabrina. "She'd be good for you, Son. Don't make the same mistake I did with Lenore. Don't let her slip through your fingers...not for any reason."

A nurse quietly entered the room. David knew she wanted them to leave. Leaning down, he kissed Shelby's forehead. "I'll be right outside. Get some sleep now."

"Wait," Shelby murmured, "all of you. I want you to promise me that what we've discussed here will be kept to ourselves until after the election. I don't want Julie paying for something she had no say in. The scandal—along with the investigation going on now—would destroy the political career she wants so badly. I...I don't even want Julie to know until after the election." His voice rose in pitch. "Promise me...all of you...promise me!"

The three of them glanced at each other, then nodded their heads and saw that their promise relaxed Shelby a little.

"Good," he whispered and closed his eyes.

The short time spent in the hospital room seemed endless to Sabrina, but she felt a great sense of relief now that Hester's secret was finally out. Once they were in the hospital corridor, though, her feeling of relief was shattered by the piercing look in David's eyes.

He moved close to her and took her arm in a firm grasp. "You knew all along, didn't you?"

CHAPTER SIXTEEN

SABRINA'S BLOOD FROZE as she looked into David's pained and accusing eyes. She had often dreaded the moment when he would find out that Hester had confided in her, but the past few hours had been so hectic, she really hadn't had time to prepare herself.

The chill between them seemed to grow at an alarming rate, and finally he appeared ready to say something, but then she saw him glance over her shoulder. Turning, she faced Julie and Brian. Sabrina looked around for Hester, who had taken a seat along the corridor wall. Her face was drained of color; her fingers twitched nervously. After taking a hesitant glance at David, Sabrina sat down next to Hester.

Julie looked at the two women sitting nearby, then asked David, "How is he?"

Sabrina knew Julie was wondering what she and Hester were doing at the hospital, and she was able to hear the three of them as they talked.

"He's sleeping now." David's cold eyes settled on Brian's. "This damn business at the plant is wearing him down. You're sure that Mansfield Chemicals isn't mixed up in anything illegal? You are going by the book, aren't you?"

With palms upright Brian answered defensively. "How many times do I have to tell you? Mansfield Chemicals is clean!" One hand went to his forehead.

"God knows I'm as upset as Shelby is about it. I don't need you to hassle me."

"David," Julie said, coming to her fiancé's defense, "if Brian says he's checked the situation out at the plant, he has. Why can't you let it go at that? Let's accept the fact that we're all upset right now and try not to make matters worse."

Her brother took a deep breath. "I'm sorry, Brian. Julie's right. We shouldn't be at each other's throats."

Brian shrugged his shoulders. "No problem. The papers are having a field day, though, what with Julie and the campaign. The whole thing is probably a political maneuver to defeat her at the polls."

"Maybe," David said halfheartedly and looked over at Sabrina and Hester.

Confusion and irritation were eating away at him as he tried to accept the fact that Hester Devereaux was actually his sister—half sister, anyway. Mixed in with the shock of that was a gnawing suspicion that Sabrina had known and had not had the decency to tell him. Why hadn't she?

As Sabrina lifted her eyes to meet David's, she saw his features harden. She could guess at what was going on in his mind as he stood there with his hands shoved in his pants pockets. He looked tired and tense, and she believed he was struggling with the promise he had made his father, that the three of them had. Knowing David, she could imagine the conflict that silence would cost him.

Turning to Julie, David suggested, "Why don't you and Brian go on home. You've been here all night. I'm going to stay a while longer."

"That makes sense," Brian agreed and took Julie's arm.

She asked, "You'll phone if...if his condition changes?"

David nodded, and Julie and Brian left him standing there alone.

Sabrina's heart went out to him. She wanted to go to him, to comfort the man she loved, but she wasn't sure if, in his present mood, he would be receptive of her attempt. She was certain of one thing, however, that David would again ask her that troubling question.

"Hester," she said softly, "you need to get some rest. Would you mind taking a cab home? I want to stay with David."

"Yes," she said weakly as she stood up, "I think I will go home. I am tired."

David went to her and placed his hands on her shoulders. Then he took her in his arms. "We have a lot of talking to do, Hester, a lot of years to make up for." Drawing back, he added, "You will take care of yourself now, won't you?"

She took in the sincerity on his face and tried to smile. "I will, David. You do the same."

His gaze then settled on Sabrina. "I'll see Hester to a cab. We need to talk, too."

Sabrina followed them with her eyes as they went toward the elevator and then she looked around for a water fountain. Her mouth was dry, her spirits, sagging. She saw one at the opposite end of the corridor, went to it and felt the cold water cool her throat.

Her ears picked up the rasping sound of a buzzer followed by the scurrying of steps behind her. She turned and saw several people in white, one pushing a cart, all rushing down the corridor. "Shelby!" she screamed. Then she calmed, seeing them enter the room next to his. Suddenly the odor of sickness and disinfectant became overpowering. She took another drink from the fountain.

All was quiet again as she returned to the chair she had previously occupied. Minutes later she heard the elevator doors open and saw David coming toward her.

Sitting down next to her, he leaned forward and rested his arms on his knees. As he stared down at the tile floor he asked, "You did know, didn't you...about Hester?"

In a wisp of a voice she replied, "Yes."

"Before Atlanta?" He looked at her.

She nodded.

"Before that night in the cottage?"

"Yes," she whispered.

He mustered all the control he could. "Why in God's name didn't you tell me? Why did I have to find out like this?"

Depending on his sense of fairness, she measured her words carefully. "Why haven't you told Julie?"

His eyes narrowed. "You know why I can't. I promised Shelby." He studied her face for a moment and answered his own question. "And Hester made you promise."

Again Sabrina only nodded and watched as David's fingers intertwined firmly.

"Why?" he asked as though to himself. "Why do people do these things? We burden others with damn secrets and then make them promise to suffer in silence, knowing the pain that silence will bring with it." He leaned back, bracing his shoulders against the wall. "Is there anything else I should know?"

She averted her eyes and studied her own hands. "No." In an attempt to distract him from his troubling thoughts, she said, "I couldn't help but overhear your conversation with Brian. He said your father's plant is in the clear.''

Exhausted, David widened his eyes, trying to stay awake. "It has to be. Shelby would never condone a thing like the dumping of hazardous wastes.''

"Isn't Brian the acting president now?''

He looked at her strangely. "He's not crazy enough to pull something like that. Why would he? To save a few lousy dollars?''

"Obviously somebody's doing it,'' she reminded him. "Who do you think is responsible?''

He crossed his arms over his chest. "One of the other chemical plants. Might even be one that's not under investigation. Smaller firms handling chemicals aren't under scrutiny like the big ones. Or it could be drivers who are sometimes sub-contracted to haul waste out of state to legal landfills. By dumping earlier, they could save time, do double duty carting other freight.''

"Then why is the State Attorney's office—''

The approach of a doctor interrupted her. "David, your father is sleeping. Why don't you go home and do the same? There's nothing you can do sitting here the rest of the night. We'll call you if there's any change.''

Looking up, David nodded slowly, knowing that the doctor was right. After patting David on the shoulder, the man in the white jacket went to the nurses' station.

SABRINA PARKED THE BRONCO in front of Belleamie and looked over at David. He'd flown from Atlanta to Shreveport and had taken a taxi from there directly to the hospital after Julie had phoned to tell him of Shelby's attack. As she looked at his still profile, she felt a resurgence of love and sympathy for him. Not wanting him to be alone in the dark mood he was in, she had asked him that he stop and have coffee with her before she drove him home. She was certain Hester would be asleep.

"How about that coffee?" she asked, breaking into the thoughts that were obviously disturbing him.

He turned and gave her a weak smile. "Right," he answered and opened the car door.

While Sabrina fixed the coffee, David used the phone in the kitchen to check with the hospital. Shelby's condition was stable, and he was still sleeping, he told her with relief after he'd hung up. She suggested they take their coffee out into the garden; although it was November, the night was balmy, and she thought the fresh air would be good for both of them.

In the garden Sabrina led him to the newly painted gazebo that glistened in the pale moonlight. It was set off from the path and now graced with young magnolia trees. David followed her up its two wooden steps, took another swallow of coffee and set the mug down on the white railing. He removed his jacket and placed it on the railing, also. Then he leaned over, and looked out over the gardens, listening to the night sounds around them. "It's so peaceful out here," he whispered.

Sabrina put her coffee mug down and walked over to him. It was peaceful, and she knew that he was tense. David turned to her and she slipped her arms around his waist and leaned toward him, resting her forehead against his cheek. "Right now you need to feel some peace. This has been a trying night for you, David."

His arms encircled her, and he began a slow, soothing massage on her back. "It hasn't exactly been a piece of cake for you, either." Then he closed his eyes, rethinking the things his father had said. "I still can't take in the fact that Shelby had an affair with Lenore Devereaux, that she bore his child. Knowing him as I do, it's almost impossible to see him ever doing anything that wasn't calculated and preplanned." He laughed in a low tone. "Shelby...a man of passion?"

Holding him close, Sabrina quietly told him, "There are different kinds of passion, David. Shelby also has a passion for power, just as Brian does, and Julie has a passion for politics. Even Hester is passionate about the memory of her mother and Belleamie."

Sabrina drew her head back and looked up at him. "My great passion is for Michael's future. And yours? I haven't really decided yet. Perhaps it has to do with Mantek."

Although he was exhausted, David's eyes were filled with love and caring as he told her, "Isn't it obvious to you, love? You're the only real passion I have in my life now." He shook his head slowly. "What would I do without you?"

The kiss he gave her was tender and gentle, and it confirmed what both of them knew: that they needed to be with one another now, to share their strength and to support the other against the ill winds that were battering them.

Sabrina retrieved David's jacket and, leaving the coffee mugs behind, she led him up the stairs at the side of the house to the second floor balcony and through the French doors into her bedroom.

Minutes later, in bed, she held him in her arms, his face resting on her bosom, his leg over hers. Gently she stroked his back while her other hand touched his temple, her fingers moving softly as she tried to comfort the man she loved with all her heart.

And David needed her sweet solace, the consolation and understanding that Sabrina was offering so freely. In her arms it seemed to him that the cares of the world were far away, giving him time to fortify himself for their inevitable return. As he lay there, absorbing her warmth and soothing strokes, he felt a welcome energy flow from her body into his, and he knew that with her at his side he would be able to surmount any obstacles that might come their way in life.

Slowly David's breathing deepened, and Sabrina felt his breath waft across her breast. The feel of him in her arms filled her with peacefulness and contentment. The closeness, the touching, as well as the knowledge that he loved her and needed her gave her an extraordinary sense of pleasure as she lay there in the darkness. And not unlike David, she began to feel a renewed strength permeate her body and soul. Little by little, her eyelids closed, and she, too, slept.

As dawn moved over Belleamie, David rose from Sabrina's arms and dressed. He kissed her softly, left quietly through the French doors and headed for his own home.

During the remainder of the week, he kept Sabrina and Hester informed of Shelby's condition, but on Friday, after Sabrina had left for New Orleans, Shelby went into a coma. On Saturday evening David phoned her. Shelby had died.

"We all knew it was coming," David told her over the phone, trying to sound as though he had fully accepted the fact. "He asked for you, Sabrina."

"He did?"

David's voice brightened. "He'd taken quite a fancy to you. I'm just glad he wasn't twenty years younger...probably would have given me a run for my money."

"I miss you, David."

"No more than I miss you. Sabrina, we never did talk about our plans for Thanksgiving with Michael. You're still bringing him up here, aren't you?"

"Yes," she said happily. "Todd and I worked it out today. He'll bring Michael here tomorrow, and on Monday we'll both drive to Greensboro. I've arranged for him to miss three days from school, but he'll have no trouble catching up."

"Great. Then we'll have an entire week together. I'll make sure the cottage is ready for you two."

His enthusiasm touched her heart, and she wondered how Michael could help but like him. "I'm looking forward to it," she told him, then asked, "How's Hester taking it?"

"I went to see her this morning...I wanted to tell her personally. We're both still trying to deal with our new relationship, but things will work out." He paused. "You know, since she met you, Hester has gone through some remarkable changes. She not only looks better, she seems to be taking real control of her life. And the house looks wonderful. I know she's proud of that, and I'm so proud of you."

Sabrina picked up the phone and carried it to the easy chair nearby and sat down. "I've grown to love the place."

"Hey, I met Ernest Fundy at Hester's. What do you think of him? I know he's got a good business going in town."

"He's a fine man, David. I'm hoping that he and Hester will think of sharing their lives together."

David chuckled. "First a new sister, now maybe a new brother-in-law." His voice lowered. "I told Hester the funeral will be this Tuesday, said I thought she should attend, but she thinks it would be better if she didn't. She doesn't want Julie to see that Shelby's death has upset her so. You'll come, won't you?"

Thinking of Hester, Sabrina hesitated. "David . . . I think I should be with Hester on Tuesday. Even though she won't be at the service or the cemetery, I'm sure she'll be thinking about it, and it will be difficult for her. She's had to make such a quick turnaround in her feelings."

"Oh . . . I guess you're right."

Sabrina heard the disappointment in his voice. "But you know my thoughts will be with you, David." Then she asked, "How is Julie doing?"

"She's taking it a lot harder than I thought she would, but," he reminded himself, "she was always closer to Shelby than I was."

"The hurt will pass. Julie has a full life ahead of her."

"So do we, love," David told her with a smile in his voice. "Listen, I've got a million things to do. I'll see you and Michael Monday, right?"

"We'll stop at Hester's first. She'd never forgive me if we didn't. I'll phone you when we arrive. Will you be at home?"

"No, call me at my office. I have to get things organized there fast and furiously. Shelby told me he was leaving the house and plant to me, and the stock portfolio to Julie, so right now I'll have to spend some time at Mansfield Chemicals, as well." He laughed. "That wily old fox got his way finally, didn't he?"

"Are you actually going to stay on at the plant?" she asked, knowing he wouldn't want to.

"For the time being, until this investigation business is settled. Then Julie and I will decide what we want to do with it. I'd just as soon sell it. Sabrina, I really have to get busy now. See you and Michael Monday."

"I love you, David," she said quickly.

"Love you, too."

A lot was happening, Sabrina told herself as she went into the kitchen to put a dinner in the microwave. Then she poured herself a glass of red wine, went back into the living room and sat down on the sofa. She took a sip of the light Bordeaux and checked her watch, telling herself she'd have to get a move on if she was going to make it to the symphony on time.

When she had arrived home last evening, Ina had made her promise to attend tonight's performance of Berlioz's *Symphonie fantastique*, in which Eugene had several bassoon solos. Sabrina smiled, remembering Ina's delight when she showed her the engagement ring he'd given her.

Ina and Eugene, Hester and Ernest, David and her, Sabrina thought, rising as the beep of the microwave sounded. "A regular season for love, and it's not even springtime. Springtime?" she added on her way to the kitchen. "Let's get through Thanksgiving first."

ON MONDAY, she and Michael were driving north to Greensboro. Realizing how hard it would be for a seven-year-old to be restrained by a seat belt for the four-hour trip, Sabrina had made sure he had some of his favorite things with him in the car. At the moment he was trying to reassemble his plastic model of a space station.

She glanced over at him. "How's it going, Tiger?"

"This dumb thing doesn't want to fit right." He reached into the open bag on the seat divider between them and pulled out a chocolate chip cookie. "Hey, Mom, Eddie's going to Camp Indian Head next summer. Can I go, too?"

Sabrina knew the camp was located just across the state line in Mississippi. Ralph's boys went there every year. It seemed to her at the moment that something always loomed up to separate her and her son. "Summer's a long way off, but we'll see."

"Eddie said you gotta apply early, or they'd be filled up."

"How early?"

"By January."

"Has he been there before?"

"Yeah . . . he likes it."

"Well, I'll talk to Eddie's mother when we get back to New Orleans."

"You won't forget?"

She glanced down at his freckled face. "You'd let me?"

His giggle was music to her ears. "No way." Then he dipped into the bag for another cookie.

"I think you'll like Miss Devereaux," she said, wanting to ease the conversation toward the inhabitants of Greensboro, one in particular.

"You like her?" he asked as he munched.

"Very much."

"Does she have a dog?"

"No, but the people where we'll be staying do. They have an Irish Wolfhound named Tara, and she's just had puppies."

"Puppies! How many?"

"Seven."

"Wow! Will I get to play with them?"

"I'm sure David will let you, but you can't be rough with them. I'm not sure if their eyes are even open yet." She glanced at him again. "David said that while I'm busy working, he'd like to show you some of Greensboro. There's a park where they have paddleboats. Interested?" she asked hopefully.

"You like David, too...as much as Miss Devereaux?"

"Well...yes, but in a different way."

His little feet started pumping. "A lot?"

Sabrina swallowed with difficulty and found her voice, a low one. "Yes, Tiger, I do...and I like Julie, his sister, a lot, also."

She noted the foot pumping, knew that was a habit he had when he felt nervous. She was becoming nervous, too.

"Mom, is Ina going to marry Eugene?"

"Yes, she is."

Michael's voice took on a subdued tone. "She'd move away then...just like Dad did."

Her nervousness increased. "Yes, she would. She and Eugene would live together."

He set his model aside. "I'm never gonna get married."

Sabrina smiled. "You certainly don't have to decide right now."

"I don't like marriage."

Her smile disintegrated. "Why not, Tiger?"

"Cause married people always argue a lot. Dad and Ann do."

And Todd and I did, she moaned inwardly, feeling devastated. She tried to explain. "Not all married couples argue a lot, and when they do it doesn't mean they don't love each other."

He tilted his face up toward his mother and squinted. "Then why do they do it? It just makes everybody unhappy."

"Tiger, if I could answer that, we'd both be rich." His next question floored her.

"You really like this David?"

Cautiously she answered, "Uh-huh."

"Enough to marry him?"

Hold on, Sabrina, she cautioned. "I'd certainly have to talk it over with you first, wouldn't I?"

"I s'pose."

"You suppose right. What you think would make all the difference in the world to me. You know that."

"It would?"

"Of course it would."

"Well, I like it being just you and me, Mom. We don't need anybody else."

The lump in Sabrina's throat just about choked her, and she had to fight to hold back the tears. She felt stupid and miserable for having brought up the subject at all. Why hadn't she just waited until after Michael met him? How could she tell her son that she had needs he couldn't fully comprehend right now? How could she explain how hopelessly she was in love with David?

Hopelessly. Quite the appropriate word, she thought as she quickly dabbed at her eyes. Smiling through the moisture in them, she tried to agree with her son. "No, Tiger, we don't need anybody else."

"Promise?" he asked.

The jolt in her heart felt like physical pain, but in spite of it she quietly assured him. "I promise."

Sabrina pushed at the small triangular side window to let cold air blow across her face. She tried to ignore the heavy thumping of her heart as her promise to Michael echoed in her thoughts, thoughts that were interrupted by words David had whispered to her in moments of sweet intimacy, words that she now had to dutifully dismiss. If it had to come to making a decision between Michael and David, as it now appeared it did, there was not the slightest need for consideration. Her first priority was and would always be Michael.

"Mom, can I spend Christmas vacation with you, too?"

That came as a shock, but a pleasant one. "I'd love it, but what about your father?"

"He won't care, and all that yelling makes me feel bad."

The shock changed to an extremely disturbing feeling. She didn't want Michael living in that type of atmosphere. Todd's constant arguing had been one of the reasons for the divorce, and apparently he was at it again. Sabrina's thoughts raced furiously. She wondered how long Ann would put up with it. What if she didn't? Would Todd still want joint custody of Michael?

Todd now struck Sabrina as the type of man who would go through five wives or more, casting aside each one as soon as he realized his word was not the only law in his household. He would never be able to accept that today's woman wanted to be considered an equal partner in marriage. There was even a chance that maybe Michael wouldn't have to return to his father after the Christmas holidays.

To answer her son's question more exactly, she told him, "I'll talk to your father, Tiger...about Christmas. I'll tell him it's all my idea."

Her thoughts started like the wind again. She'd been thinking of having Michael transferred to a school in Greensboro in January. Belleamie would be almost finished by then, and she'd been hoping to get an apartment for her and Michael in town. But that had depended on Michael's liking David. And she already knew what her son thought about another man in his life. Besides, her assignment for Delta Associates would be over by then. What would she do to earn a living in Greensboro? Well, she decided, if time was going to take care of everything, it had better start doing so—and soon.

CHAPTER SEVENTEEN

WHEN SABRINA AND MICHAEL ARRIVED at Belleamie, Hester fairly doted on the boy. She was lavish with praise, telling Sabrina how healthy and attractive he was, how intelligence was so obvious in his eyes. And Michael liked her, too—and the homemade peach pie and ice cream she served him.

While Hester kept Michael occupied in the kitchen, Sabrina phoned David at his office, and he told her he would leave immediately and be waiting for them when they arrived at his home.

Sabrina then went to check on the bedrooms upstairs to see if a section of carpet in the Blue Room had been replaced as she had ordered. It had been. Her next stop was the library to check with Ed. She found that his men were putting the finishing touches on the one section of paneling that had to be matched, since the electricians had all but demolished the original piece.

Meanwhile, she found herself becoming more nervous by the minute, wondering what Michael's meeting with David would be like. She checked her watch and decided that he wouldn't have had sufficient time to get from his office to his home yet, and she did want David to be there when she and Michael showed up.

Knowing her son was in good hands with Hester, she checked on all the guest bedrooms. Sabrina had decided to make the fireplace the focal point of each room. There were spacious sitting areas in front of the fireplaces, and over the Italian marble mantels she'd had antique mirrors and matching sconces installed. On the mantels she had set the porcelain figurines she and Hester had discovered in the attic.

The bedrooms were now painted a soft white, and with their new carpets, each room was cheerful and welcoming, even though they were still drapeless and the huge four-posters remained uncovered, Sabrina knew the rooms would be friendly and beautiful when they were finished.

With steps lacking her usual springy bounce, she went to the window in the green room and looked down at the gardens. She could see the gazebo, and instantly her thoughts were of David and the night, or the morning, rather, that she and he had embraced in the light of the descending moon. A warm and tender heat touched her face, but then her cheeks chilled when she reminded herself of the duty she had to her son.

Then she saw Michael. He was walking with Hester and Ernest. Well, they were walking, but Michael, with all his bursting energy, was darting first in one direction and then the other as Ernest pointed out different plants for the boy to inspect.

She looked at her watch again and decided David would have gotten home by now. As she walked down the walnut staircase, her mind was a crazy mixture of hope and fear.

As the Bronco neared the front of the Mansfield estate, Sabrina saw that David was outside, waiting for them. She wondered if he had been pacing, fighting the same nervousness she had been feeling for days.

"There's David," she said, looking over at her son, but the boy showed no interest.

When she helped Michael down from the Bronco, she saw his eyes look up at the man coming toward them. His expression didn't bode well.

David crouched down so that he would be on eye level with him. Extending his hand, he said cheerfully, "Hi, Mike!" He was just as aware as Sabrina that so much rested on whether or not the boy would be receptive to him.

Michael looked at David's extended hand, then up to his mother, who nodded at him. As though not wanting to, he placed his little hand in the large one offered, but withdrew it quickly. Then he hooked his thumbs onto the back pockets of his jeans. "My name's Michael," he said quietly, not looking up.

David gently raised the boy's chin with one finger so that their eyes met. "All right . . . Michael. My name's David."

Michael remained quiet.

Sabrina looked at David as he glanced up at her, and in his eyes she saw the desperate hurt.

When Michael stepped back toward his mother and positioned himself in front of her, David stood up, and his voice took on an animated tone. "Got something here for you, Michael." He went back toward the front of the house, and in seconds he was wheeling a green-and-white bicycle toward them.

Instinctively the boy went to it and ran his fingers over the chrome-plated spoke wheels and the green-colored tires and seat.

David smiled. "It's got coaster brakes, too."

Michael looked up at him and stuck his hands back into his pockets. "I already have a bike, back home."

Sabrina saw the depth of disappointment in David's eyes. Quickly she told her son, "While we're here,

Tiger, we'll have a house all to ourselves. Would you like to see it?''

The boy nodded.

''It's right around the back.''

When he had darted ahead of them, David asked, ''Why do I feel like I've just stepped on his favorite toy?''

''It's not you, David. He's just frightened right now. I think he's afraid you might come between him and me.''

Wanting to believe it, David said hopefully, ''I guess he'll come around...eventually.'' Then he stopped, remembering the luggage in the Bronco. ''You go on ahead. I'll drive the car around. Are the keys in it?''

''Yes.''

He started toward the car, but turned. ''For God's sake, tell him I don't bite.''

He arrived momentarily with the luggage and Sabrina took about twenty minutes to get them settled in the cottage. Then she asked David, ''Is Tara ready for visitors yet?''

Understanding her tactic, his eyes lit up. ''How about it, Michael. Would you like to see my wolfhound's puppies?''

Another pair of eyes lit up—smaller hazel ones. ''Sure.''

David took them to a screened-in area at the back of the main house. He and Sabrina both watched Michael closely as his interest was captured by the large box. The boy lay on his stomach, his eyes wide and curious. On top of a blanket, huddled against one another, were seven Irish wolfhound puppies. Most of them were asleep, but one whimpered at him.

''Where's Tara?'' he asked.

"Cora, our maid, has her out for a walk. She needs the exercise."

"Who? Cora?"

"Tara," Sabrina told him.

Just then Cora came through the screen door with the puppies' mother. David took hold of the dog's collar and sat her down next to him and began to stroke her.

Tara's silver-gray head lowered, all 125 pounds of her alert as she intently eyed the boy staring at her litter. Michael looked over at David who was now crouched down next to Tara. He asked, "Can I pick one up?"

Hooking his fingers under the dog's collar, he said, "You'll have to ask their mother."

"Okay, Tara?" he asked, looking into the huge dog's shining amber eyes.

David bent his head to check her response. "She thinks it's okay."

Carefully Michael lifted one of the soft balls of warm movement and held it against his sweater, listening to the little whimpering noise it made. "Have you named them yet?"

Continuing to pet the wary Tara, David told Michael, "No, we'll just name the ones we're going to keep."

The boy's eyes went from the puppy to David. "You're not going to keep all of them?"

"All seven? That's a lot of dogs to take care of, and I don't have the time to give them. They like to have someone to play with, especially when they're puppies. Tara can't do it all the time...not with all of them."

The dog emitted a low whine of concern as she stared at her puppy in Michael's arms. David knew she wouldn't hurt the boy. The only reason he'd held her back until now was so that she wouldn't scare Michael. He asked, "Okay if Tara checks you out, Michael?"

"Sure it is."

David let her loose, and she plodded over to where he was sitting. She sniffed her puppy and then him. He giggled when her soft tongue lapped at his ear. Ducking his head so he could see past the dog, he asked, "Won't Tara miss them when they're gone?"

Sabrina glanced at David, and he winked at her. "I'm afraid she will."

"Would you keep them if you had someone to help with them?" Michael asked, exchanging one puppy for another under watchful amber eyes.

"I would in a minute."

"Well—" he looked at his mom "—couldn't I help, Mom, for a while, anyway?"

"That's up to David," she told him and sat down next to him.

"Could I, David?"

"Boy, I'd really appreciate that, Michael."

He glanced up at David and studied his face for a few moments. "You can call me Mike if you want."

"Okay...Mike."

Visiting the puppies turned out to be an all-afternoon affair as Michael bombarded David with questions about Irish wolfhounds, and he in turn regaled the boy with stories of how the muscular, graceful dogs, who rarely barked, had once been the hounds of Irish kings. Gentle giants, David called them. Tara, standing on her hind legs with her paws on David's shoulders, was more than six feet tall. Michael couldn't get enough of watching the dogs, especially when it was time for Tara to nurse her brood.

Sabrina's heart brightened as she sat quietly watching the two of them. At one point David was lying down next to her son, propped up on his elbows, talking up a storm. And her heart gladdened even more when, after Cora served them cheeseburgers, David brought in the bike Michael had refused earlier.

"How about taking Tara for a run, Mike? She's a natural-born chaser, gives her the feeling she's out hunting, and the exercise is very important for her right now."

Sabrina and David watched Michael ride the bike around the estate, Tara prancing beside him. David said, "Those puppies aren't going anywhere." He put his arm around Sabrina. "I hope you and Michael aren't, either."

For Sabrina, Monday ended better than it had started, but Tuesday, the day of Shelby's funeral, was a nightmare for everyone. A depressed mood hung heavily over the Mansfield and Devereaux estates, but she tried not to let it affect her son.

She felt deeply for both David and Hester, but took some comfort in the knowledge that he, at least, had come to terms with the problems he'd had with his father. Sadly, the death had cheated Hester out of a true reconciliation with her father. The brief moments they had spent at his hospital bedside couldn't possibly erase Hester's long and lonely years, but Sabrina was grateful for the exchange that had taken place.

On Tuesday afternoon, while Michael was busy with the puppies, Sabrina decided to phone her father in Connecticut, to try to restore the closer bond they once had. It wasn't easy, but when Sabrina finally put the receiver down, she was glad she had taken that first step.

That evening, David took Sabrina and Michael to a rodeo exhibition, and on Wednesday he and the boy took off early on their own. First they went paddle-boating, and in the afternoon Michael was treated to an air show, where stunt pilots brought gasps from the crowd below. On Thanksgiving Day morning, while Cora, Julie and Sabrina worked in the kitchen, the two "men" headed for a nearby lake to go bass fishing.

While they sat on the river bank, holding their rods, David brought up the subject of Michael's father.

"Does your father ever take you fishing, Mike?"

"Uh-uh. We do some things together . . . sometimes. That's when he pays a lot of attention to me, but most of the time I don't see him very much."

"Oh . . . well, I guess that being a marine biologist and everything, his work must keep him pretty busy."

"I guess."

They were sitting under a huge oak tree, and now Michael shifted his back from the oak and leaned against David's arm. "At school, some of the kids tell me about the things they do with their dads, but it doesn't bother me when they do."

"You know, Mike, when I was your age my father was always busy, too. I think that sometimes all fathers get busy." He saw that the boy seemed to have to mull that over. Then he said, "Your mom tells me you want to go to camp this summer."

"Yeah . . . with Eddie. He's my best friend."

"Ahhh . . . and I bet you like to be with him. In fact, I bet you miss him right now."

Holding his fishing rod with both hands now, Michael told him, "Sure, that's what best friends do."

"Think we could ever be best friends, Mike . . . after Eddie, I mean? There are lots of things we could do together if you wanted to." He took hold of the line on Michael's rod. "Here, tug it like this . . . just a little."

He did. Then Michael said, "We could be good friends, but you can only have one best friend."

"I'd sure settle for that." David leaned back against the oak tree again, feeling a warm glow in his heart. He had thought that he only had enough love in him for Sabrina, but now he knew there was plenty left over for her son.

Michael swatted at a fly and then tilted his face toward David's. "Could my mom do things with us, too?"

"Of course. In fact, your mom and I are kinda like best friends. When she's in New Orleans I really miss her, and I'm pretty sure she misses me." Gently he placed his arm around Michael and patted him. "And now that you and I are good friends, I'm sure gonna miss you, too."

BEFORE THEY SAT DOWN to Thanksgiving dinner, David told Sabrina of the day's events.

"You're looking at a good friend of his," David told her proudly. "Not his best friend, of course. That's Eddie, but a *good* one."

"He never stood a chance, did he? You can be such a charmer," she teased.

"He's a great kid, Sabrina, and he'd have a wonderful time living here. Those wolfhounds would run him ragged." He smiled broadly. "And Julie adores him, so does Cora."

"And Hester," Sabrina added. "If she asks once more if Michael and I are staying in Greensboro, I'll—"

"You are staying," he told her. "I'm not going to let you or Michael get away from me. And you've got your work cut out for you here. The town's growing fast and becoming modernized. You could start your own architectural firm. It might begin small, but I have faith in your abilities. With my love and support, you could develop your own firm into whatever you want."

Sabrina wasn't sure she could take much more happiness. The picture David was painting was a beautiful one. Little by little things did seem to be settling into place for them.

And their Thanksgiving dinner was so very special. David had insisted that Cora join them, and all seemed happy that Brian had begged off, citing stomach problems as the reason. Ernest, bless him, had invited Hester to have dinner with him and his mother. Yes, everything was going so well.

Too well. On Saturday morning David was arrested.

CHAPTER EIGHTEEN

A DRUM CONTAINING HAZARDOUS WASTE with a Mansfield Chemicals identification number on it had been found dumped in northern Louisiana. It was early Saturday afternoon when Julie phoned Sabrina at Belleamie. Hester and Ernest had taken Michael into town to show him the botanical gardens and to have dinner with Lucille. Sabrina had stayed at Belleamie to catch up on some work she had let slip by this holiday week. David had said he was going in to his office at Mantek to do the same. Sabrina's face paled as she listened to Julie's voice on the phone:

"He was at the office when the police took him into custody. I'm here at the station now, trying to get him released. There shouldn't be any problems."

"You're sure about that, Julie?"

"Yes. I talked to Judge Greenleigh. He agrees that it's absurd to think David had anything to do with it, but someone at Mansfield Chemicals had to be held responsible. As legal owner, David is it, right now."

"Who could have done it?"

Julie heard the terror in her voice. "Calm down. We'll take one problem at a time. Getting David out of jail is top priority. The judge is doing some checking, and then I'm sure he'll release David on his own recognizance."

"I'll come down there."

"Don't. There are reporters all over the place. It would just make for more sensationalistic pictures. Wait for us at the house. We should be there in about an hour."

Sabrina charged back to the Mansfield home. After declining refreshments from Cora, she started to pace, peering out at the driveway every few minutes. Suddenly all the plans she and David had been making for the future seemed in dire jeopardy.

She waited for what seemed like hours, but finally heard a car door slam. Her heartbeat seemed to stop for seconds. Only Julie and Brian got out of the car, but then she saw David, and air rushed into her lungs.

Running, she headed for the front door. David was the first to enter, and she rushed into his arms and held him as though her body could protect him from all that threatened him.

Brian followed him. "I don't know about you people, but I need a drink." He took quick steps toward the salon, and when the rest of them entered, he was already pouring himself a hefty shot.

"It's a little early, but I think I'll join you," David said. "How about you ladies?"

They declined and as Sabrina watched David pour his, she thought, *Jail. If he's sent to jail, I'll die!* Her insides jerked again.

"The court hearing is Monday morning," Julie told her as she slumped into a chair.

"Meaning," David added, "that I've got until then to find out what the hell's going on." His first swallow was a long one. Then he sent daggers over to the man refilling his glass. "Brian, friend, I thought you told me everything was on the up-and-up at the plant!"

The man's face flushed, and he pulled at his tie to loosen it. ''Don't be climbing all over me, David. How the hell do I know how that drum got there?''

More than concerned, Sabrina asked, ''Aren't there records to show where the drum was supposed to be shipped?''

Julie let out a long, depressed sigh, and Sabrina saw her sitting there, holding her head with one hand. ''At the same time they arrested David, the judge issued a search warrant for Mansfield Chemicals. The records concerning that particular drum are missing.''

Moving next to David, Sabrina asked, ''What do we do now?''

He poured himself another bourbon. ''Those records didn't just get up and take a walk by themselves. Someone's out to get me, and I want to find out why.''

''No one's out to get you,'' Brian insisted. ''Haven't you heard of misplaced or misfiled papers?''

''Easy for you to say. You're not facing the likelihood of prison food for the next few years.''

Sabrina's fingers grabbed his arm. ''Don't even think that . . . please.''

Julie said, ''If only there were duplicates somewhere.''

David stared at Brian again. ''Shelby had wanted to have computerized copies made of all transactions, but Brian here convinced him it would be a needless expense, would cut down on the profits!''

Sabrina felt her stomach churn with anxiety and fear for David. Desperately she tried to think. Then: ''David, if identification numbers can be filed off, couldn't a false number be imprinted?''

"I brought that possibility up, but the EPA had already had their lab boys check it out. No evidence of that. They said it's ours."

Julie asked, "Who at the plant would be dumping the waste, and why?"

"Damned if I know," David told her. "Either that drum being left with our number on it was a slipup, or somebody wanted that drum traced to us. Sitting in that cell, I racked my brain, trying to figure it out. Could it be some kind of revenge? For what? Shelby was a hard businessman, but he'd been respected for it. He didn't have enemies who would want to see his reputation or his firm ruined."

"Do you?" Sabrina asked, grabbing at straws.

That he hadn't thought through. "Not that I know of. One thing is sure, though, Julie's political future is going downhill fast. That one drum." He shook his head. "I can't help wondering if all of the others came from our plant, too. The hell of it is that by tomorrow all of Greensboro will think that the Mansfields are 'public enemy number one' types."

"Make that by tonight," Julie suggested.

David looked over at Brian again. "You certainly turned out to be a hero. I thought you were going to pass out when the State Attorney's office brought you in to take a deposition."

The man's eyes twitched. "Well, I am the acting president."

"No more you're not. I'm closing the damn plant down, and if I can find anyone to buy the place, I'm going to sell it!"

"But you . . . you're throwing away everything I've worked for . . . and tossing a lot of money out the window along with it. David, please . . . be sensible. We've got contracts to fulfill!''

''We'll buy a release from them. I'm closing, Brian. Selling. *Finito!* You got that? The name Mansfield is not going to be remembered for this dumping crap!'' David pounded his fist on the table. ''How the hell did one of our drums get there?'' His arm shot out and he pointed a finger at Brian. ''You, acting president, why don't you tell us how?''

Brian put his glass down. ''You've never liked me, have you? And you've always hated the plant.''

''Please, Brian,'' Julie told him, ''don't whine.''

''Well, maybe he's the one who put the drum there...to have an excuse for shutting down the plant.''

''Now you're being stupid. Why would my brother risk having himself thrown in jail?''

''Don't worry, sis. I'm not going to jail, not if I can help it.''

Sabrina asked him, ''What are you going to do?''

''I'm going to the plant, see if I can find something the police have overlooked.''

''Now?'' Brian asked as a muscle in his jaw quivered.

''Maybe you think I should wait until Monday, after my chitchat with Judge Greenleigh.''

Julie saw the strained look in her fiancé's face. ''Are you all right?''

He shook his head. ''No, I've got this stomach pain. I think I'm getting a bleeding ulcer over all this.''

Bitterly David suggested, ''Try cutting down on the booze.''

Sabrina asked, ''Can we get you something, Brian?''

''No, no. I think I'll go home. Peace and quiet seems to do the trick.''

"Go home, Brian," Julie told him a little impatiently. "Try to take care of yourself." Then she walked him to the door.

When she returned, David asked, "Julie, are you actually going to marry that . . . that—"

Julie's hand went up. "There are two ladies present, and no, I'm not sure I am. In any case, Brian is not at his best in emergency situations."

David's laugh was low and cutting. "When is he?"

"Lately, not very often," Julie commented, the irritation in her voice apparent. "I don't know what the problem is, but he's changed enough to make me decide to postpone any thoughts of marriage. If I have a political career left after this, it's going to take every bit of energy I have, and I don't think I want to go through life holding Brian's hand." She looked directly at her brother. "Are you really going to the plant now?"

"I have to."

Sabrina said quite firmly, "Then I'm going with you." She knew Hester and Michael wouldn't be returning until early evening.

"No, you're not. I don't want you anywhere near that place. It's jinxed."

Sabrina told Julie, "Your brother has a lot to learn about women, doesn't he?"

"Especially a woman in love," Julie responded. Then she patted his back.

"Sabrina, I just don't like the idea of—"

"One car or two, David?"

A suspicious line developed at the corners of his mouth. "Is this what I'm going to have to contend with from now on?"

"One car, I take it," she said, and he nodded. She turned toward Julie. "Michael is with Hester and Ernest Fundy, Julie. I'm sure we'll be back before they return to Hester's house, but if she does call, will you tell her I'll be there as soon as I can?''

"Sure I will. You two be careful, though."

IT WAS BEGINNING to get dark when they arrived at Mansfield Chemicals. David left the chain-link gate unlocked and drove past the long warehouse toward the new concrete office building at the far end of the property. He noticed the dark clouds that rolled rapidly overhead and heard the wind picking up.

"Ugh!...what's that smell?" Sabrina asked, wrinkling her nose.

"The chemicals. Wonderful, isn't it?"

David parked near the entrance, but when he put his key into the lock, he found that the door was open. "Who the hell—"

"What's the matter?"

"The door...it's been left unlocked." Shoving it open for her, he joked, "You go to jail for one day and there goes discipline."

He flicked the light switch on and fluorescent bulbs sputtered overhead. The reception area filled with light. Sabrina followed him down a corridor to the elevator, and they went up to the fourth floor.

Using a key from the ring he'd taken from his glove compartment, David started to unlock the door marked "File Room," but that, also, was unlocked. He pulled it open.

Sabrina saw the concern in his eyes. "The police...maybe they forgot to lock it."

"Maybe," he repeated while scanning the long corridor. "Wait here." He entered the file room and switched on the lights. A moment later he said, "Okay."

Sabrina went inside and closed the door behind her. She glanced around at the rows of four-drawer file cabinets. "What first?"

"We look for a drawer marked 'Out-of-state Shipping Invoices.' I saw it somewhere when Shelby's secretary gave me the grand tour." He started down one row; Sabrina took the other side. "Has to be here somewhere," he mumbled as he checked the last cabinet and started up the next row. Sabrina was close behind.

Halfway up the narrow aisle she said, "Here it is," and pulled the drawer open.

David had already reached for the office key ring in his pocket. Seeing the look on his face, Sabrina pulled on a drawer in the adjacent cabinet. It was locked.

Warily David told her, "The police are getting pretty sloppy, aren't they?"

They went through the top drawer and the next. In the third he found the folder that should have included information on "M1738," the ID number on the drum in question.

After ruffling through several pages, David's voice rose in pitch. "It's here! M1738 . . . signed for on November second by the agent at the landfill."

Checking David's dubious expression, Sabrina said, "That means it wasn't a Mansfield drum they found, doesn't it?"

He checked the yellow form again. "It should . . . but why does this seem too damn easy?"

Sabrina reached for the paper and examined it. Then she looked at the next sheet in the folder and compared the two of them. "David, are these forms filled out here before shipment?"

"Yes, why?"

She examined a few more sheets. "Why is the one we're interested in different from the others? Look—" she handed him two forms "—the one we were looking for was typed with a Nylon ribbon. All the others were typed with a carbon ribbon. I bet the secretaries here at the plant use carbon ribbons. Just about everyone does now."

"Except maybe someone who has a typewriter at home that they don't use much." His brain clicked into gear. *The front door was unlocked. Just one file cabinet was open.* "Someone's been working overtime, Sabrina, and I'm starting to get a funny feeling I know who it is."

On a hunch, she suggested, "Let's check the signature for the M1738 with the other forms."

They both did and nodded at the same time. "A forgery," David said. "An attempt to clear me...or an attempt to make it look like I've falsified government mandated records."

"David, who do—" She stopped and again wrinkled her nose. "That's not the same smell."

His head jerked toward the closed door of the file room. "Hell no...that's smoke!" He rushed to the door and grabbed the knob. "It's locked from the outside."

He started pounding against it with his shoulder, but the locked door wouldn't budge. Smoke started to pour in from the crack under it, and he coughed. "It must be jammed with something!"

Sabrina's eyes shot around the room over the tops of the cabinets. The only windows were wide, thick single panes, not constructed to open. David lunged again, but the door held firm. The room was filling with smoke. By now they were both coughing.

"The window, David!" Sabrina hollered, looking around for something to break it with. "There...the paper cutter!"

David grabbed the heavy wooden square. "Get back!" He hopped up on top of the file cabinet under the end window.

Using his jacket to cover his hands, he took hold of the cutter. Closing his eyes for protection, he began banging it against the window. Nothing happened. He banged again and again, coughing as he did.

Sabrina started to gag, then put her hands over her ears as the shrill sound of a fire alarm went off. Even with her ears covered she heard the shattering of glass as the window gave way under David's forceful pounding.

"Be careful," she yelled as he started to widen the hole he'd made in the window.

When he had cleared glass from one side of the window pane, he tossed down the cutter and let his jacket fall to the floor with it.

"Come on!" He reached for her hands as he bent down from the top of the file cabinet. When he held them securely he said, "Ready?" and then raised himself up. In one powerful lift, he pulled her up next to him.

After a quick glance at the room now filled with smoke, he said, "Hope you're not afraid of heights." Then he stepped out onto the concrete ledge that wasn't more than a foot wide—and four floors up. "C'mon," he called to her once he was on the ledge.

Sabrina bent her head to avoid the sharp edges of glass still hanging from above, but the moment her head was outside the window, she gaped at the concrete pavement below. Her stomach wrenched; her head went into a momentary spin.

Smoke was pouring out the window from behind her. She coughed again. David reached out for her hand. "Sabrina...come on, hurry!"

Trying to calm herself, she tilted her face up toward him. The wind had picked up. She saw it blowing his hair as he reached down to take her hand.

"Easy now," he said in a controlled tone and held her hand firmly. Slowly and carefully he eased her up beside him on the ledge. "Don't look down. Good. Okay, we're going to make our way along this ledge. There's a fire escape in the back of the building. Ready?"

A gust of wind caught her dress, and she cursed the high heels she was wearing. At the same time, David looked down at her feet.

"Can you kick those shoes off? We'll get them later."

Sabrina eased one foot up—very slowly—and shook it. She felt the shoe slip off and heard the frightening echo of it hitting the pavement below. The other followed. Now the wind really picked up, and the ledge underfoot felt like ice.

"Okay, love, here we go."

She felt her hand being tugged and her arm stretched out. Her other palm flattened against the rough concrete behind her. Then she moved her right foot a little and planted it solidly on the ledge. Thank God the left knew to follow!

As she attempted another step a gust of wind hit her. She began to lose her balance, but David's arm flew out in front of her, smacking her back against the hard, damp concrete.

Sabrina stood there frozen, inhaling deep breaths of air. The cooler wind snapped at her hair, but she wasn't about to raise a hand to push it back. Then the blare of distant fire trucks sounded in her ears as David cautiously started along the ledge again.

"I'm going to turn the corner now," he warned.

He did and she felt a strong pull on her arm. Sabrina looked over at him—or where he had been a moment ago. All she saw now was his hand holding hers; all she heard was his voice over the wind.

"Easy now ... put your right foot around first, get a good feel on the ledge. Then think like a ballet dancer and float around the corner. I've got a good hold on you."

Her heart sank as she thought, *And who's got a good hold on you?* She felt dizzy again.

David felt Sabrina's icy grip on his hand, sensed her hesitation. "C'mon now ... you can make it! I can see the fire escape from this side!"

She opened her eyes and saw the smoke billowing around them. At that moment she also heard a terrible crash just inside the building behind her. The roar of fire engine noises came closer. She felt as though her blood had turned to ice water.

"Ready, love?"

David's voice warmed her a little; his hand warmed her a lot. "Ready," she said and took a deep breath while she felt for the corner of the building with her shoulder. Pinning herself back against it, she slowly moved her right foot around and felt for the ledge with her stockinged foot. *Like a ballet dancer!* she ordered herself. Desperately she tried to suspend all feeling. Then, as David pulled her ever so gently, she took a deep breath and eased her body around the corner of the building.

The concrete wall behind her felt like a second skin as she exhaled into the night wind. Then David urged her on again.

"We're almost there, love . . . just a little more."

As they inched toward the fire escape, Sabrina's ears—her eyes were closed—picked up the sound of screeching wheels and then the hubbub of men and equipment below. Suddenly she felt David's arm around her waist. Then she was being pulled up and through space. Feeling the fire escape beneath her feet, she let her body sink into the hard contours of his.

He kissed her face once and then again. Holding her tightly, he said, "Guess this rules out mountain climbing on our honeymoon." He could feel her heart pounding against his. "You all right?"

Feeling as if all the air in her lungs had escaped in one single gush, she nodded against the curve of his shoulder.

Minutes later, after David had retrieved her shoes and moved the car, he and Sabrina watched as the firemen began to get the situation under control. He had already told one of the fire fighters that dangerous chemicals were stored in the warehouse. He'd also showed him his identification and said he would contact the police to give them a full report on what had happened.

The car wheels screeched as they pulled out of the parking lot. Sabrina didn't like the expression on David's face. "Where are we going?"

"I'm taking you home," he said abruptly.

"And you?"

"I'm going to have a little talk with Brian."

Knowing that Michael was safe with Hester, she told him, "Then I'm going with you." The quick look he gave her said he wasn't going to argue this time. "Why Brian?" she asked.

David's eyes darkened dangerously. "Julie's political ambitions are down the drain. Who benefits?"

"Brian."

"All it took was one lousy drum with the Mansfield number on it to see to that. He knew Shelby wasn't going to last much longer, and even before Shelby had his heart attack, Brian must have known he'd planned to leave the plant to me. He wanted the presidency so badly he could taste it, probably guessed I would have brought in a new president. He had to get at me somehow."

"So, that one drum killed two birds with one stone...Julie's political career and setting you up to take the responsibility for dumping hazardous waste."

"As they say, the buck stops here." He rounded a corner on two wheels. "And if the investigators find more of those forged shipment records, they're going to throw away the key on me."

Sabrina's thoughts settled on one horrible fact. "David, he's not just an ambitious man. He tried to kill you!"

"Both of us. We must have interrupted him, and he locked the file room door from the outside and barricaded it."

Clasping her hands tightly, she continued to guess at the rest of the scenario. "Julie would not only be out of politics, but with you dead she'd be a much wealthier wife, and he probably thought he'd end up as co-owner and president of a damaged plant that could easily be put back in operation. But how do we prove all this?''

"Don't worry about that. When I get through with that sucker, jail is going to be the only safe place for him." His eyes shifted to her for a moment, then returned to the road. "Trying to get rid of me is one thing, but when he goes after you—''

Sabrina had never seen David like this before, and she was a little frightened of what he might do to Brian. "Maybe we should just tell the police. I remember a case in New Orleans where a contractor set fire to his own office to try to destroy evidence, but he wound up in prison eventually."

"Uh-uh. I'm all for law and order, but the police haven't exactly been rooting for me so far. They've been taking a lot of heat because of the dumping, and they're happy to have someone to blame." With veins standing out on his forehead, David screeched the car to a stop in front of Brian's apartment building. "You wait here."

"Not on your life. If he does admit to anything, you're going to need a witness." She hopped out of the car, and with heels clicking on the walkway to keep up with him, she followed as fast as she could.

At the door to Brian's apartment, David listened for a few seconds. In a whisper he said, "He's in there." Cautiously he tried the knob. The door was locked. He took hold of Sabrina's arm and moved her to the side. Then he stepped back to the opposite wall.

If asked at this moment, Sabrina would have sworn David had inhaled pure energy. It actually looked as though his white shirt would burst as he reared back and charged toward the door. He raised a foot and crashed it near the lock, battering the door open with a huge thud!

They rushed in. On the other side of the living room stood Brian, his mouth agape. He'd obviously been shoving papers into the briefcase that was open on his desk. A wall safe next to it was open, too.

David stopped midway, his arms hanging tensely at his sides, his fists tight. "Cleaning house?" he asked in a threatening voice.

Brian's face contorted to an expression of sheer fear. Panic loomed in his eyes as he stammered, "Listen...I...I didn't mean for things to go this far. I only—"

"You only tried to kill us! You're garbage!" He started to lunge for Brian, who grabbed a long, sharp letter opener from the desk, crouched and jabbed at David, slashing him on the arm. David parried the next swing of the knifelike opener and began tracking Brian as he circled the desk backward, all the while continuing to thrust at David to ward him off.

Sabrina saw the bloodstain growing on his shirt; fear for him rioted within her. Primitive courage guided her as she lunged at Brian. His back was to her now. With all her energy she kicked him in the back of one knee. His leg buckled; his arms flew out to the sides as he reached for nonexistent support. David's movement was swift. His fist flew fast in Brian's face, sending him stumbling backward. Then he lay on the floor, still and unconscious.

Rubbing his hand, David looked over at Sabrina and smiled, "You know, lady, if you ever tire of architecture, you'd make a helluva policewoman. Believe me, after we're married I'm not ever going to try to put anything over on you."

She glanced down at Brian's bruised face. "Same here."

She and David checked the briefcase and the wall safe and found the original documents that had been missing from the Mansfield Chemicals files, the ones the State Attorney's office believed David had destroyed. The Mansfield drum, M1738, had not been shipped to the out-of-state landfill. David phoned the police, who promptly came and took Brian into custody.

At the station, Brian couldn't talk fast enough. He admitted to having dumped the Mansfield drum himself. His motive had been to destroy Julie's chances at the mayoralty and that fear of being caught had made him try to throw the blame onto David. He knew nothing about the other illegally dumped drums, however. He had gotten his idea when the EPA had discovered them. He told the investigating team that a thorough check of the records at the plant would put Mansfield Chemicals in the clear.

Both Sabrina and David were surprised at how easily Julie took the news of Brian's arrest. She was more angry than disappointed. Almost at once she began to make phone calls to get her campaign geared up again. Yes, Sabrina thought, Julie was going to make a fine politician.

While Julie was busy on the phone, David took Sabrina in his arms. "One problem out of the way, love. On to the next. I'm going to tell Julie that Hester is our half sister. I can't go on pretending that the woman is just a neighbor. It's not fair to Hester; she's been through enough."

"How do you think Julie will take it?"

"She'll be shocked at first, as I was, but she's made of good stuff. After it sinks in, she'll welcome Hester into the family. We all will."

As David predicted, Julie was stunned when she learned of the love affair between her father and Lenore Devereaux and that Hester was, in reality, a Mansfield. David was so proud of Julie, though, when she insisted on going directly to Belleamie with Sabrina and David, to begin, she told them, the process of making up for the years of sisterhood she and Hester had lost.

And in the weeks that followed, time did indeed seem to set Sabrina's life in order.

EPILOGUE

ON CHRISTMAS MORNING at the Mansfield home, Sabrina and her son, along with David, Julie and Hester, opened the gifts that had been piled around the huge tree strung with popcorn, cranberries and multicolored lights. It glistened with decorations that David had first noticed when he was Michael's age.

And Sabrina's heart was happy as her son oohed and aahed over one gift after another. She had worried when she'd felt Todd was spoiling Michael, but she wasn't worried now. Each gift was given with so much love that she could only feel that Michael was being given so much more than the gifts themselves. And she beamed when he proudly handed out the presents he had personally selected for his new friends. She almost cried when Michael gave David the carefully wrapped rocket model he had assembled in New Orleans.

This was indeed a very special Christmas, she thought as she glanced over at Hester. The woman was so different from the frightened individual she had met when she had first arrived at Belleamie. Her face now shone with life and love. She would be having Christmas dinner with Ernest and Lucille.

"Now for your present, Mike," David told him and stood up.

Michael jumped up next to him, and Sabrina felt a lump in her throat when her son thrust out his hand for David to take.

She followed them outside to the front of the house where David told them both to wait, and in minutes he was back, leading a tan-colored Shetland pony by the reins.

Michael rushed to him. "For me?"

Crouching down, David said, "All yours, Mike. Merry Christmas."

Impulsively Michael threw his arms around David's neck. David looked up at Sabrina, and they exchanged a warm, lingering glance.

Pulling away, Michael asked, "Can I ride him now?"

"Sure you can. He belongs to you." He lifted the boy up and set him down on the shiny leather saddle. Then David guided the pony toward Sabrina and took her by the hand.

This Christmas Day was clear, pleasantly cool and so special, Sabrina thought when they rounded the corner of the house. As Michael and David considered different names for the pony, they neared the guest cottage, and she heard the sweet tinkling of the wind chimes, thinking it the loveliest of music.

Sabrina glanced back at the smile on her son's face as he busily stroked the pony's mane, then she looked up at David. "Now that Todd and Ann are separating, I'm thinking about transferring Michael to a school here in Greensboro."

"Do you think he meant it when he told you that you could keep Mike with you permanently? He could change his mind."

"No, I know Todd. He'll be content with just seeing him every now and then, when it's convenient for him."

"What about the lease on your apartment?"

"Ina's already asked me to sublet it to her and Eugene if I did move here."

"Which you *are* going to do."

"Yes," she told him, knowing that her ties to New Orleans had already dissolved, and that much stronger bonds now claimed her in Greensboro. "Hester will be opening her home in the spring, and she's going to need some guidance and support. In just this short time she's grown to depend on me, and I've become very fond of her, David."

"We'll all be here to help her get started." He laughed softly. "Not that she needs the money, but it will be good for her to become involved with people again. I've already suggested that she take it slow, accept only a few guests at first."

Tara came bounding out, and David knew she wanted to romp with Michael and the pony, but he held firmly onto the reins.

As they rounded the back corner of the house, Sabrina looked in the distance toward Belleamie. "Hester is so proud of Lenore's home, and I am, too."

"What you've done to it has already made you famous around here. You're not going to have any trouble getting clients when you do open your own office. That space in the mall is still available. You've only got to decide what you're going to name your business... Hutchins or Mansfield."

That had been bothering Sabrina, too, but before she could respond, Michael hollered up to them. "David, can I keep my pony here when Mom and I have to go back to New Orleans? Would you take care of him for me?''

They stopped and waited until Michael was next to them. Then David asked him, "How would you like to stay right here and take care of him yourself, Mike? I need your help with Tara's puppies more than ever, now. They're going to be running all around this place pretty soon."

Holding her breath, Sabrina waited for her son's response. She knew that everything depended on what he would say. It was almost too much for her when she saw his face turn radiant.

"You mean for good?!"

"If that's what you want, Mike . . . for good."

"Mom, could we?"

"That's up to you, Tiger."

Placing his hand on Michael's shoulder, David told him, "I need your help with something else, too...man-to-man stuff. You see...I love your mom, and I want to marry her, but . . . well, I'm kind of bashful about asking her."

"Just ask her. Best friends can ask anything!" Not waiting for David to do so, Michael turned to his mother. "Mom, will you marry David?"

Sabrina already felt the pounding of her heart, and now the tears began to form. She raised a finger to brush under her eyelids. "Tiger," she said almost choking with happiness, "I guess I'm a little bashful, too. Would you tell David I will?"

"Hey, David," Michael bellowed, "looks like we're gonna move in on you!"

David extended his hand and Sabrina took it in hers. Then he kissed her softly and whispered, "This is where you both always belonged. Welcome home, Sabrina.''

Together they walked hand in hand beside Michael. So much had happened, she thought, feeling the wonderful comfort and warmth of David's hand holding hers. But it had all ended well. Exceedingly well. David squeezed her fingers and she looked up into his smiling face. In that moment, Sabrina knew that she and her son were truly ''home'' now and that love would abound forever.

**He could torment her days with doubts
and her nights with desires that fired her soul.**

Ride the Eagle

VITA VENDRESHA

He was everything she ever wanted. But they were opponents in
a labor dispute, each fighting to win. Would she risk her brilliant
career for the promise of love?

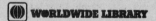

**For the millions who can't read
Give the Gift of Literacy**

One out of five adults in North America
cannot read or write well enough
to fill out a job application
or understand the directions on a bottle of medicine.

**You can change all this by joining the fight
against illiteracy.**

For more information write to:
Contact, Box 81826, Lincoln, Neb. 68501
In the United States, call toll free: 1-800-228-8813

**The only degree you need
is a degree of caring**

LIT-A-1R

Harlequin Intrigue
Adopts a New Cover Story!

We are proud to present to you the new Harlequin Intrigue cover design.

Look for two exciting new stories each month, which mix a contemporary, sophisticated romance with the surprising twists and turns of a puzzler . . . romance with "something more."

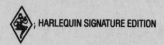
CAROLE MORTIMER

JUST ONE NIGHT

Hawk Sinclair—Texas millionaire and owner of the exclusive Sinclair hotels, determined to protect his son's inheritance. Leonie Spencer—desperate to protect her sister's happiness.

They were together for just one night.
The night their daughter was conceived.

Blackmail, kidnapping and attempted murder add suspense to passion in this exciting bestseller.

The success story of Carole Mortimer continues with *Just One Night*, a captivating romance from the author of the bestselling novels, *Gypsy* and *Merlyn's Magic*.

**Available in March
wherever paperbacks are sold.**